EVER SINCE WE SMALL

MORE PRAISE FOR *EVER SINCE WE SMALL*

"*Ever Since We Small* is an astonishing accomplishment. This epic tale spans generations of an Indo-Trinidadian family and serves as a timely indictment of the legacy of colonialism in the Caribbean. It is a critical and necessary book for those interested in understanding how the past wrestles with our present moment, and why hope is our most transcendental inheritance."
—**Cleyvis Natera**, award-winning author of *Neruda on the Park* and *The Grand Paloma Resort*

"*Ever Since We Small* raises powerful nuanced questions: What does it mean to carry forward the memory of a people? Where does duty end and desire begin? And how do women shape their own lives in the shadows of history? This is a book about many things, foremost among them a tale of lives bound by blood and silence, a story that unearths the emotional aftermath of tragedies, threading it with the intimate, often unspoken realities of motherhood, longing, and survival. A sweeping, necessary novel on what it means to be human."—**Krystal A. Sital**, author of *Secrets We Kept: Three Women of Trinidad*

"In this intimate exploration of voices and pain, Celeste Mohammed weaves all of the complexities and contradictions of Indo-Caribbean identity and expression into some unforgettable characters. Through generations of loss and gain we are carried along in language as varied and important as the span of time and influences themselves. Ultimately enriched. *Ever Since We Small* wraps truths and trauma with loving care."
—**Oonya Kempadoo**, winner of the 2024 Guyana Prize for Literature, past winner of the Casa de las Américas Prize

"Celeste Mohammed's *Ever Since We Small* is searing family saga rooted in indenture and its postcolonial fallout. Destitution, family dynamics, substance abuse all swirl around together to present a hard and unflinching look at one family's generational struggles through bondage into the decolonization and neocolonization of Trinidad and Tobago. I am amazed by the research into the languages and multiple ethnic and linguistic heritages of T&T, handled with grace and expertise. Celeste Mohammed is a writer with the feminist magic of beholding many generations in a single glance. I have needed this book for years."—**Rajiv Mohabir**, author of *Seabeast and Antiman: A Hybrid Memoir*

"Let us allow that the rich, ripe language of Celeste Mohammed's ten narrative stories is an innovative kind of brilliant poetic rendering, and say that *Ever Since We Small* is an epic work that fleshes out and completes Harold Sonny Ladoo's *No Pain Like this Body*. She has accomplished the portrayal of a legacy of drama begun, in this case, with one woman's *kala pani* crossing and worked through generations, culminating in the unique and too-real racial complexities of a Caribbean present. Her empathetic handling of voice and crystal-clear imagery speak of a writer we must watch closely and treasure."—**Shani Mootoo**, author of *Oh Witness Dey!* and *Polar Vortex*

"Mohammed's skill as an astute observer and keeper of memory, shines through in *Ever Since We Small*, which is a searing triumph! Occupying every beating register of emotion, *Ever Since We Small* offers us irresistible interconnected stories of one Indo-Caribbean family throughout generations that are at once wholly magical, splendidly mischievous, and utterly heartbreaking. No doubt Mohammed has come to this literary landscape to conquer!"—**Lauren Francis-Sharma**, author of *Casualties of Truth*

EVER SINCE WE SMALL

CELESTE MOHAMMED

NEW YORK, NY

Ig Publishing, Inc.
Box 2547
New York, NY 10163
www.igpub.com

ISBN: 978-1-63246-176-6

Printed in the United States of America
First US edition
Manufactuer: Lightning Source

For my great-grandmothers,
Kairoon Mohammed and Popo Mano,
And their daughters.

scream
so that one day
a hundred years from now
another sister will not have to
dry her tears wondering
where in history
she lost her voice.

—Jasmin Kaur

CONTENTS

FOREWORD

What are the inheritances of women's suffering? Of their being brutally policed into smaller versions of themselves that are deemed more socially acceptable and easily dispensable via emotional and physical violence? Celeste Mohammed's novel, *Ever Since We Small*, offers a sweeping landscape for considering these questions, leading us from 1899 to 2017, from Bihar Province in India to Trinidad, as she follows the path of a young Indian woman, Jayanti, and the generations of men and women that she gives life to, after her journey into Trinidadian indentureship.

Mohammed's opening chapter tells the tale of Jayanti being forced to commit *sati* to preserve the honor of her husband's family. Her dramatic struggle, with both herself and with community and colonial expectations, sets the stage for envisaging the various types of self-immolation possible within the conditions of poverty and indentureship, and in the aftermath of trauma. In Mohammed's skilled hands, the horrific moment of death by fire is rendered as a moment of communion between the powerful feminine divine and the vulnerable human female corporeal form, offering a literal tempering by fire of a female will to survive, reject patriarchal control, and thrive in the new uncertain terrain which ensues. Leading as it does into Jayanti's decision to indenture herself to a plantation in Trinidad, Mohammed's is a particularly evocative imagining of the birth of an Indo-Caribbean feminist impulse. Subverting the colonial fantasy of white men saving brown women from brown men (an idea explored by Gayatri Spivak in her famed essay "Can the Subaltern Speak?"), here it is: women and divine maternal forces who encourage other women and lead them to redemption.

Mohammed then moves forward in time to depict the terrain of modern Caribbean living in the wake of these histories. With her keen ear for the rich cadences of Caribbean speech and her astute noting of both the mundane and magical elements of quotidian Trinidadian life, Mohammed's novel is a testimony to the vibrant culture that exists in the region which, though informed by Indian, African, Chinese, Indigenous and other ancestral origins, is no longer constrained by them and instead abounds in the ever-unfolding fruits of layered languages, traditions, and faiths that are not solely the inheritances of the past but indices of bold new futures. Yet Jayanti's freedom at the end of her chapter does not translate into happiness for her descendants. The titular phrase "ever since we small" echoes many times in the text, hinting at both entangled lines of relation and potential solidarities, but also at the recurrence of cycles of abuse and violence and heavy cultural and gendered expectations for both women and men.

There are many versions of the walking wounded in the novel, of those who have returned from the edge of destruction and who carry both external and internal scars. Mohammed is particularly deft at weaving strands of interconnectivity in her writing. In the memorable chapter, "The Visitation," which serves as a tender romance embedded in an overall framework of inherited trauma and its ripple effects, a severely scarred American soldier forges a relationship built on mutual acceptance with a survivor of domestic violence who is burdened with additional self-hatred over her dark skin. The comparison of Abby's anxiety with a PTSD-affiicted American soldier is at once an expansive gesture of solidarity, a reworking of older tropes of white male American military encounters with Trinidadian women, and a commentary on how much surviving a Caribbean landscape of gendered violence, colorism and desperate social aspirations is like war.

Here though, and in the overall structure of the book, Mohammed subverts the marriage plot. Despite her sensitive and insightful representation of various romantic relationships with the potential to disrupt painful patterns, it is not marriage that ends these chapters and resolves personal and generational curses. Rather, it is the reestablishing of broken family and community ties, of forgiveness and acceptance at multiple levels in the human and natural world that must come to pass before healing can be achieved at both personal and community levels. The text beautifully conveys the need for others to hold our memories, for intimate witnesses, for ones who share in our suffering and joy and with whom our faiths are intertwined. This extends well beyond the limits of the human, challenging lines typically drawn between the living and dead, the "real" and the mythical, the mundane and the magical, the secular and the sacred.

Mohammed employs both human and non-human voices in the text: Papa Bois, the Divine Mother (in her many forms) and forests are all given narrative authority in the various chapters of *Ever Since We Small*. In "Outsiders," it is the trees that are our guides. There is a lyricism, a surefootedness whenever Mohammed turns her attention to the varied landscapes of Trinidad, both rural and urban. Here, she personifies woods as spaces that bear the potential for both contemporary freedom/healing and the memories of conquistadores, Black

Power struggles, Indigenous knowledge and all sorts of past revolutionary action against the state and oppressive hierarchies.

Folkloric figures recur frequently in *Ever Since We Small* too—in the form of the diablesse, the saapin, the soucouyant, the lagahoo. The murdered Salma is evoked specifically as a churile haunting the minds and paths of her grieving family. In the novel, as in Caribbean culture more generally, female folklore figures serve as indices of women's pain and marginalization, and as evidence of the ways in which their personal choices are violently policed by social norms and maligned as abnormal. With her vision of a Divine Mother as "a dark-skinned Madonna," Mohammed offers a particularly powerful rejection of the insidious life and strength of colorism in the region, where love for others and self-love are all compromised by enduring ideas around lightness and darkness. This manichaeism though is of course also reflective of what Mohammed celebrates about the Trinidadian landscape, with its spaces of both darkness and of light, of both hope and despair. While conveying a keen awareness of the class, race and gender divides by which Trinidadian society is riven, hers is an upending of hierarchies, an embracing of the imperfect as worthy, a lifting up of denigrated belief systems, of new liberatory versions of Indo-Caribbean femininities and masculinities, of the rich tapestries of Caribbean creole, and of phoenix-like emergence from experiences of destitution and violence that make up the scarred beauty of a place. The purifying fire which starts off this novel burns away ever-pervasive shame to reveal enduring beauty and effervescent hope.

—Lisa Outar Rome

EVER SINCE WE SMALL

THEN

1899-2000

THE LEGEND OF JAYANTI

1899, City of Patna, Bihar District, India

Legend says it happened one night, within a house which stood upon the banks of the Ganga, a rupee's throw from the walls of the East India Company. A beautiful woman—a lovely *suhagin*—appeared to young Jayanti in a dream, offering two silver bracelets so thick that the girl mistook them for shackles, and promptly refused the adornment. That was her first mistake. Her second occurred the next day when, just to counter the infernal whirring of the millstone as she squatted beside it grinding grain into flour, Jayanti mentioned the dream to Beena, her senior sister-in-law.

"Aiyo! What if it is Chamunda Maa coming to warn us of great evil?" Beena exclaimed, yanking the *ghunghat* of her *sari* even tighter around her face, as if the veil could become a shield.

"Not every dream is an omen, *bhauji*," Jayanti scoffed. "We have both dreamt of many handsome princes with hearts bursting from love, haven't we? And yet, are we not still here… doing this?" She poured another handful of grain into the hole of the mill, and wondered if Beena harbored, as she did, a secret discontent with this cloistered life in the *zanana*, the women's quarters. But Jayanti could not risk the question, lest it get back to their mother-in-law.

"Besides, why would the family's *kuldevi* goddess come to *me*, the newest and lowest daughter-in-law? I am only eighteen. If there was something important to be said, would she not go to

Anjali, who is old and wise and whom our mother-in-law favors above us all?" Jayanti said, trying but failing this time to hide the soreness in her tone.

"Still, you must tell our mother-in-law," Beena persisted. "Perhaps *devi* is displeased. Perhaps you made a little mistake during our last family *puja*, or maybe one of our women consumed meat during the last Navratri fast, perhaps there is still time to fix this."

Jayanti make a mistake? Never. She had been raised and trained for marriage, in much the same way as the bullock in her father's yard had been trained for cart-bearing. She always knew that one day she'd leave her family and enter a husband's, and that at her in-laws' house she was meant to tread with silent dignity and obedience while bearing the load of her wifely responsibilities: produce children for her husband, attend to his needs, serve his family, and worship his family's gods. And if she discharged these duties faithfully—which she'd been doing, as far as she was aware, since marriage two years ago to Pratap Singh, a widower twice her age—she would have fulfilled the singular and overarching purpose of her life: securing her husband's divine protection and prosperity. And so, having performed every *vrat*, vow and fast required, Jayanti had no reason to fear *devi*, or to interpret her own dreams inauspiciously. Except, maybe, if the gods paid attention not only to rites and rituals but to secret fantasies of living another life, elsewhere, in the arms of some handsome, young, lovelorn *rajah*.

"Please do not say anything, Beena. You know our mother-in-law has not yet grown so fond of me, as she is of you two."

In truth, there had been a time when the mother-in-law had fawned over Jayanti, back when she'd first left her father's village and joined this household as a virgin bride from a high-caste (if not exactly wealthy) Rajput family. But, of course, that was before she'd disappointed everyone by failing to produce the son—or any child, for that matter—which Pratap Singh, part-heir to his father's corn chandler empire, so desperately craved. Over these two fruitless years, her in-laws"favor had soured like *dahi.* Jayanti was unwilling to further sacrifice her status by now being the harbinger of might-be-omens.

"I swear I will tell if the *suhagin* comes again," she promised Beena, then hurried off to slip her neck under the yoke of a junior daughter-in-law's schedule: laundry, cooking, as well as child-minding (which extended beyond her husband's four daughters from his deceased wife, to all the children of the household). Within an hour, Jayanti had forgotten the dream.

However, a few weeks later, it recurred. This time there were *four* bracelets—three silver and one gold—and the smiling *suhagin*, who wore a beautiful red dress with fine shimmering beadwork, informed Jayanti that she would keep returning, every night, and Jayanti would know no rest, until the bracelets were accepted. So Jayanti held out her tender wrists. They sagged as the heavy bracelets were clasped. Then, the *suhagin* burst into a flame which became a wild conflagration of colors in the sky—purple, red and ochre *abir*—like a sunset over the Ganga on a Holi day. It was the heat that woke Jayanti. Her bed was drenched with sweat, while Pratap Singh continued in a dead sleep beside her, insensible—as usual—to the clamors of her heart.

Later, as she lay out his clothing for the office—a fresh *dhoti* and *kameez*—she timorously relayed the dream. He responded with a deep chuckle that made his grey handlebar moustache twitch and his substantial belly quiver.

"This is good, very good," he said.

"How so, my husband?"

"Have I not promised you a golden bracelet for each son you bear me? I think Mata Ji foretells of children. And, as a businessman, I am proud that my wife did not accept her first offer of only silver—which might have been daughters—but has waited for the deal to be gilded with a son."

"Do you truly believe this, *pati*? Did my predecessor, your venerable first wife, experience anything like this before she…"

"I assure you." He smiled. "She did not, on any of the four occasions that her lap was filled, including the last which claimed her life. *You* are specially chosen by *devi*. I will tell my mother that from now on you must be given extra rice and meat, you must be fattened and healthy for what is to come. The rest is up to you, Jayanti. You are young but I have always seen in you the makings of an excellent wife, a true *pativrata*. You know what must be done."

Jayanti wasn't sure she believed her husband's interpretation of the dream, but all that mattered was what *he* believed, and what she'd been taught to do with *his* belief.

Immediately after his departure, she dashed across the courtyard of the *zanana*, wanting to be first in the *thapana* room. There, inset within the wall, was the place where the *kuldevi* had been located and worshipped by all the women for as long as the family had existed—three centuries, according to her eldest brother-in-law, Hari Singh, who headed the household since his father's brain had become addled. There, before the trident drawn in vermilion, Jayanti performed not only the daily prayers to Mata Ji and to all the family *satimatas* and *ishtadevtas*, but also began a special veneration before the shrine of Pratap Singh's deceased wife, so that she would not become jealous or mischievous toward the impending pregnancy. At first, Jayanti prayed by rote, with half a mind on the chores awaiting her, but somewhere during her chant of the Gayatri Mantra, she felt herself swept up by a monsoon of emotion she hadn't forecast, and the baby suddenly became very real and very dear to her.

Oh, Jayanti's heart cried to the Divine, let this be true! Oh, to have someone in my life who will love me! She recalled the looks that passed every day between her sisters-in-law and their chubby little children, she saw how they clung to each other on their mats, laughed and cuddled as if in their own worlds—even as they were ignored by the men of the family. She'd been hoping for new sweet feelings to arise and blossom, lotus-like, from the thick drudgery of her marriage but, as yet, that hadn't happened. Perhaps she and Pratap Singh hadn't been long enough in each other's lives, or beds, or maybe it would never happen? But with a child, her *own* child, she would at least have what her sisters-in-law had: love in its purest form, love that would need and adore her instantly. She would no longer have to wait.

"Beti."

A whisper, someone calling her "daughter"; she almost believed it was the goddess herself. But then came Beena's excited tone: "Ahhh, sister, Pratap Singh has told! I knew that dream was a message." And there was their mother-in-law in the doorway beside Beena.

"Beti," the old woman said again, with a lilt of tenderness Jayanti hadn't detected in a long time. She shuffled closer, dipped into her brass *lota* and showered holy water upon the girl's head, muttering blessings and congratulations.

From that moment, the mood and spirit of the household changed. The rest of that day passed differently, with the crackle of portents and miracles electrifying the air, with lightheartedness and laughter, and with Jayanti being given rare assistance with her workload from Beena and even Anjali. Then, that one auspicious day spawned several others. Pratap Singh even made three consecutive sleeps in Jayanti's bed and was gentler with her than ever he'd been since their wedding night. So gentle, that she wondered was this now the beginnings of that elusive love?

Several days later, however, Pratap Singh came home from the corn business, staggered into the *mardana*, the men's quarters, and took to his bed, feeling unwell. His eyes were bloodshot. When he spoke, it was with some effort and his tongue could be seen floating, heavy and greyish, like a river porpoise, in his mouth. The family doctor came and mumbled a diagnosis of bowel impaction. Pratap Singh was to be given only vegetarian meals for the next week, to ease these unfortunate stoppages.

At first, the diagnosis seemed accurate, because over the next few days, the patient soiled himself with the force of the Ganga in flood season, and had to be moved outdoors, onto a pallet in the courtyard. But then he began to refuse all food. He did not sleep, he just lay there groaning.

Jayanti spent all her time either at his bedside—cleaning him, lifting his head to sip water, anointing his body—or in the *thapana* room, praying for his recovery. "Save his life, save his life," her supplication always began, before derailing itself into an interrogation of the gods: Why was *her* husband stricken like this? Why now, when they were on the cusp of marital bliss? Was this a divine test of her wifely faith? Did this have anything to do with her dreams? In the doorway of that prayer room, she crouched and watched the succession of ayurvedic gurus and other healers summoned by her in-laws. She watched with a quivering heart, she chanted her mantras, she clutched at the string necklace from which her *pala*, a silver likeness of Chamunda Maa, hung. Pratap Singh would get better, he must get better, because she, like everyone else knew: a husband's health was as strong as his wife's *pala* necklace was unbroken.

Yet, with every hour, every passing day, every medicine-man's visit, the sickness seemed to worsen. Remedies grew progressively expensive, until one evening when an ointment laced with gold dust and powdered ivory was prescribed, Jayanti was asked to surrender her wedding jewellery so that her in-laws might purchase the balm. Although she knew her father-in-law was still very wealthy, and the family could well have afforded the medicine without her help, Jayanti understood she was being called beyond mere lip-service and prayer, to the highest plane of wifely devotion: the realm of self-sacrifice, to prove herself a true *pativrata* and husband-protector. She surrendered the items eagerly and was left with only a few glass bangles on her wrists. She would have sacrificed those too, if necessary—and everything else she owned—to restore Pratap Singh to good health. Because, she knew, if these minor sacrifices proved ineffective, a much greater one would be expected of her: *sati.* She needed only to glance around the *thapana* room at the several keepsakes and little *murtis* of the five previous *satimatas* of Pratap Singh's family, wives who'd agreed to burn themselves on their husband's funeral pyres to prove eternal devotion and saintliness. At eighteen years old, Jayanti was not ready to become a *satimata.* In fact, she could not believe the gods would be so cruel.

But after a week, Pratap Singh's condition had worsened to include a fever which caused him to drift in and out of consciousness, to rage at anyone who came near, and to even fight with Jayanti—pulling at her hair and clothes—whenever she tried to help him.

Her in-laws sent for a special *sadhu*, the most powerful exorcist that side of the District, who claimed to embrace the tenets of all religions. And on the morning of the tenth day, the holy man arrived in a fragrant cloud of sandalwood, with dreadlocks hanging near his ankles, and clad only in a mustard *dhoti* and long string of beads. Beneath a matted beard, his face was as dark, sharp and pointy as some ancient flinty spearhead. He made seven circles, poking his wooden staff around Pratap Singh's pallet, then he bent and grabbed what seemed to be a handful of dust from the courtyard floor. He then straightened, raked his slitty eyes around the perimeter of the yard and, ignoring every other veiled woman peeking out of the shadows, he pointed the blackened nail of a talon-like finger at Jayanti, half-hidden in the doorway of the *thapana* room.

To Pratap Singh's brother, Hari Singh, he said, "The wife. Bring her."

Behind the *ghunghat* of her *sari*, a trembling Jayanti kept her gaze low as she approached the *sadhu*. She wished that the thin veil was made of some sturdier material, thicker and more opaque, like those worn by Muslimah women. Maybe then she would feel less afraid, less exposed and less scorched by the heat of the *sadhu's* eyes as they traveled from the *sindur* on her scalp, to her bare feet, then back up again. It seemed no one, not even Pratap Singh who lay on the floor between her and the holy man, dared even to breathe.

"Show me your *pala*," the *sadhu* demanded.

Was that all? Jayanti almost smiled as she reached beneath her *ghunghat* seeking the necklace she'd worn since the day she'd performed her first wifely *puja* within this household.

But—where was it?

Her fingers scrambled around her clavicle like starving rats in a gully. Panicked, she broke *purdah* and looked up immodestly, straight into the dread face of the holy man. And there he stood, holding *her* necklace by its broken string as the pendant dangled accusingly. Everyone in the courtyard, indeed the entire house, emitted a gasp of horror.

"Your marriage is how old?" the *sadhu's* voice boomed.

"Two years only," Hari Singh replied on her behalf.

"Did you renew your *vrat* for the second year? Did you replace the old necklace thread with a new one, thereby refreshing your commitment to your husband's health? Did you… did you…" he went on and on, listing her wifely rituals.

Jayanti knew she'd done all these things under the watchful eye of her mother-in-law, but was it possible she'd made some inadvertent mistake? Sometimes, she became distracted while chanting mantras, sometimes she drifted into memories of her home village and her father's house, her nieces left behind, her days of playing guessing games, giggling endlessly and dancing with them before her betrothal at twelve years old.

"It was here, below his pallet," the *sadhu* announced. "How could you not see it, if you'd been caring for your husband as you should?"

"Please, sometimes he struggles with me when I… Perhaps that's when the string—"

"*Suwar ke bacha, gadha ke beti*! You dare blame your husband for his own ill-fate? It is your failure of character that has caused this. Your insufficient devotion to him and your lackluster obeisance to his gods. *You* are to blame!"

Jayanti burst into tears. He was right! Her devotion *had* been lacking because for two years she'd lacked any feeling, any true love for her husband. She'd daydreamed about returning to her father's house; she'd fantasized about young handsome princes coming to save her; she'd grimaced under Pratap Singh's weight, cringed at the prickle of his moustache, scorned his eel-like tongue and his thick yellow corn-cob fingers. Duty was not the same as devotion, she now saw, and so with no heart in any of her *vrats*, vows, fasts or promises, she had mocked the gods and doomed her husband. If he was not precious to her, why would he be precious to them?

She clutched her stomach and, like a slashed bamboo, crumpled in the middle. She fell to the floor.

Pratap Singh expressed a loud groan then, through the torn parchment of his lips, but no one could glean if it was in exoneration or condemnation of his wife. The effort proved too much though, and he was soon overcome by a seizure that flung him from the pallet and had him thrashing all over the floor. His mother collapsed and began wailing. As if on cue, the daughters-in-law and children of the compound joined in the ululations, while a sobbing Jayanti struggled to restrain her husband from swallowing his own tongue.

Just a little before sundown, Dr. Parker, having received an urgent request from businessman, Hari Singh, hurried from the compound of the East India Company and headed for the wealthy family's home. He was greeted by a deep rumbling chant of "Ram, Ram," echoing up, as if from a dark chasm of the earth itself, to reverberate within his own lily-white soul. His hair stood on end, and he knew at once: the patient was gone. Yes, Pratap Singh had passed away but five minutes earlier, the doctor was told, and his wife had already smashed her glass bangles and announced her *vrat* to become a *sati*, to burn along with him, on his funeral pyre at sunrise.

"Will you not dissuade her?" the doctor asked, as Hari Singh hurried the *ftrangi* Englishman from the courtyard entrance, back to the waiting carriage.

With a sneer that seemed to hoist his moustache as high as his eyebrows, Hari Singh replied, "Parker-*sahib*, the women of my family have all been *satis*, why should Jayanti bring disgrace upon them by refusing to follow? She too must prove herself innocent of her husband's death. This is our way, you must understand."

Immediately upon his return to the Company's compound, Dr. Parker reported the matter to Magistrate Robertson, who declared that the godly might of English justice would intervene to save the poor girl, body and soul, from "these uncivilized Hindoos." However, the Magistrate made no mention of his other, career-oriented, motivations. There'd been four instances of *sati* in the District during the past year—it was almost as if the passing of a law prohibiting the practice had spurred the natives to more frequent bouts of madness. He'd looked the other way—as he often did with their strange heathenistic beliefs—but he'd promised himself he wouldn't let it get to five. *Five* cases of *sati* would draw attention, five would be an embarrassment to the East India Company, five would be enough to get him tossed from the palanquin heights he enjoyed here in Patna, to some dung-caked outpost of the District. In short, Robertson could not let this girl kill herself on his watch, in his city. He sent for the police captain to hatch a rescue plan overnight.

Meanwhile, two streets away, the family priest and a cluster of menfolk attended to Pratap Singh's body. Jayanti changed into the pink wedding clothes she'd tucked into her trunk. They fit looser than two years ago—she had to make a few more folds to get the *sari* just right—but she wanted to wear them, so to be, in the end, as she had been in the beginning with Pratap Singh, before she had failed him so horribly. She deserved to die.

Then, she approached the grass mat in the center of the courtyard where they had laid out her husband. She cast a long look upon his four children seated there, singing their hymns. If she did not pay for whatever cosmic wrong she had precipitated, they would grow up being told that their mother, Pratap Singh's first wife, was a saint, while she, his second wife, was the demon who had killed him. Jayanti sat, lifted his head onto her lap, shut her eyes and whispered, "My husband, I am sorry. I will prove the innocence of my heart… I will prove my devotion… I will do this for your sake, for your sake." Her body, a thin line, wafted as she passed the several hours of night, insensible to everything but Pratap Singh's body. Twice he seemed to perspire and twice she wiped him down saying, "I am going with you. Be calm. The sun's first rays are still to come."

Over and over, upon the purple fabric of her mind's eye, Jayanti projected her *suhagin* dreams again, with new clearer understanding. She was the *suhagin*, the beautiful married woman, not so? It was *she* who was destined to burst into flame—the ultimate wifely sacrifice. *She* who would be consumed by holy fire. It was *she* who was fated to become *satimata*, mother goddess, to save and intercede for generations to come. Or maybe, she would visit heaven, only to reappear on earth and be married to an upper-caste brahmin and have her lap filled with many royal priestly sons. All night, Jayanti swayed and sang and anticipated her saintliness. Oh how it beckoned, just within reach, assuring her she would be loved most deeply when she was dead.

Then, as the sharp *khanda* of morning opened its first pink slits in the dark skin of the sky, Jayanti was roused from her meditations by the growl of Hari Singh.

"All is now ready," he said.

She nodded without opening her eyes.

"When you leave this house today, know that you shall not return. There is only the pyre, no longer is there a place for you here."

She nodded again.

"Look at me!" he snapped, and when she did, he continued, "If you lose heart and shame my family today, I will kill you myself. I will run my own sword through your belly. Do you understand, child?"

She stretched across, placed her hand directly over the flame of the lamp which they'd kept burning near the corpse. She held her palm there, without flinching from the fire, until Hari Singh said, "I am satisfied. Let us proceed."

Outside the family compound, a great crowd of villagers, draped in funereal white, surged and jostled, flooding the path from the house to the banks of the great Ganga. There was much rejoicing—tom-toms, drums, and other musical instruments—because Pratap Singh's widow had sworn a *vrat* to perform *sati*, to give the village another blessed female martyr. His body had already been removed from the house, on a bier of bamboo, and placed on a platform atop the pyre of wood and straw.

However, Jayanti's procession from the house was proving slower. A curtain had been rigged around the bullock cart in which she sat, so she could maintain *purdah* until the moment of her great triumph. That did nothing, though, to discourage villagers from calling to her, begging her to employ her new supernatural powers as a *sativrata* to bless them or curse their enemies. They tossed garlands and trinkets over the curtain to attain her favor; they climbed on each other's shoulders to get an early glimpse of her soon-to-be sainted face. But Jayanti sat wide-eyed and mute as the cart ambled along. In a way, she'd left this world; she was already envisioning the little cenotaph, a mound of earth the villagers would raise by the riverside in her honor, so that everyone who passed would have to bow to it—a high tribute to her husband's family, possibly the greatest recompense for the trouble she'd caused them. She hoped, too, that one day her own family, her father and brothers maybe, would also come and venerate her for doing them proud, for being a most honorable daughter to the end. Oh how she wished she could see them, her mother, her dear nieces, one last time!

A tear escaped the brim of her gaping eyes just as the cart lurched in front of the English compound. Jayanti peeped out and saw that two white soldiers had stepped into the road. Parker-*sahib* and Magistrate Robertson, whom she recognized from his dinner visits to Hari Singh, swooped forward in their dark English suits, looking like the carrion crows that circled the riverbank. The Magistrate extended his arm, as if he meant to reach her curtain.

Hari Singh intercepted and blocked his path.

At first, no words were exchanged, but from the Magistrate's adamant pointing, Jayanti guessed he was demanding she be taken into the courthouse behind him. Hari Singh kept shaking his head in defiance.

The Magistrate's jowls became puffy like a cobra, then he spat out some words Jayanti did not understand. Instantly, more guards appeared: a motley mix of senior white men and junior Indian *duffadars* surrounded the bullock cart. The crowd fell silent. So silent that everyone heard when Hari Singh stepped aside and said in his best English, "But sir, please sir, can be only-speaking through veil, please."

The magistrate gave a curt nod then drew close to Jayanti's curtain, but didn't disturb it. Using Dr. Parker as interpreter, he tried many arguments, hoping to cause Jayanti to recant her vow; he even offered her money, and yet she shut her eyes and shook her head in solemn and stubborn refusal. What could he offer her on earth that would be better than the veneration she would receive when in the heavens? What good were his hard cold rupees when lamps would soon be lit, incense raised, and bells rung in her honor? When she was now destined to have her own devotees, who would offer garlands and plates of honey, sugar, milk, curd, and richest ghee. She pictured it all in her mind, like some intricate, brightly colored, *rangoli* tableau, as the Magistrate spoke. Then finally, in exasperation, he threatened arrest, informing her that *sati* was "quite simply illegal" under English law.

Jayanti, who'd never in life spoken more than three words to a male, now surprised herself by the boldness of her answer to this important *ftrangi* man: "If you will not let me burn with my husband, I will hang myself in your jail. Is that legal, *sahib*?" Would now come the shackles of which she'd dreamt? She was ready.

But the magistrate rocked on his boot heels for a bit, then said, "Very well. Proceed. But my men will guard the pyre. They will keep you safe if you decide to change your mind, which I hope you will, young lady. So help you God." He gave a hand signal, and though the guards stepped aside to let the bullock cart pass, they ran ahead to reassemble themselves around the looming, yet unlit, cremation stack.

Jayanti submerged herself in the holy waters of Ganga Ma for the last time, and came out of the embrace feeling purposeful, strong, and anointed. Then, as she was ascending the *ghat* from the river, Hari Singh came, put a clay vessel to her lips and told her to sip. From the smell alone she knew it was *bhang*, the potent drink made of spiced milk and cannabis—she understood he was trying to help her face the anguish of slow death. She drank deeply then returned the vessel with a grateful smile. She recalled the story her chillum-puffing father had taught her as a child, of when the gods had stirred the heavenly ocean causing a drop of sacred nectar to fall from the sky and sprout the very first cannabis plant. Oh, this unexpected blessing, having fallen upon her, soft and dewlike on this her last morning, that Hari Singh was not as hard a man as she'd always thought him. It was an auspicious omen: the gods were with her, she would endure the burn, and her beloved family would hear only one story—of her bravery and devotion—not the other story of her being a bad wife.

She lit a brand, and began walking around the pyre, setting it ablaze. Then she mounted the platform, and as the flames caught and stretched upward, she sat, placed Pratap Singh's head on her lap, shut her eyes and began chanting, "*Ram, Ram, sati… Ram, Ram, sati…* God, God, I am chaste."

However, as the wind drove the fire nearer, she felt its climbing heat; she struggled to breathe in the scorching air, and she began to doubt her anointing. Her arms and legs grew so hot that instinctively she shook them and groaned as if that would cool her body. Then, just at the moment when she decided to fling herself into the thickest flames and end her life as quickly as possible, she heard within the roaring blaze the small voice of a woman whispering her name: *Jayanti… Jayanti.* She opened her eyes, and there was the *suhagin* from her dream, now wearing the flames themselves as if they were a saffron *sari*.

"I am Sati, wife of Lord Shiva," the woman said with a gentle smile.

Jayanti gasped, and the onlookers heard her exclaim, "Oh Mata, you have come to give me courage to do as you did for your husband's sake," which caused much exultation among the crowd. "She is chaste, she is chaste! Sati herself has manifested to her!" they cheered.

The goddess shook her head *no*, and from her flowing black hair floated a cloud of white smoke which formed itself into another, lighter-skinned woman. By her crimson *sari*, the items clutched in three of her hands—trident, sword, dish—and the way her fourth hand was positioned in a *mudra* of blessing, Jayanti recognized immediately the goddess Parvati.

"Oh Gauri, most perfect and nurturing wife of our Lord, let me return as you did to be helpmeet to a royal husband, and mother to many royal sons," Jayanti called out, and the crowd roared again. "Hear how she speaks to Parvati now! She is chaste, she is chaste!"

In a voice so musical Jayanti wasn't sure whether the words were being spoken or sung, the second goddess replied, "We shawl their failings, we buttress their weakness, we crawl so they may conquer. We burn so they are warm, we drown so they may breathe."

Who was the "they," Jayanti wondered, and who was the "we?"

Then the wind seemed to cleave in two, parting the flames and pushing them in opposite directions, away from the fabric of Jayanti's *sari* which had begun to smolder. Through the corridor of smoke strode a third goddess. The whole pyre shook with the thundering of her feet—or was it Jayanti's head throbbing from the force of the *bhang*? And as this third goddess came to stand astride pale and pretty Parvati, the contrast was frightening. Her skin, deepest black as if charred, hung loosely on her bones. Her blood red eyes were sunken and a third eye flamed brilliantly from her forehead. She carried a skull-topped staff, a noose, and a sword. Her entangled black hair blew wildly about her shoulders.

"Maha Kali!" Jayanti screamed and cowered over her husband's body, which was now alight at the feet. At the name of the demon-goddess, the crowd screamed too, and stampeded in different directions.

Yet within the fire, there was a quiet calm.

"Fear not, *beti*," Parvati whispered to Jayanti, "Do you not remember *she* is also me? When, to save the world, I jumped into Shiva's throat and combined myself with the poison he had swallowed, *I* became Kali. I am she, and she is what is hidden within a woman like me, who has sacrificed too much." Then, Sati stroked Jayanti's cheek, while Kali danced *tatkars... ta thei thei tat...* and Parvati sang a joyous *bhajan*, "*Jayanti zindabad...* Long live Jayanti! Three generations of silver, one generation gold. *Jayanti zindabad...* Long live Jayanti!"

And why shouldn't she live long? What had she done that was so wrong? Yes, her mind had wandered during *puja*, yes, she'd dreamt of other men—hadn't Beena done the same? Why wasn't Beena here on this pyre? Why wasn't her husband taken early? Could it be that death chose men by some other criteria than the simple failings of their wives? And what did the goddess mean by generations of silver and gold? Was that the dream's message? A promise of a new husband and family? A promise of fruitful love?

Subtly, languorously, in the same way that smoke from Sati's hair had wafted and curled and reformed into Parvati, Jayanti's commitment to die transformed into a commitment to live, a hope and curiosity for her future that she'd never felt before.

What need had she of the afterlife if happiness awaited in this one?

She sprang up and lunged to one side of the pyre, seeking escape. The *duffadar* stationed there raised his sword, causing her to shrink back into the flames, where her lower half caught fire in earnest now. She screamed again. The magistrate, who had been watching from atop his own carriage, ordered the swordsman seized, and while the crowd was distracted with the wrangling of guards, Jayanti dove through the other side of the pyre and ran into the quenching waters of the Ganga a few yards away.

The crowd and the family of Pratap Singh set off after her like hornets. "Cut her down! Knock her head! Tie her and throw her in again!" they jeered at Hari Singh, who rushed down the *ghat* to carry out these murderous intentions. But, with swords and rifles, the English soldiers held everyone at bay.

Jayanti, who was miraculously not much burned except for some areas of her arms and legs, managed to stagger back up the steps of the *ghat*. However, at the sight of the seething crowd, she was weakened by a heady cocktail of fear, *bhang*, and the delirium which often accompanies near-death. She swooned. A soldier caught her tiny frame. Then Magistrate Robertson appeared and, with great ceremony, placed his heavy hand on her shoulder and said, "By your own law, having once quitted the pile you cannot ascend again. And by my touch now, your *purdah* is broken and you are impure. You are now an outcast from the Hindoos, but I promise: The East India Company will protect you, and you shall never want for food, clothing or the love of our Christian God." He then sent her, in a palanquin, under armed escort, to the English hospital—the only place she would be safe from the vengeance of her husband's family and the ridicule of the affronted village.

Jayanti's three days in the hospital bed were not unpleasant. She was attended to by Dr. Parker and mostly local nurses, all of whom made a great effort to keep her comfortable. Between the morphine and the unfamiliar sludge of daily "porridges," she slept for long dreamless stretches, and when she was awake, she never once asked—as some patients did—about the caste of the cooks preparing her food or the nurses touching her bowl and body. What did it matter now? She could not fall further from grace. And even on the first day, when they'd presented her with a replacement *sari* and *ghunghat*, she'd refused the latter, declaring, "No more *purdah*. Mata Ji saved me to make me free."

On her fourth day of convalescence, she awoke to an emptied ward and the surprising news that Magistrate Robertson would be paying her a confidential visit.

He arrived with Dr. Parker and a fat well-dressed *babu* in tow, who looked quite wealthy in a fine muslin *dhoti* and *kurta*, a *jamawar* shawl with brocade border, and gold embroidered *juttis* on his feet. Almost like Pratap Singh at their wedding. Jayanti felt the prickle of her old doubts—Was she really, truly, innocent of her husband's death? Or had she caused it by wanting more from life than him only?

She shrank herself into the sheets as the three men loomed over her bed with accusing eyes. At a hand flick from Dr. Parker, the ward nurse removed herself to the far corner of the room. Jayanti wondered what ill-words or curses these *sahibs* had come to pronounce upon her. But then she remembered the three goddesses of the fire and drew strength from the fact that *they* had called on her to live and that *they*—not these men—had the divine and decisive say over her future.

The Magistrate began. To her, his English sounded like a dog barking in fits and starts at something in the bushes outside the window. But Dr. Parker, always clean shaven with kind eyes, massaged every raspy outburst of the Magistrate into gentle, even if badly accented, Urdu. He said that the Company could not keep her there much longer and wished to make arrangements for her continued welfare and safety. The Magistrate had come himself, as "the incarnation of English Justice and Mercy," to offer what her native laws and traditions could not: "the power of choice."

Then he explained her three options.

"Firstly, you should be made aware that your in-laws, led by one, Hari Singh, have threatened to file suit for your return to their custody. They argue that you are, in effect, their property."

"But they will kill me," Jayanti pleaded, clutching the bed sheet at her neck. She glanced at the local man for corroboration but, with a quarter-smile of polite disdain, he kept his attention fixed on the white men.

"Actually," the doctor said, inclining his head and giving a satisfied smirk, "Magistrate Robertson here has prevailed upon your in-laws to spare your life. Of course, all your worldly possessions will pass to them, for the upkeep of your dead husband's children, but no physical harm will come to you. Rather, you will be dispatched to an *ashram* in Vrindaban to live out your days in widowhood."

Jayanti shook her head as if trying to unscrew it from her neck. She felt sure Hari Singh would not keep his promise to spare her life, and even if he did, what life was that? At eighteen years old, to have her hair shaved, to don the drab clothing of a widow, to become estranged from color, spice, laughter, and everything except the holy texts. To be confined to a monastic cell, entombed alive in a state of penance and privation, and never able to remarry or love. Had she rejected the pyre for this other death? No, she would not do it. Besides, such a life did not accord with the dynastic predictions the goddesses had uttered over her. No, she would not go.

"What else?" she asked.

Here, the magistrate cleared his throat before expelling another cluster of shaggy sentences, which the doctor then translated, but with a reddening face.

"Magistrate Robertson is willing to make... how shall we say... *accommodation* for you, at a guarded compound not more than a day's journey from here, where you would enjoy the company of other Hindoo ladies—among them widows, like yourself. You would have a small allowance to see to your needs and, in exchange, you would be required to... *entertain*... the Magistrate—and him *only,* I might add—upon the occasion of his weekly visit to you."

As he was speaking, Jayanti's gaze had rickshawed between the doctor's flushed face and the *babu's* brown one, which had hardened like fired clay. Between these reactions, she understood what was being offered: the same kind of loveless nights she'd shared with Pratap Singh galloping between her legs, the same kind of immobility she'd experienced under him and in his home—except, now, within the walls of a *ftrangi* man's compound.

"No," she half-whispered.

"Might you take time to consider the advantages of such a—"

She sat upright in the bed. "Never!" Her answer shot out like the crack of a whip, then recoiled and seemed to shatter the earthen vessel of her own heart. Words—more than she'd strung together since the funeral pyre, more than she remembered speaking since the day of her wedding—began to gush from her. She didn't even care if these English men understood what she was saying, but she had to say it anyway. Maybe the *babu* would understand, or maybe the nurse in the corner, if she spoke loudly enough. She had to profess to someone what she had seen on the pyre. How the Divine Mother had appeared to her in three different incarnations at once, and how the trio of goddesses had corroborated all she'd felt about wife-hood, and how they hadn't blamed her for discontent, but had changed the way she viewed her own purpose and enlarged her with such *shakti* that she'd loved herself enough to not want to die, but to want to live… *free*… to be the mother of generations. For the first time in her life, she had true faith.

She ended, breathless, and sat with eyes bulging, chest heaving, hair wild and uncombed around her damp face. After a long moment, the doctor double-cocked his head in her direction, tapped his forehead as if to indicate she was deranged, and mumbled a few words (she understood "jadoo," black magic) to the Magistrate, who then pivoted on his heel and fled the ward.

Dr. Parker gave a slight bow and said, "Magistrate Robertson accepts your decision. However, on the day he saved you, he made an oath to secure your welfare. The English justice system is founded upon the sanctity of one's *vrat*. So, he commends to you a third choice, which will be detailed by this good man here, a licensed *arkatti*, working under the auspices of the Agent General of Immigration. You can trust him. Farewell, Miss."

The doctor left, and Jayanti remained alone with the *babu*, whose face softened into an oily smile that made her think of rancid coconuts. Out of the corner of her eye, she saw the nurse move closer.

The man introduced himself as Gupta and said he had come

to make sure she never again had to turn a millstone.

"What then, Gupta-ji?" she asked.

The man explained that he could take her to a beautiful *tapu*, an island, far away, where no one had heard of her dead husband or her failed *sati* and no one would cause her shame. She would be fed, clothed, and housed generously, and all she would have to do was *cheenee chalay*—sift some sugar—then collect her own big, big salary of sixteen cents a day. She could live free of all the rituals of widowhood, if she wanted to. Or she could marry again—the island was teeming with Brahmin men eager for Indian wives—so she could easily start over and find love. And if she didn't like it there, she could simply say so and come home in one year. All she had to do right now, Gupta stressed, was put her thumbprint on this *girmit*—he pulled the document from under his shawl—and the matter would be settled.

"Please excuse. Time for her medicine." The nurse tramped loudly toward the bed carrying a tray of bottles and jars that Jayanti had not seen since her arrival at the hospital.

"Just a moment longer," Gupta said in an irritated tone. "She must sign, and I will be done here."

"Yes, most honorable Gupta-ji," the nurse replied. "You may stay, if it pleases you, while I perform certain daily matters of a female nature. Unless to look upon such would render you ritually impure, in which case there is a bench just outside the door where you may wait. I won't be long." With a flourish, the nurse began to peel away Jayanti's bedsheet, which caused the man to wheel in disgust and hurry toward the door.

The moment it swung shut, the nurse grabbed Jayanti's hand. "Do not sign," she begged. "This man is always in here, talking to patients—both men and women—waving around his *girmits* and forcing them to sign."

"He's not forcing me."

"Then they disappear and no one knows what happens to them. I have heard stories though. In your husband's house, maybe you never heard them... but I have. They will take you down-river and lock you up inside a big boat, they will feed you unclean and polluted things and force you to accept their white god. Can you not return instead to your father's house?"

Had the news of her "failure"reached her home village yet? Had her father and brothers cursed at the banana tree beneath which her navel-string was buried? Had they disowned her? Even if they hadn't, even if they'd let her return, all they would be able to offer was a daily plate of food and a shelter, not true redemption. And all she would be bringing to them was the stench and shame of her husband's untimely death and her failed *sati*. She loved her family too much to subject them to such ridicule. "I have neither father nor brother,"she lied. "So I have to go to this new place, this island. I want to go and have a new life, *bhauji*."

"*Are bap re*!"the nurse replied. "They will make you cross the dark waters, and you will be cursed forever, with no caste or protection from our gods. You will die in a strange land, among strange people and your body will not know the dignity of fire, they will throw you into a pit."

At this Jayanti laughed. It started as a guttural chuckle and then her whole body became so wracked by amusement that it shook tears, as fat and viscous as nectar, from her eyes. She snorted, "So, I will lose nothing then."

The English sub-agent sat in his sweltering Calcutta office. Behind him, just outside a small window but within speaking distance, the *punkah-wallah* worked the rope controlling the linen blades of a ceiling fan. Unfortunately, the bloody thing seemed to be emitting only hot air today as the Sub-Agent perused the latest manifest: a cargo of coolies, who'd just been brought down the Hoogly River on Gupta's *pulwar* vessel. Alas, only five women among them—which was surprising because he'd promised Gupta a higher-than-normal rate for "good females." When added to the sixty this depot had amassed from other recruiters, the tally was still short. By law, *The Hummingbird* could not sail for the West Indies without forty indentured women per hundred indentured men.

Typically, most indentureship rules resembled white threads that could be tinted, by personal interpretation, to be any color a sub-agent wanted (make the doctor examine them "thoroughly"... make sure to feed them "regularly"... keep the men and women "separately"); but with numbers and quotas there was no leeway. His boss, the Agent General of Immigration ("Toppy"as he was commonly referred to among sub-agents), was fastidious and known for revoking a man's appointment because of sloppy numbers and breached quotas.

"For godssake, bring *pani*!" the sub-agent called out, causing another turbaned native, seated outside the door, to enter and refill the brass jar of drinking water on the desk. The sub-agent poured some into a mono-grammed goblet and sipped slowly, contemplating the stack of leather-bound books beside the water—coolie registration book, depot accounts books. Would *they* be the death of him, or would it be this oppressive heat or some heathen sickness? The longer a ship was delayed, the longer these recruited coolies would continue eating, pissing, shitting, and spreading their diseases around. And almost as costly was their spreading of virulent lies about the indentureship—that they were being collected for torture rituals, that they'd be hung by their heels and oil extracted from their heads—which caused the weak-minded recruits to grow frightened and, every now and then, run away. Last month, one hapless soul had even slit his own throat, right there in the depot yard. Every delayed coolie, every dead coolie, strained the depot's fraying budget just a little bit more.

"Pull harder, man!" the sub-agent, desperate for cool untainted air, barked at the *punkah-wallah* as the fan slowed. One could never be sure if these bloody natives were doing their best or just pretending, so as to dupe unsuspecting Englishmen. Take Gupta, for instance: the slick-tongued *arkatti* had promised to deliver a *pulwar* full of good women, a promise which the sub-agent had, in turn, relayed to Toppy ("I assure you, sir, *The Hummingbird* shall sail at this month's end.") But now, Gupta had reneged. The only way the shipment might yet prove valuable is if the five new women were of sufficiently high quality: something other than prostitutes and the immoral, low-caste women who usually passed through.

Adjusting his sweat-soaked collar, the sub-agent returned his full concentration to the manifest, trying to decipher the appalling penmanship of this bugger, Gupta, who harbored illusions of being fluent in English. One entry did look interesting: a widow, of good Rajput caste, who'd attempted *sati*—which meant she possessed some virtue. In fact, see here: Gupta had made notes on her *girmit*, describing her as "holy"and "comely." In other words, exactly the type of woman he'd been told to find. The sub-agent rifled through his desk, looking for the *girmit* of another recruit, a male, whom Gupta had brought in last week on an earlier shipment. The man had asked to be married before leaving India. "Perhaps he's gotten whiff of the quim-shortage in the sugar-colonies," the sub-agent chuckled to himself. Apparently, according to Toppy's most recent communique, there was an ongoing "wave of unrest among Indian indentured men." The poor blokes had become so desperate for cunny that they'd started sharing women and then killing each other in jealous fits of rage. The last thing His Majesty needed was a tribe of horny barbarian men, with sharp agricultural implements, roving the islands. An influx of "good" Indian females, who could not only work the fields, but also be paired off to help "engender secure family life," would defuse the problem, Toppy had written.

"Ah-ha!" Here was the man's *girmit*. The sub-agent's chest ballooned as he reflected on the awesome scope of his saving power. He could protect this Rajput woman. She was in grave danger. Everyone knew that coolie women were ravenously sexual creatures, made manageable only by the strictures of religion and family. Being newly outcast, if she was subjected to the conditions of plantation life and the competition for her affections, she would surely plummet into the depths of her heathen nature. She had to be married off now, *before* arrival in the colonies. And such a marriage would also keep this lonely male recruit from meeting a violent end, amidst the cane stalks of a faraway land.

"Bring *them* to me!" the sub-agent called to the "water-boy" who, to save money, often doubled as interpreter and office assistant because, if nothing else, the sub-agent was an honorable Christian and a fine Civil Servant, always about His Majesty's business.

For Jayanti, it had been one thing to talk boldly while in the hospital: to declare herself free of *ghunghats* and veils, to claim she belonged nowhere and was willing to go anywhere. But it had been another thing altogether to step into the street and have the unforgiving sun slap the bare skin of her face, and to endure the equally hostile glares of those village people who'd happened to be there when she'd been escorted from the hospital, down the *ghat*, to the waiting *pulwar* of Gupta-ji. In the darkness of the boat's hull, greeted by the whites of so many eyes, she'd almost screamed and clambered back up the ladder; but thankfully, she'd been hurried behind a heavy curtain, to an area where only she and four other women were housed for the duration of their river journey down to Calcutta. After several weeks—she wasn't sure how many—they'd arrived today, joining the clog of boats upon the flattest part of the Hoogly River. Jayanti had peered through the porthole at this muddy ant-nest of scurrying bodies, noxious smells, and clanging unintelligible voices. She'd felt nauseous for the first time since boarding the boat, and terrified to leave its dark and close-walled interior.

But then the *pulwar* had turned, taken a different tributary, and the clutter of vessels had thinned. Along one bank of the river, lush, manicured gardens came into view—like something from her dreams, the kind of place she'd once imagined her handsome savior-prince taking her to live. She'd thought again of Pratap Singh then, and felt her insides prickled by thorns of guilt. Could she have done anything differently?

One of the other women, seemingly entranced by the beautiful scenery, had begun to sing in her own language, and although Jayanti hadn't understood the words, she'd recognized in the tune notes of lamentation and regret. She'd wept openly then, sobbing into her loosened scarf. All the women had wept, but none had said why.

Then, suddenly, the *pulwar* had docked at a jetty on the opposite bank from the gardens. Jayanti and the other *girmityas* had been led off by one of Gupta's boatmen, taken through an open yard, past a temple, into a large shed where the five women had been herded to an inner room. They were told they'd remain there until the *malik* could complete their intake and registration. It could be days, the boatman had said. Weeks, even.

Yet, the goddesses were still with Jayanti, for here she was, only a few hours later, seated on a mat in the office of the sweaty white *malik* who talked and talked and, despite having an interpreter, kept pronouncing her name as "Shanti."

Beside her, on his own mat, was another man. Indian, like her. The *malik* called him "Joe Paul," but who knew what his name actually was—Gopal... Chapal... Trupal? He was very dark-skinned, long and lean—his wrists fine, his knees and elbows knobby as if he'd been hungry for a long, long time. An ex-convict, Jayanti guessed. With those gangly arms, probably a thief. What had he stolen? Grain, flour, corn, rupees? The harvests had been bad these last few years, Pratap Singh had often said. She could not see the man's face well, as they were both facing the *malik*, but she could feel that the scrawny soul was also assessing her, as best he could under the circumstances.

A shout came from outside in the yard. There was some ruckus—wailing, cursing, even cheering—then Gupta's boatman ran in calling, "*Malik! Malik!* An escape! In the river but his swimming is not good!" The white man and his assistant ran to the other side of the office, where a large window gave full view of the yard, its pier, the *pulwar*, and the river. Without turning around, Jayanti guessed the escapee was heading for the gardens on the other side—that's what she would do, if she had to, if the nurse's warnings of torture turned out to be true.

Then, in the quiet below all the clamor, the man next to her whispered, "May the Lord of Crossings give our brother strength. *Jaya Hanuman Jaya, Jaya Hanuman.*" He spoke the Bhojpuri dialect of her father's village. And although she knew the prayer had not been for her, hearing it in her mother-tongue made Jayanti feel as if the goddesses themselves had sent a message of support, through this humble emaciated man.

She turned to him. "I am Jayanti. What are you called?"

"I am Gopal," he said solemnly, eyes downcast as he picked at a raggedy toenail. "I am seeking a wife."

"I am not seeking a husband," she replied, suddenly understanding why she'd been called to this office.

Then Gopal laughed with no trace of irony or derision, simply threw his head back, and such merriment filled his eyes and his cheeks that he no longer seemed as gaunt. Jayanti's mind flew over her two years with Pratap Singh: she'd only ever seen him laugh like this with his brothers, never with her; and had she spoken to him as she'd just done to this man, more than likely he or his mother would have smacked her.

Jayanti closed her eyes and shook her head as the last broken threads of her marriage, tinted red with regret, now seemed to leach their color and float away. She felt free to join Gopal in his muted but shoulder-heaving laughter. And for a moment, it was as if she had never been on the pyre, never been betrothed, never left the hut where she'd slept and played with her nieces. For a moment, she was an innocent girl again.

"I will wait," Gopal said to her, with a gleam of admiration in his eyes, and he repeated these words to the *malik* and interpreter when they returned. "I will wait for this one."

Yet two weeks later, when Jayanti boarded the *jahaj*, the biggest ship she had ever seen, she did so not as some broken rudderless female being forced by a tide of misfortune, or as a bow-headed obedient wife, but with the volition of a free, single and casteless woman.

She made neither objection nor correction when the new white man on board read her registration card, haphazardly scribbled by the depot *malik*, and accounted for her as "Shanti." Instead, she made a choice to become this new woman, this Shanti, crosser of forbidden oceans. She did not join those *jahajis* who tried to linger on the top deck or rush to a porthole below to watch, with wails, prayers, and breast-beating, as India, their *bhaarat maata*, receded. She, Shanti, stood aside, with her friend Gopal who had left the ranks of male *jahajis* to find her on the crowded deck. Together, they craned for a glimpse of the fiercely naked horizon ahead, believing and assuring each other that the Lord of Crossings... *Jaya Hanuman*... was with them. She hadn't been surprised when Gopal, despite all the commotion on board, had almost miraculously manifested at her side. He'd done the same, for the past fourteen days, protecting her from the lechery of the depot yard and from its often-violent competition for food rations—even though she'd steadfastly refused to become his bride.

And almost with clockwork choreography, they fell into the same pattern of interaction as the *jahaj* sailed toward the Cape of Good Hope, and the days at sea turned into weeks. Despite their separation "tween decks"—he with the single men in the fore, she with the single women in the aft—Gopal never seemed to be far from the corner of her eyes. He materialized even nearer at mealtimes when they could chat a little, and at tense moments when other *jahaji* men ventured too close, or when she was headed for the latrines and had to walk past the sailors lingering outside. Shanti was grateful, because within days of boarding, it had become apparent that the latrine-walk was where the seamen, both the whites and the dark ones with woolly hair ("negroes," she was told, from the same *tapu* to which they were sailing), seduced or baited *jahaji* women. The white officers were even bolder, coming below deck at night and grabbing whomever they wanted. But thanks to Gopal, everyone seemed to assume she was spoken for, and she'd been left alone.

But one night, following a meal of mutton that had smelled spoilt and had roiled her stomach all evening, Shanti asked the *sirdar's* permission to go to the bathroom. Gopal was already asleep, so she hastened past him and up the hatch. It was during her return that it happened. So quickly—a shove against the wall, a hand over her mouth, a deep stab into her belly, a twitching throb, his skin so black that he was invisible except for the yellowish whites of his eyes—that she decided to believe she was still asleep and it had been nothing more than a dream, nothing more than the dark Lord, Krishna mistaking her for one of his *gopis*. And it felt so similar to what she'd known with Pratap Singh, that she assumed this searing pain, this sensation of being cleaved and hacked, was how congress always felt for a woman, and that there was nothing inauspicious about this "dream."

When her nausea began during the fifth week aboard, she told herself it was the food; and when the retching wouldn't abate, she told herself it was the effects of the *Pagal Samundar* they'd all been warned about, the mad seas where two oceans met. And when the fullness began to make her breathing difficult, she told herself it was because of the woolen petticoat, worsted stockings, and flannel jacket she'd been made to wear for the weather. But when the distended heaviness in her mid-section began to make it impossible for her to sleep on her tummy, she conceded to herself that no god or spirit had raped her, it had been a mortal man.

A negro sailor? An Indian *jahaji*? She did not know.

"And now my lap has been filled," she confessed to Gopal, with tears in her eyes as they squatted on the top deck, picking through the edible bits of some rotten potatoes. "But I did not want for it to happen in this way, *bhai*."

"Can you show who it is? For I will gladly kill him and throw my soul into the *kala pani* afterward. I will do it tonight, I will—"

"Then what will become of me… and this child?" She grabbed his hand—yes, touched him, for the first time. It was her way of finally accepting the awkward marriage proposal he had made so many weeks ago in the office of the depot *malik*. But would Gopal be offended now, she worried, would he withdraw the offer, believing that it was only her change in circumstances and not a change of heart precipitating her yes?

When he stood and walked away from her without saying a word, she took it as an answer. Her tears flowed faster, and she looked across to the edge of the deck and pictured herself running toward it and doing just as Gopal had threatened, releasing both her soul and the child's to the dark waters. But then, gurgling somewhere in the recesses of her mind, she heard again the goddess' song and knew that with or without Gopal, she would survive this odyssey.

It was only later that night, at dinner, she learnt that he'd gone straight to the *sirdar* and made his request for marriage officially known. Gopal had told her this with a beaming smile and they'd held hands again, for longer. And during week-nine, as *The Hummingbird* glided into the warmer waters of the open Atlantic, she and Gopal exchanged vows publicly before the ship's captain, who pronounced her, "Mrs. Shanti Gopaul."

No one heard, though, the *vrats* the couple made privately to each other on their wedding night, lying on side-by-side mats now, in the middle, married-section of the hold. No longer, they swore with clasped hands, would they depend on fickle deities; this journey was the last time they would let themselves be tossed and tumbled at the whim of unseen forces. In the new land ahead, they and their no-caste children—the one in her belly and the others to come—would choose their own gods and make their own luck. But, unknown to Gopal (because all women have their secrets), Shanti kept one vestige of her old life tucked away, in the innermost pocket of her heart. It was the divine promise—*three generations of silver, one generation gold*—which would ever remain the source of her personal faith and *dharma*, until a tropical night, a half-century later, when her soul would leave a cane-cutting village in South Trinidad and make its longest and last crossing.

After her final breath, as Gopal sat at her bedside, surrounded by their eleven no caste children and thirty-six grandchildren, he recited, yet again, this story. It had grown longer, more intricate and more embellished over their years in the New World, until no one—not even he—knew what was true and what was not, what memories were pure and what had been polluted.

And when he was finished speaking, one little grandson named Lall jumped up, drew a cardboard sword from his waist, aimed it to the heavens, and declared: *Jayanti zindabad! Long live Jayanti*!

OUTSIDERS

1973, Bagatelle, Trinidad, West Indies

Behold, we are *bois*. We've always existed and we were once everywhere. Now, although carved from the southern continent and pushed back to the fringes of this island, still we see and listen and know—anything we don't know must've occurred in a city or town far from forest. Here, though, on this Trinidad mountain wrapped in an ever-climbing vine of squatter settlements, we know *all* things. We stand, a proud infantry, shielding ganja fields, bootlegging stills, and Black Power camps. We are no less noble than our cousins, Sierra Maestra and Andes, who've hidden generations of freedom fighters. In that honorable tradition, we shapeshift, confusing army and police, tripping their heavy black boots, delaying their discovery of camouflage fluttering above bagfuls of weevilled rice and box-crates of ammunition. For we believe, as the revolutionaries do, that this land belongs to "the people," and that outsiders bring discord. Watch us bristle now, as reporters from television—*state*-owned—enter this village called Bagatelle.

Their van has exhausted the paved road. The lady and two men alight, shoulder cords and cameras, and start climbing the steep track. Some of us find it amusing how the trio eeks and shrieks, slips and slides, like incompetent *bachac* ants. But the oldest among us shakes royal fronds resembling dreadlocks and cautions, "Laugh today, cry tomorrow," recalling the gutting and felling, the shooting and dying, that always results from strangers entering our woods.

"Morning! Anybody home?" the reporters shout at each shack. They receive, mostly, the doleful blinking of bare-chested, underwear-clad children seated on rickety stairs, sucking mangoes or digging noses.

The reporters resort to patois, calling, "*Bonjou! Bonjou, tout moun*!" as if these people would fall for some mangled *kwéyòl.*

Yet some squatters do emerge. Not the men. They are either in the city working, or inside sleeping off last night's babash rum, or outside behind the plywood houses smoking and staring into our verdant lushness, wondering if they too should join the guerillas and if Black Power will make them as wealthy as white people.

It is the squatter-women—ever practical—who face the outsiders. With old skirts pulled up like armor over sagging breasts, thick-soled feet shod with righteous indignation, mahogany legs planted like fenceposts, arms squared like gates.

"*Koté ou sòti*?" each woman asks.

"Ma'am, we're from TTT News. We have unconfirmed reports of a "buck" here in Bagatelle. Have you seen a tiny man lurking? And if so, do you believe he's a buck?"

A *buck*? The women wonder if that's really what this posh-looking reporter just said? She doesn't seem the type to believe a midget-demon can live in a bottle and bring wealth or destruction, depending on how much milk and bananas you feed him.

Some make the sign of the cross and whisper, "*Bondjé-Oh*," backpedaling inside.

But a *grappe* of women remain and profess they *have* seen a short ugly man entering the forest, his stature too small and his hair too straight to be a Black Power soldier.

This, yes *this*, is the *commess* the reporters are seeking! The camera clicks and, on cue, the residents molt from cagey to charismatic, performing for the lens, hoping there might be a lil *cacadah*—maybe five or ten dollars—in exchange for sufficiently dramatic material. Watch them hand-chopping their legs, at varying levels, indicating the buck's height: thigh high; no, some say knee; others say mid-calf.

We know they are all lying: he's even shorter than that. We know his name is Godfrey. He's asleep right now, concealed within us like a primal memory, in the shelter he and the Indian boy, Shiva, have fashioned from the twisted remnants of a gilded cage. They meet secretly, at night. And because we've heard all their plans, we tremble when the reporters arrive at Shiva's house.

We rock ourselves, cedars creaking, bamboo clattering warily as, to everyone's surprise, the crew is invited inside by the Gopauls—the only Indians on this mountain—who've seemed content to remain outsiders: old-thief Lall, thirteen-year-old Shiva, and That Town Woman who whores in the city and who only lives here a few months at a time before disappearing for longer stretches. Nobody knows where she goes. But the boy calls her "Mammy," and the only time he seems happy, eats well, and goes to school, is when she's here.

This wayward, *vaykivay*, family are the last people on God's green earth who should risk talking to reporters. *Ki mélè zé nan kalenda wòch*? What business have eggs in the dance of stones?

Through their chicken-wire windows, we have a clear view as the cameraman positions the Gopauls on a faded love seat, Lall center-frame. Insufficient room for shoulders and elbows, so the family sits hunched in awkward intimacy, afraid to betray anything other than the unity expected in Indian homes. Oh how shameful, should viewers conclude that living amongst blacks has somehow eroded their values. In fact, Lall has consistenly reminded Shiva that, despite their roast *baigan* skin, curly (almost kinky) hair, and wide-ish nostrils, they are pure. He is proud that, unlike negroes, he can name his immigrant grandparents—Shanti and Gopal—and say from where in the motherland they'd come. "So don't let no creole fool you with Black Power talk," he drills into Shiva's head, "that's a scam to use Indians against the white man, and then turn 'round and continue calling we 'coolie' afterwards. Is *we* must outsmart *them*!"

Lall does all the talking with the reporters. "One day, outta nowhere, a voice start abusing my good wife: saying she bottom rosy, and if is good sex and plenty money she want… come go back Guyana with he."

That Town Woman sighs, cinches her blouse, impersonates a virtuous *dulahin*. Shiva, meanwhile, stares at the knees of his school pants and hopes not to be called upon to bad-talk the buck, his new secret friend. He knows Godfrey doesn't really mean those words, but how else can a lil, two-by-four man hurt a giant prideful bully?

Lall continues his buck-story like it's a sequel to *The Ramayana* and he is the great Lord Rama himself. "So I grab my *pooyah*… the blade always sharp… and I threaten him, 'Come out, if you name man!' I search too, shine torchlight everywhere, but I never see nobody. Still, the voice keep coming back, cussing we stink… especially me."

Then Lall pivots from vedic hero to victim. "Me eh know why this buck hate me so. Is because I's a Indian? Maybe he pushing a Black Power head? But I does steady tell my son, "If yuh not white, yuh black. All of we—Indian and creole—is one.

So I asking the neighbors, police, soldier-man-and-them, even freedom-fighters… Comrades, if allyuh spot this buck, kill 'im dead one-shot, before he kill *me*, Lall Gopaul, a brother after your own heart."

He raises a fight-the-power fist. Yet despite what he's said, Lall knows *exactly* why Godfrey hates him; that's why he wants Godfrey silenced. *We* know this and Shiva knows it too, so he slices eyes at his father, in disgust. Only That Town Woman is clueless: she wasn't here two weeks ago when Lall came home, out of breath, squeezing the knot of a garbage bag. "Move fast," he'd gasped, almost kicking Shiva off the cinder blocks stacked as stairs at the front door. "Come inside now!"

Shiva had been waiting for their down-the-hill neighbor, Miss Jackie, to signal from her window that he could pass for a plate of *pelau*. She was one of the negro women who took pity whenever Lall left him with nothing but salt-biscuit and water. But, Shiva knew, Lall would put a good cutarse on him if he learned the boy was accepting charity from black people.

Obediently, Shiva closed the door.

"Lock it," Lall said, setting the bag down near the back door, in a cool, shadowy spot. "Don't touch this. Is a parrot I selling Chang, the hardware-man."

"Ok," Shiva shrugged, picturing another blue-and-yellow macaw or other smuggled Amazonian bird. Those were big-money or big-jail, so Lall was careful with them.

"I goin and sleep." Lall's eyes were indeed red, as they typically were after several nightshifts on Farfan Estate, but he had an alert, almost fearful expression. "Don't open for nobody, don't even answer, you hear?"

Oh, but at his father's first snores, we spied Shiva slinking out to Miss Jackie.

On his tip-toed return…*singing*? An Indian song Lall liked, but this voice was lower. And was it coming from the eight-track player? No, from the garbage bag, and without the nasal monotone of parrot-singing. Sure, Lall sometimes caught other birds on the estate, but no *picoplat* or *chickichong* could croon like this—too real, too sad, and too human-like.

Gently, Shiva loosed the bag. Wow! A cage unlike any he'd seen, a dome of golden metal, a house for a very rich bird. Except that *thing* inside, wearing a white vest and khaki shorts, was no bird. It was a… man? As tall as a twelve-inch ruler, round head on a rounder body, but spindly limbs.

"W-w-hat you is?" Shiva asked.

"What *I* is?" the creature scoffed. "*You* is a son-of-a… thief."

"I know, but who you is? Chang family?" The little man had a toasty complexion and his lank hair hung over oblique eyes and a wide flat nose, as if he were a miniature version of the half-Chinese-half-Indian hardware proprietor.

In two bow-legged waddles, he crossed the cage and raised himself onto the golden bird-swing. "I's Godfrey, Mr. Farfan buck. I sure your father mention me. Boy… bacchanal on the estate today! Farfan send the estate manager, Persad, to let-go your father and some others. He say was for thiefing, nah. But everybody know Farfan done sell-out the land… quiet, quiet… to them British white people, and planning to fire every-damn-body, with no severance pay. Well, Lall decide he hadda leave with something after so much years. So, when Persad gone, Lall break the office window and *raff* me. He threaten to strangle me if I bawl, *oui*."

Shiva dropped to his stomach, eye-level with the creature, and asked, "So-o-o… you's a *real* buck, then?"

Godfrey swung forward and seized the golden bars on

either side of Shiva's nose. "You deaf ? Yes! Now, come, let we go. I sure Persad done call police. Them looking for your father already. If he make a jail, who go mind you? Everybody know your mother don't be around. Carry me back, quick. For your own sake, *bai*. Before you remain with only these *kapar* people you can't trust."

The buck's prediction made the boy quiver. Lall was a country-bookie-come-to-Town from some southern village packed tight with cane-cutting Indians, yet he'd never spoken of family—except the grandparents from India, who he esteemed like deities. So, for Shiva, other relatives were make-believe creatures. And his mother was just an occasional apparition. Bad as he was, only Lall was real. And now, this buck—this Godfrey, with his forecast of orphanhood—he was *real.*

Shiva jumped up and unlatched the back door, then re-tied the bag while explaining to Godfrey, "We go pass through the forest, follow the treeline down to the main road and..." He was about to say, "catch the bus to the estate," when he remembered he had no passage-money.

"Well, find some. Police coming," Godfrey urged, thinking of Farfan's imported milk and Lacatan bananas.

Shiva dashed to Lall's bedroom, then followed a tried-and-true process: ease door, step inside, gauge Lall's breath, move to the rhythm. He'd done this countless times, for the sake of trifles like snacks and comic books. *This* time his cause was important, he believed.

But alas, a *dotish* mistake: he dropped Lall's pants. We say "dotish" because we know that *he*, more than anyone else, more than That Town Woman, more than any of the other women who visited that bedroom while That Town Woman was away, *he* who had borne the hot imprint of Lall's belt most often, *he* should have remembered the sound the buckle would make on the wooden floor.

Like an un-dead corpse, Lall arose and seized Shiva's wrist. "Aye! What you doing!"

Luckily, a hammock is no easy thing to exit, stale-drunk. Shiva slipped from Lall, then sprinted to the back door and snatched the bag, reckoning he could lose his father in the bush (*Truly, we would have helped!*), make it to Farfan Estate and return Godfrey, thus saving everyone before nightfall. But halfway out the door, Lall bulldozed the boy's skinny, sapling spine. They wrestled... son over father, father over son... while the bag bounced away and came to settle in our midst.

The black plastic was shredded, the golden metal was dented, the little door dangled. Godfrey was ejected onto our leaf-littered soil, his feet connecting as if by magnetism. We knew at once he was no demon, but rather a man who'd lived within us before, in a different place. We welcomed him with blossoms of immortelle and poui. And when he hungered that night, we lowered *barbadine*, *caimate* and some *sikea* fig; we echoed the gush of Blue Basin Falls, from bark to bark, so he could follow and quench his thirst. By dawn, he was already forgetting Farfan's full-cream milk and spotless bananas, as he recollected a different island. A fragment of rainforest floating in a tributary of the mighty Orinoco, the only place he'd ever walked free, where he'd once been a chief among a tribe of men his own size; the place he'd had to forget in order to survive within a golden cage.

"Things does just be disinappearing," That Town Woman is telling the camera. She claims that, last week, a *roti* towel sailed out the backdoor while her back was turned, cooking. Shiva had given chase and saw the towel drop into the bush, but he'd returned saying, "It just gone—*poof!*— when I reach it."

While she talks, the boy sits wide-eyed, recalling all he's stolen for Godfrey since the fight with Lall: that towel, to use as a sheet; two washrags to fold into a pillow; a cigarette lighter, a can opener…

"Oh God, watch how my son trembling, nah! Like we frightening the child with all this demon-talk?" Still performing for the cameras, That Town Woman massages Shiva's knee. His thigh muscles retract. When was the last time his mother touched him so tenderly? Maybe he was a baby? He is relieved when Lall finally shoves her aside and retakes the spotlight.

"Every time I buy grocery, something gone from the cupboard next day." Lall talks as if he regularly buys food, as if he's had a job these last two weeks. In fact, it was That Town Woman who coincidentally arrived, the morning after Godfrey's escape, with a box of groceries and her usual greeting, "Lall! Shiva! Look I reach!"

At her voice, Lall had frantically unlocked the back door and summoned Shiva from the forest where he'd banished him the night before: *Don't come back here until you find that buck! If you make me loss that sale, I go kill your ungrateful backside.*

Shiva had slept on cardboard under the house. Then, around dawn, we watched with Godfrey as the tear-stained boy staggered toward us and sank onto a mossy boulder. He surveyed our crowded undergrowth, contemplated our canopy, then studied our hanging lianas and scrotum-like bird nests, wondering where to find the buck.

From within the flames of a nearby *balisier* bush, Godfrey spoke. "Me eh know your father so brutal. He does tell everybody on the estate how he love he son so much. Me never thought he does beat you so."

"Only sometimes," Shiva said, not understanding why he felt the need to defend his father and explain that Lall *did* show him love. Lall was generous after every big pay-day, taking him into Town, treating him to new shoes from Bata or clothes from Woolworth's or ice cream from Dairy Queen. And Lall had pawned his gold chain to buy high school books and uniforms last year. And he'd even poisoned the dog belonging to those people up the hill who'd spit on Shiva and called him a "coconut oil coolie."

"Daddy not that bad," Shiva insisted.

Godfrey's gusty sigh disturbed the ferns at Shiva's ankles. "True, nobody born bad. I born since that first Victoria-queen. I see plenty things, *bai*. So I could tell you: loneliness does twist-up and bitter man heart like ginger. God never make nothing to live by theyself. We 'pose to be part of something bigger. That's the first mistake your father did make: leaving the village to come out here by he-self, with people who not cut from the same *sari* cloth."

Shiva grunted, unconvinced that these musings bore any relevance to *his* problem: how to recapture this blasted buck *and* his father's favor.

Then Godfrey added, "A good woman could turn a man life into something bigger. But that's the second mistake your father make: he choose to love That Town Woman, that scunt who born up-this-side, so she don't know nothing 'bout *pyar* and duty and sacrifice, she only know black people ways."

But Shiva loved that "scunt." She was his mother—and, unlike Lall, he'd been given no choice in the matter—so it seemed *he* also had a twisted-heart problem. He sniffied and smashed his heels harder against the rockface, trying to create some other explanation for his tears.

"I could still carry you back by Farfan," he mumbled, feeling a fresh urge to spite Lall.

"Nah. After all this *jhanjhat* today, I going home. A place with only tall forest, small people, and woman my size. The one time in my life I ever leave, I wake up in a cage, on a boat heading here. Trini-people does pay big-money for Guyanese buck, but I never thought them smugglers woulda ever catch *me.* My luck change now, though: I free. And I could change your luck, too, Shiva. For only three hundred dollars, we could be free together, far from Bagatelle."

"And we missing the eight-track player and some cartridge."

"And my expensive picture of Christ that does light up."

"And money, and—"

Lall and That Town Woman are growing staler and staler on camera.

The reporter-lady's gaze meanders to Shiva, who's been compulsively swallowing, his throat writhing like a provoked *macajuel.* This boy has something to say, she decides.

"Have you seen the buck?" she asks kindly.

To Shiva, her face is too wide and eager, like a spring-trap for *lappe* and *agouti.* He feels cornered and has to look away as he mumbles, "Yeahhh, but…" Should he cover-up his father stealing Godfrey? Should he blame Godfrey for all the things he himself has taken and sold in an effort to raise three hundred dollars? The boy feels drained by weeks of lies and secret-keeping.

"He don't cuss *me*," he continues, but then… the Freudian slip, "He does sing for me. Since the first day Daddy bring him here he been singing in Indian, Spanish, Warahoon—all kinda South-American language."

"Boy!" Lall reaches over and clouts Shiva twice. "What chupidness you talking! I never bring no buck here!"

"Mr Gopaul!"

"Lady, this buck bewitching my son. He need knocking back to he senses, that's all!"

Then, seeing no sympathy on the woman's face, Lall begins to sniffle. "I eh thief no buck, ma'am. Is *he*-self follow *me* from work, saying I hadda mind him or something bad go happen. Oh God! My father did always say bad things does follow we Gopaul-family! Daiz why I did left the village and come Town to live, thinking the curse woulda remain behind. But look at the trouble I end up in. Me can't afford to mind no buck. Anybody who catch him, could keep him. Let him make *them* rich, I just don't want him here. I frighten for my family!"

Lall collapses into That Town Woman's lap, wailing. For Shiva, Lall's humiliation is a dream come true; he launches from the love seat, eager to kick a man while he's down. "Daddy, is you-self thief Godfrey! You always thiefing!"

Then, Shiva faces his mother and demands that she justify the warm tracks her fingertips have left upon his skin. "And *you*, Mammy? You have a heart? Who does bring a living thing in this world, just to love it now-and-again and once-in-a-while? *Who?*"

Since the broadcast, journalists have descended upon the Gopaul house like pothounds on a rubbish heap. The viewing public, enthralled by the buck-story, has hardly noticed the nation's Black Power Revolution fizzling out like a wet flambeau over the last fortnight: the forest camp was razed by government gunfire. Meanwhile, Lall has done wonders for race-relations among "the people." After repenting, he became the first Indian "Shango

Baptist"at Ezekiel Tabernacle, where Reverend Ethelbert, an Afro-haired, dashiki-wearing clergyman, has hired him as night watchman. And from all over the island, Baptist visionaries—all black—have been moved by "the spirit of doption" to visit the Gopauls and bless them with cash, groceries, and prayers of exorcism.

Godfrey's all but gone.

Shiva has raised the cash for their escape: some for the guard at Caricom Jetty, some for the super-cargo, Prakash, who loads Persad's smuggling boat and minds its cargo until Guyana, and some for pocket change on the mainland. Godfrey knows, from years in the estate office, that the boat leaves every Thursday at 5:00 a.m. and that Prakash will stowaway anything, even a boy with a talking backpack, if the price is right.

Shiva is hiding in a quayside shed. Through wide doors, he spies the black-and-white length of the boat, *Indira*, lying in beside the quay wall. All night, he's crouched, hugging the backpack, dozing on-and-off to the buck's excited prattle: "After we find-back my people on the island, I go carry you Mahaica, where it have plenty pure Indian and no Black Power stupidness. You go fit in, man. You go see real power—how them does take care of they own. You go turn *bigsawatee*, with money and friends and gyal for so! You go breed, make endless children, and start your own new tribe. I promising you."

At 4:30, Prakash wakes Shiva. "Come, *bai*. Customs gone. We pushing off."

Shiva zips the bag, follows Prakash. The boat looms larger and larger. Can he turn back? Now, after all he's stolen? His cheek is cold and clammy. Dew, he tells himself because he won't admit tears as he arrives at the quay's edge. Not a big gap between wall and boat; he's jumped wider puddles in Bagatelle. And yet, he's terrified. Nearby, within the mist, a boat bellows a sound that makes his skin prickle. Daylight is coming. If he jumps now, day-after-tomorrow he'll be in Guyana, starting that better life Godfrey's promised. Better how? He cares nothing for tribes or purity! His belly roils as he rocks from leg to leg, slow-dancing with *Indira.*

"Come!" Prakash calls from the deck.

Shiva pictures himself leaping, but not clearing the gap.

"Jump, *bai*!" Godfrey demands, within the bag.

But Shiva's knees are knots and his toes have rooted. Twisting, he looks back at the shed. Then his eyes move beyond and climb the twinkling ridge of the mountain, to where his parents lie entwined on their new four-poster bed. His mother has seemed happier these days. Maybe she will stay? Maybe "better" is here?

"Shiva!" cries Godfrey. "Jump, you scunt! Or me go *bad-luck* you whole fuckin family: you mudda, you fadda, all you pickney and grand-pickney dem. Jump now!"

We are here too, tangled mangrove at port's edge. Our leaves plead with Shiva in an almost-forgotten tongue: *Kouwi pa lèd, tan lafòs pa la…* To run away is not ugly, when one has no strength.

Yet even *we* do not see the end coming.

The boy's heart surges so suddenly that all we know is what *you* know now: he has flung the bag mightily toward the deck but, as he races away, the wind—that holy, unseen hand—pushes it far and plunges it down into the *kala pani*, the vast and moody Caribbean Sea.

EVER SINCE WE SMALL

1987, Barrackpore Village, Trinidad, West Indies

That August holidays, after a year of matchmaking *commess* in the family, Pa did send me and Salma by Mammy sister, Tanty Nazroon, for she to learn we 'bout business-and-thing, just in case nobody ever ask again for we to marrid.

Nazroon shop was two streets away, we used to walk from home every day. But we did notice, early o'clock, Tanty couldn't do maths to save she life. And we did wonder how she manage to stay in business so long, and what *she* coulda ever teach *we*. And we did feel sorry-too-bad for she, so we did bring a lil calculator from home for she to use, but she say she didn't trust them small, small number that keep appearing and disin-appearing by theyself. That's how old people was in them days: you couldn't argue with them. You had was to swallow whatever they tell you. Otherwise, was cuss in your tail, or worse yet, two *cocoyea* broom on your back.

That's why we did take a good long while before we interrupt Tanty and the young, handsome stranger-man who did waltz in the shop, on that rainy Tuesday morning, trying to pay with a hundred-dollars bill. We did spend a good-few minutes watching one-another, back and forth, talking with we eyebrow, until we decide that is *Salma* who should *chook* she-self in the big-people conversation. Like how she did smarter in schoolwork—even though she did only thirteen years and I was done fifteen—we know Tanty woulda accept *she* maths much quicker than mines. You see, I was always the black sheep of the Mohammed family. Why? All because I did look scary when I born: tar-color skin, with long hair, long nails and two newborn teeth. Mammy say the midwife did tell she I woulda be a greedy child who woulda cause plenty grief. And she and Pa used to pound that talk in me and Salma head ever since we did small: one of we had blight, and one of we had *barakat.* Sometimes, I does feel things mighta turn out better for we, if only they did tell we something different 'bout we-self.

So that day, in the shop, I did keep my tail quiet and let Salma argue with Nazroon.

"Tanty, excuse, he check right. Is two dollars you have for the Mister," Salma did say, from where we did sit-down, on the stack of sweet-drink case, like two pigeon on a wall.

The *madrassi*-looking stranger-man—skin blue-black and shiny like them kaka-roller beetle—did just call for five *aloo* pie, two *saheena*, two b*aiganee*, plus three red sweet-drink, three banana sweet-drink, two cream soda, and one Express and one *Guardian* newspaper. In truth, that was more action than the lil village shop ever see on a Tuesday morning, but was still easy sums for we to check in we head—twenty dollars, total—so we didn't know how the hell Tanty get twenty-two.

"Look the calculator. You want it?" Salma say.

Steups! Tanty suck she teeth and say, "Keep that. I wukkin it out here the proper way, with pen-and-paper. This big-money he bring here, this hour of the morning, trying to addle my old-brain… and he watching me like I's a big thief, too."

"No Ma'am," the fella answer, and he drag he fingers through that pretty, curly hair he had. "I just sayin is a lil mistake, nah. I didn't mean to give you so much trouble with the hundred-dollars, but that's what the bossman gimme to pay with. But is ok, don't worry yourself. When you work it out, give she the two dollars to buy something nice."

He did point he lip in we direction then. "Hello, *sundar larki.* You beautiful just like your Mammy," he did say. And we did know one-time which one-ah-we he mean, because that's how it was in them days: everybody used to make the same comment 'bout Salma—*that smaller sister over-pretty. Oh God, she pretty-for-so!*—and then play like them ain't see nobody else right-dey next to she. In fact, the onliest person who did ever overlook Salma for me was the old-ass, grey-beard Imam from Woodland who did approach Pa, the year before, looking for a second wife: *Yasmeen have the right age. She might be ugly, but I go still take she off your hand. My madam too sickly for housework now, but this gyul big-and-strong like cattle, she make for labor.*

So, yes, we did know right away, was Salma that this young man in the parlor was asking 'bout.

Tanty Nazroon did rest down the pencil and turn to watch we. "Nah, them is my sister chirren. They helping me for the holidays. But you right: from since that lil one born, I did tell she mother: this child is me in print. We's the onliest fair-skin girls in the family, and with the same kinda pretty eye… like cat, nah."

Is true: Salma eye-them did really look greyish—a throwback, Mammy did tell we, to a Pakistani great-grandfather. But Tanty Nazroon eye was no closer to grey than goat shit, just like everybody else in the family. So we nearly buss-out laughing when she say that chupidness.

The young fella, too. If you see how he twist-up he two lip like he tying cow, just to hold back a laugh. But then he drop a sweet piece of *mamaguy* on Tanty when he say, "Oh gosh, yes, I seeing the resemblance plain, plain."

Well with that, Tanty start to blush down the place. She tone wasn't dry and grainy no more—it had plenty *surwah*—when she lean across the counter and say, "Here, take the two dollars, nah son."And when he ask what Salma name, Tanty force the girl to answer.

But the fella never take the money. He push it back and say, "No, give the *larki*,"and he tell we how he name Shiva Gopaul and how he working on the crew that fixing Rochard-Douglas Road.

Tanty Nazroon did have a way she used to waggle she head, to show she mean what she saying, nah. We notice how she well waggle it up when she tell the fella, "I's Tanty Naz, and my next niece over there name Yasmeen. Come back and ask we for anything allyuh fellas need, okay *son-ah?*"—that's how we did know Tanty blood really take to Shiva.

And he did waggle-back he own head, too, when he answer, "Okay, tomorrow then, Tanty," before he dart out in the rain.

But believe-you-me, if we coulda only know then, the *koochoor* Shiva woulda cause in we *cutiya,* we woulda run he ass out and lock the door that very first, fateful day. That blasted Shiva Gopaul mash-up we whole Mohammed family. You hear what I saying: wherever that man walk, he bring trouble like trouble is he birthright.

Anyway, let me slow down and take my time with the story, to make you understand.

After lunch, when was just two-ah-we alone in the shop, me and Salma did crouch down on the floor with a dog-ears Mills & Booms name *Duskftre.* We did find it couple days before, under Tanty old accounts book-and-them. Salma was the one who coulda read lil better, so every day, while Tanty pulling a sleep, Salma used to read two-three page, in a Radio Trinidad accent. From ever since we small, that girl did always like to put on airs and talk highfalutin. She did always feel she *dey* like white people, just because of she high-color skin and eye. But, then again, if I did look nice like she, I mighta do the same thing, *oui*.

So, Salma was speechifying one sexy, rip-blouse scene that had both-ah-we giggling down the place, when Shiva voice blast from the doorway like bamboo bussing on Divali night.

"Where Tanty? How come allyuh here by allyuh-self?"

We scramble up, and Salma push the book in she skirt waist, under she blouse; and like fright did make she tongue ready to sting like *jep*. She bawl, "Slow down your volume nah, man! Tanty pulling-a-five right in the hammock back dey. You go wake she up."

But then the two of we hang we head, waiting to see if Shiva mention the lovey-dovey book cover. If he did notice it, that woulda pour a fresh bucket of shame on we family—imagine a stranger-man mistaking we for two force-ripe *zaboca*—and worse yet, if he went and run he mouth in the village that we reading sex-book. Back then, them kinda bad-name on a young-girl in Barrackpore did worse than the AIDS-thing we did hearing 'bout on TV: one rumor, and nobody want you when time to marrid. We did see that happen to a few girls already. Like we cousin, Farida: somebody did see she with a boy behind the Form 4 Block, and the boy did boast up-and-down the village how he well feel-she-up and do rude-things to she body; but he refuse to marrid, so she father pluck she outta school and send she quite-to-hell Mayaro to marrid some fisherman who did never hear she history. She remain like a scary bedtime story in everybody head—something you does tell lil chirren to frighten them—like a *douen* or a *lagahoo* tale. And me and Salma did feel like we was one slip away from sliding down the same kinda hill.

Anyway, Shiva act like he never even notice the book. He only smile and push three dollars across Tanty Nazroon counter. "This for *you*, big sister," he say. "Me don't operate with favoritism at all, at all, at all. I done see too much of that in this work: the bossman paying them creole better than all the lil coolie fellas like me. He say we born to dig dirt and tote load. *Steups!* Anyway, hold this, big sister. You older than she, so is only fair you should get more."

With that, he leave the shop, but keep glancing back at we, the same way how the sun was playing hide-and-seek with the clouds that day, the same way how lovers does flirt-up in a Indian movie scene. We couldn't tell, though, which one-ah-we he did watching.

But—*papayo!*—one thing was for sure. I had three dollars to Salma two! For me to out-do my pretty-face sister in this stranger-man eyes, it did make me feel nice and shiny, like them penny and shilling and bob that Tanty used to bring home from NCB Bank. The onliest thing woulda feel more satisfying, is if Salma did get-on like she digging-a-horrors. But nah: she wasn't vex; she just pull out the Mills & Booms, and we jump right back inside the romance again, happy like pappy.

But now I look back and I could tell you plain: we was dotish. Oh God, we was over-too-dotish! We never even stop to wonder if was bad karma to take Shiva money, or why he hand was so free with he money, or what he did want back in exchange for he money. We was lil girls then, with nothing in we head except what Pa and Mammy did plant there since we born. We did trust every-shittin-body—yes, every man-jack-and-they-brother. But, most of all, we did trust one-another because we was *sisters*. We was the same two who did band together and call hunger strike for almost a week (although we did keep hiding Crix biscuit and eating in we bedroom) after Pa did say he go marrid me to the Imam. We did think we was invincible together and no stranger-man coulda ever come in-between we.

Then Shiva start showing up in the shop, every single day, during Tanty Nazroon naptime. He fix he lunch break to suit, he did say. For that hour, he and we used to cock-up there, on opposite side of the counter, and well chat we head off—not Salma so much, though, to be honest; she was always a quiet girl. Mostly, he used to talk to me—politics and thing—maybe because I was the bigger one, he must be thought I coulda understand them things better. But still, whatever he reason, it did make me feel special to have a handsome fella focusing on *me.* Half the time, me didn't know what the ass he saying, but to sound smart I used to just parrot-off the things that Pa and Mammy used to say in the house 'bout the government.

And, Lord, when it wasn't politics, Shiva did like to talk 'bout he-self. Is how much time-after-time he tell we he's a North-boy from up Diego Martin side. We never dream to know where that was, but we always nod we head like we understanding. And he say how he father, Lall, did born in South, but went North to sell in Port of Spain market, fall in love with woman and bright lights and never leave Town. And he tell we how during the week, he does beg-a-lodging by some people in San'do, but every weekend he does travel back North to see 'bout the father—buy lil food and medication and thing.

He never once mention he mother. We did wonder, eh. But we was lil girls, we wasn't supposed to cross-question a big, hardstones man like he.

If we coulda talk plain, maybe we mighta ask, and maybe we mighta see something on he face or hear something in he voice that woulda warn we how much hate he did have inside for women. But that wasn't we luck.

Instead, we end up asking him other kinda questions. Easier ones. Like, one Friday, we did ask him if the people where he staying does treat him good (because we did notice from day one how he always looking like a stray way *maaga* dog, like them people never used to feed him.) We did notice how, every morning, he used to buy breakfast and lunch from we shop, and then before he leave work in the evening, he used to buy whatever stale food we had—thing we woulda give the animal-them in the backyard—to carry home for he supper.

"Yeah, they does treat me nice," he say. But he did answer too quick, and he face did suddenly look dent-up like the old Klim pan we used to knock to call fowl.

So we just let that talk dead right dey.

Then, next Monday, is *he* who come back and revive it again; but this time, singing a different tune.

"*Humph!* Bachelor life not easy, girls. It hard to depend on them people where I staying. That's why my father say is time for me to marrid. He say to look for a nice Indian girl from South. He say they not bright and fast like North 'oman. They simple and humble and know how to keep husband and mind chirren and thing—just like he grandmother from India, Shanti, who was the perfect kinda wife. That's true? Allyuh South girls perfect?"

He make a kinda laugh that sound like when dog trying to hawk up bone. And he look even more like a pothound the way how he hang he head and watch we, like he think we woulda bawl *Mash*! and run him from the shop door.

But when we just remain there, smiling bright bright, he add on in a braver voice, "So now, I's twenty-six years. I lookin for my *dulahin*. Allyuh know any nice girl for me?"

We didn't answer him, but as sisters we was thinking one-another thoughts and squeezing one another hand under the counter. And the moment he leave to go back to work—he shadow was still warming the doorway—we start discussing.

"I feel he like you, Yaz!" Salma say. "He does well much-you-up every day. You like him back or what?"

"Well... I not sure." I was so damn frighten to admit it, out loud. I did frighten to want anything in life. I did hear Mammy and Pa say it so much times: *Yasmeen, she blight from she born... Yasmeen, if that girl only watch a cup of milk too hard, it does sour and turn dahee...*

But Salma was like a tick jookin me in my ass. "Yes, he dark, dark, dark and yes, he hair so curly you could make mistake and think he have lil creole blood in him, but the man still real handsome. You don't find so, Yaz?"

"Yeah, he nice. And is true, I getting to like him. But... I not sure if is *that* kinda "like" he feelin for *me*, Sally. Nobody don't ever really like me. They does always be watching *you*."

"Yeah, because I's dolly-on-shelf, for they to admire and say, 'She pretty, eh!' But everybody know I not ready. I's a lil chupidee girl. Is you who done train up and ready to put in house—and that's exactly what Shiva say he looking for. A perfect wife."

"Well, you have a point there." My heart did start to swell-up with hope, like a *sada roti* when you *sakay* it good on the fire.

Salma did throw she whole self on me then, and squeeze tight, tight as she say, "I pray so much and ask God to send you somebody, Yaz. Somebody nice and young, so you could be happy and Pa could forgive we for what did happen the last time."

"I know. I been praying too," I did say, hugging she back harder and thinking 'bout all the *jhanjhat* we cause after the Imam proposal. How we did make Pa cave-in and call it off with we hunger-strike. But we did end-up making things worse, in a way, because Pa get a bad name in the village. And Lord, how much time-after-time we had was to listen to Mammy crying on the phone, "You could imagine how shame we feeling, Nazroon? Yasmeen almost sixteen now, and nobody else even taking a lil interest self? And Salma coming up, right behind, in a few years. Suppose this blight rub-off on she, and nobody want she? People go say *corbeaux* pee on my two girl-chirren!"

So, we decide to notice Shiva better. Every time he step in the shop, we study him like he was some new kinda creature that did *dreevay* out the forest to feed in we yard. And that's when we start to see the man was different to all the other men we did know. He did like to sing calypso—tunes we never hear 'bout because we only had one radio home and it did always on the Indian station. And we used to ask him, "What kinda coolie you is, *bai*?" every time he fan he tongue and complain Tanty *tambran* sauce "too spicy." And he had a strange kinda ambition, too: not to buy land, cattle, or duck, like all the man-and-them in we family, but to "watch a movie in every cinema in Trinidad" and to "have ten Levi hard-pants and ten Converse jim-boots." We used to just laugh at him. Because we didn't have sense to know that North Indian like he, does operate different to South Indian like we. Them kinda Indian does see the world through creole people glasses, and think creole people thoughts: self first and family last; spend, spend, spend instead of save, save, save; easy come, easy go.

Yes, Shiva had a different sense-ah-values to we family, but we didn't understand exactly how different yet. Instead, he did convince we he had so much in common with we own Pa, that we start to feel like the two of them might be a match make in *Jannah.*

It had a day when he say, "School was never for me, girls. But I does pick-up any skill quick, quick. The Government paying good, because they want to hurry fix the road from here to Moruga. So if I work hard, the bossman say, I could get permanent and start to make *real* money on this road."

And me and Salma did watch one another; because we did remember how Pa did say nearly the same damn thing when he take we outta Comprehensive the year before: *It have no more proftt in allyuh schoolbag; the future for allyuh is either in the new road or in husband.* And Pa did say how the road go open up Barrackpore, for plenty people to drive down from San'do to watch the countryside and buy fresh vegetables and poultry and thing. And he did say that's why he sending we by Tanty: to put a business-head on we shoulders, in case marriage never come we way, so we could still help him in the farming business.

When we tell Shiva what Pa say, he agree same speed. "I like that. Woman with business-brain and common sense. That better than book sense, any day. Better than looks and pretty-face too. That kinda wife is a help to a modern man, y'know. You could close your eye and gi'she your pay, she go handle everything with a cool, cool head."

With that, he fling a *phulourie* in the air and catch it in he mouth. "And your Pa, he sounding like the best kinda father-in-law to have. One that pushing the same kinda modern vision as me."

He did wink at we then, and the two of we did blush for

him, but what he couldn't see was the setta pinching under the counter. As sisters, we was thinking with one mind: this Shiva was definitely a surprise gift from Allah—he come like a storm-shower during the heat of *petite careme* month. He come to clear Pa name and wash 'way all the shame that did latch-on to we family like locust, since the Imam-incident. He come to fix the future for everybody: Mammy and Pa go be happy, I go be marrid to a North-man, and that woulda raise-up Salma karma with the whole village, for when *she* time come to marrid in a few years.

So that night, we lie down on we bed facing one-another, resting we two head on the same middle pillow, we hair tangling-up to make one knot, and we *shoo-shoo* over everything.

And we giggle for so when Salma put-on she posh accent and say, "You go be like the Princess Margaret. Livin in Por-dah-Spain come like livin in England, girl?"

And then, we hold hands and promise one another to remain loyal sisters forever, and to still spend holidays together, no matter how far we dey from one another.

And then, was that same quiet, innocent Salma who shock me—I never know the lil girl had so much trick and chart in she pretty lil head—when she say, "Yaz, tomorrow is Friday. Dress up lil bit to go in the shop, nah. Pretend you's the lady in the Mills & Booms. Let we tie-up Shiva brain good-and-proper."

And Lawd-Faddah, I couldn't sleep whole night sake of the excitement and the new feelings that start to tremble up inside my body for the first time.

Next morning, we thief one of Mammy red lipstick, the one she used to put-on to go wedding and thing. And the moment Tanty Nazroon leave the shop to go upstairs to sleep, we start testing it out, drawing it on one-an-other mouth, seeing how it look with or without a Vaseline shine. That's the exact moment when Shiva walk in the shop for lunch break—like the man used to time Tanty as if he middle-name was "Casio." Salma grab the rag and wipe-off she lip, but I remain lookin sexy.

Shiva never once mention the lipstick, but that was the day he start treating we different. He start making a setta slack-joke and thing, telling we how "he *gutni* bend"and how that better to "swizzle the *dhal*" in we pot. Was the kinda joke we only used to hear when we uncle-and-them drinking rum and playing cards, the kinda joke we wasn't supposed to understand— we was only supposed to droop we head and look confused, like Pooja in the movie *Kabhi Kabhie*. But we did mind enough animal and read enough Mills & Booms to know was sex he talking 'bout. And to break the rules and laugh with 'im, it did feel so exciting, we did feel like big-woman instead of two dry-foot lil country-girl. So if you see how we over-do we laughter, as if Shiva was more jokey than the man, John Agitation, who used to do comedy on the TV and radio.

And is that make Shiva braver. He take two bite of he gizzard *roti*, then come out, clear as day, and ask, "It have any boy in the village who allyuh like? How come you ent marrid yet, Yasmeen? Your Pa looking?"

My guts and heart switch places right away, and my jawbone did seize up.

But quick, quick, Salma answer smart like she's the Councillor for Barrackpore. "All them fellas is we cousin. Right, Yaz? That's the onliest reason you ent make *nikah* yet, ent, Yaz? The groom hadda come from outside. Look we cousin, Farida, she not too long marrid a nice, nice fella from Mayaro. Ent, Yaz?"

"Y-y-yeah, is true."

"The boy was Muslim too?" Shiva ask. "Like how allyuh strict in the religion, nah." He point he lip to the side wall of the shop, where Tanty had she fake-velvet scroll hang-up, the one with gold Arabic letters saying the ninety-nine names of Allah.

Salma say, "We not really that strict, you know, *bai*. Ent, Yaz? Tell the man, nah."

And that was the truth, so I manage to find back my tongue and answer, "Well, we does go mosque and thing sometimes, but we father and mother have all kinda friends. Like the Chinee-man who own the shop that does sell cigarette, rum and all them *haram* things Tanty Nazroon don't sell..."

"Mmm-hmm," Salma *chook*-in, "and the negro people in Princes Town who raising pig and selling pork and *souse*. Them does buy cucumber from Pa, and he does well invite them by we house, every single year, for Eid."

Then I remember Shiva was carrying only Hindu names, so I hurry add-on a better example. "And look: we Pa does even pay a pundit-friend to make Dee-Baba puja every planting season, to pray for the crop-and-them."

"So-o-o, allyuh family wouldn't scorn somebody like me, then?" Shiva ask, with he face serious like the Chief Justice. "Because, I's not really a religious fella, nah. I's not Hindu, I's not Muslim, not even Christian. I don't believe in one damn thing except hard work."

"That's okay," Salma say, with she head bobbing like a sugarcane arrow in breeze. "All-ah-we is Indian together. And we family is open-minded, Shiva. Ask Yaz. She older, she know more things than me, and she memory better than my one. Talk to Yaz."

Salma fly up, claiming she want to pee, and run out the back door of the shop, leaving me alone with Shiva, who remain watching me hard, hard, with he eye like two drill bit.

When I tell you: I did frighten! It did seem like Salma just turn a page and—*Bam!*—I end-up starring in the most important scene in the story, the scene where somebody have to confess something to cause every other thing to happen afterwards. Otherwise, 'tory done.

Well, I grab on the counter, because my body did start to shake again with the same inside heat from the night before, and I start to feel giddy, like I coulda faint "way right there and catsprattle everything in the shop. I was so scared to say the wrong thing, but I take a deep breath, and I decide to go with my heart.

"I would never scorn you, Shiva," I tell the man. "I likes you."

He smile broad, broad then; he lean over the counter and bring he face close close to my ears. So close that I feel the warm breeze from he mouth when he whisper, "I like you too."

My knee-them give 'way but thank God for the countertop, I manage to hold up.

Same speed, Shiva pull back and start talking normal again, like the moment did never even happen. "Gimme two big-size chocolate. The Fruit & Nuts flavor." Then he say one was for me and one for Salma. Then he say, "Have a good weekend, babes," and he leave.

Babes the man call me, y'know!

Well, Lord, I clean forget Tanty Nazroon sleeping. I bawl like a cow for Salma to come back quick. And if I tell you: that day, we well hug-up and celebrate them two melt-up, deform chocolate. It was the most romantic day that ever happen in we life! And, man, let me tell you: we suck 'way that chocolate, swing we hand and sing together all the way home that evening: *Kabhi kabhie mere dil mein khayal aata hai…*

But how we was supposed to know that Shiva did done marrid, in a way? When I say "marrid," I mean he was already jamming-up with a old creole lady in Town, and he did already get tie-up and possessed by whatever jinn she did summon or whatever *obeah* she did do to keep him. By the time we did meet the fella, Shiva soul did done lost, and he did done groom-up to destroy innocent lil girls like we. The onliest thing that coulda guard and protect we, was if we still had on the *tabeej* Mammy and Pa used to pin on we clothes when we was small. But me and Salma did stop wearing them things, long long time ago, thinking we didn't need them no more, thinking we was big and coulda fend for we self, as sisters, against the rest of the whole damn world.

So Sunday, we did sit down home with Mammy, watching the after-lunch Indian movie, Tezaab. We did busy mopping we eye during the scene where Mohini escape she wicked father to be with she one-and-only, Mahesh.

But then… *bee-beep!*… a strange car horn blow outside we gate.

"Who dat is?" Mammy say, when she glance through the window. "Me eh know that numberplate from 'round here. And is 'R,' too—a rental, *oui!* Who 'round here have money to rent car and thing?"

So me and Salma did get up from the show to *macco* out the window. But thank God Mammy went back to the movie. Otherwise, she mighta notice the look on we face, or hear when Salma mumble, "Oh Gahhd," or see when we grip one-another hand and Salma bend back my middle finger.

We bawl, "Is a customer to Pa, nah."And that really wasn't

no lie, because we did know right away is Pa-self who Shiva did come to bargain with.

We leave Mammy in the drawing room and speed-walk to we bedroom. We hug-up tight, tight, chirping and trembling like two young duckling.

"Yaz, he come to ask Pa for you to marrid!"

"Oh gosh, yes, it happening! It really happening, Sally!"

And then, we use Mammy yardstick to shub the curtain one-side—just a lil bit—and we see Pa was still talking to Shiva through the gate.

And when the two of them turn suddenly and glance upstairs—we dive!—and by the time we look again, Pa did opening the gate to let Shiva in the yard.

"What allyuh doing?" Mammy bawl from the drawing room. "Allyuh missing the action. If you see big fight on the screen here."

"We comin just now!" we belt out together, like is *qaseeda* we singing in mosque.

Then we kneel, and sit down on we ankle, like is *namaz* we going and pray, but instead we start picturing all what taking place down below: Papa, that's Pa father, in one hammock; Pa settling back in he own; Shiva unrolling the third hammock from the hook on the rafters.

And we start betting whether Pa woulda call over the fence for Nana, Mammy father, to join the family *panchayat*. We listen with all we power and strength, but we couldn't hear nothing more than the low earthquake rumble from all them man-voice rolling together as one.

Salma say, "Come nah, Yaz. You know what to do. We just hadda be careful and move slo-o-ow, so wood lice don't drop on their head."

We slide 'way the bedside mat. Then, we put a fingernail each and prise up we favorite piece of wood from the old floor plank—something we did accustom doing ever since we small.

We set it aside, gentle, gentle, as if it wasn't a jagged old piece of wood but some fancy diamond we was touching. Then, like good sisters, we take turns: flattening we cheek against the floor, jamming we eye to the hole, angling, trying to see something. Then, we try a next *chart:* suctioning we ears, trying to hear something, anything. The listener, holding up she finger for silence and blinking, eye them roving like they following the numbers on a clock; and the next sister, whispering, "What going on? What they saying? Move, move, is my turn."

Is so we went, over and over, a good few times.

Then, Salma turn come again. She bend down but, in no minute, she spring up suddenly. She head did drooping like hibiscus that pick since yesterday, and she face did pull long, long, like dumpling dough.

"W 'happen, girl?"

"Ahhm… I not hearing so good but…"

"Oh God, talk fast, nah! My heart looking to jump out my chest."

"Well… I hear Papa say, 'Yes, is better she marrid now before—'

"Praise be to Allah! Finally, I—"

"Wait, Yaz, you didn't let me finish," Salma say, she eye them did look huge, round and reddish, full-to-overflowing, like the two copper we had outside catching rainwater. Then she whisper, "I feel is *me* Shiva come for, Yaz, not you."

"How the ass it could be you, *chupidee?* Ent you self say you still small and *poohar?* You can't do nothing for no man. You ever burn your hand on a *tawah?* You ever skin your knuckles jooking clothes? Catch yourself, eh, lil girl! I is the big-woman here, and is *me* the man come for, not you."

"But Papa say, "'is better she marrid now before nobody want she, like the first girl.'"

Well, right away, something shub me up from the floor and fling me down on the bed—I don't even remember moving. I only find myself there with my head under the pillow, bawling like twenty Tarzan. My shoulder and my back did shaking, and I did feel my foot-them kicking, and I did hear my ownself making that same noise like when I did nearly drown on Moruga Beach one Easter Sunday. And I did feel the same kinda strong tide pulling, separating me from my sister, from we bedroom, and from the onliest thing I did ever dare to hope for or believe in my lil life.

But Salma? She remain just so, no expression on she face except crocodile tears, as if she standing-up on the shore and she done make up she mind to stay *dey* and watch she own sister deading.

And that's what did hurt me more than anything, you know. Is how Salma, my one-and-only sister, never even put up a fight. She never once say no, she never call hunger strike, she just nod she head—yes, yes—to Pa and Shiva. Yes, to the three-thousand dowry he pay in advance; yes, to the wedding in three weeks' time; yes, to the same damn Imam doing the ceremony quick, quick and hush, hush.

And is not even that she did truly love Shiva—I did know in my heart, she didn't love the man. Is *me* who did love him. And I did feel that Salma was just spoil-up and accustom to getting the best of everything, getting first pick at everything, all because she did fair-skin and pretty, with them blasted deceitful snake-eye.

But I did blame Pa and Mammy the most.

Them did hate me since I born. And them used to always give Salma so much *dular,* full-up she head with bad-habit and high-mindedness, from ever since we small.

And so, I did make a terrible mistake. I did start praying with a vengeance every night:

God, I know you don't sleep.

I know you see what Salma and Shiva do to me,

And I know you go do back for them.

Make it ten times worser in the end.

Ameen and ameen.

So, it come like is my fault. And I go hadda live with this for the rest of my days: is *me,* Yasmeen, whey cause my sister and she husband to dead.

GODFREY'S REVENGE

1989, Bagatelle, Trinidad, West Indies

Shiva was midway down the mattress from Miss Jackie. He was pulling on a T-shirt and, though bleary-eyed and still half-sleep, wrestling with the knowledge that his performance last night had disappointed her. She didn't mention it, though. She simply stretched forward and slid the money—same "allowance" she always gave him on Monday mornings—across the soiled bedding. As he palmed the cash, a sudden madness gripped him and he said, "Gimme another hundred today," shocking himself both by the request and by the commanding tone.

"*Three* hundred dollars?" Miss Jackie asked, turning with such torque that a droopy breast which had suckled two daughters, many men, and most recently *him,* swung free of the oversized vest she'd worn as a nightie. "I give you enough for passage, food for the whole week, plus a lil extra if you feel to drink two beer Friday, before you come home. Why you need more?"

Shiva worked on a road crew during the week, boarding at a co-worker's home in San Fernando, then returning to Bagatelle on Fridays to spend the weekend with his family... and Miss Jackie.

And every week, since way back when he'd begun working at fifteen years old, Shiva brought his pay packet to this house and handed it over to this woman twice his age. She guarded every cent of it, like a brown bitch minding a litter of fat, round puppies. And over these past thirteen years, she'd ensured Shiva always had what he needed: decent clothes, groceries for the house up the hill where he lived—at first, alone with his father, Lall, who'd died of cirrhosis last year; and for two years now, with a teenaged wife, Salma, and infant son, Anand.

"I know, but the child sick," Shiva explained, recalling the baby's incessant wailing last night, which had driven him here, to Miss Jackie's house, earlier than usual. "So I want to leave a lil extra, in case she hadda take 'im doctor, nah."

Shiva had never minded Miss Jackie managing his money, he'd long ago understood it was in his best interest, so he wouldn't be tempted to "drink and piss out life, like all them other waste-ah-time man 'round here," as she'd always said. He trusted her.

In fact, more than trust, he loved Miss Jackie. She'd known him from socks to steel-toe boots. In his childhood, she'd fed him whenever his own mother disappeared and his father was too busy wallowing in flasks of white rum. In his teenage years, she'd housed him whenever he and Lall fought and he was kicked out.

And it was on one of those black-eyed and bloody-lipped nights that she'd gone further, to shelter Shiva within her body, to nurse him, to teach him there could be tenderness in this world. In the years afterward, as he grew long and *lingay,* and his muscles hardened and his hands calloused, and he learned to lift, turn, and twist her this-way-and-that to meet his desires, he'd learned, too, some inner strength. She'd made a man of him. And over years of pillow talk, he'd exposed everything down to his soul's blackest blot: as a boy, he had taken someone who'd trusted him, a friend named Godfrey, to the waters off Caricom Jetty and, after an argument, the fella had fallen into the sea... or had Shiva thrown him in?... as the years had passed it had become harder and harder to remember his own true intentions that night.

Had Godfrey lived, or had he died? Shiva never knew. But Miss Jackie had said Godfrey shouldn't have provoked Shiva, and she'd said Shiva shouldn't blame himself for what had happened, and she'd said she loved him anyway. And never having had a functional God in his life, *her* absolution had been enough to make Shiva forget almost everything about the incident, except the sound of Godfrey wailing as the tide carried him away toward the Venezuelan coast.

Since then, Shiva hated to hear crying—even on TV. It made him feel helpless and guilty, and, after his son was born, it drove him to spend more and more time here with Miss Jackie. There was no crying here, except once-in-a-while, when she babysat her granddaughter, Denyse.

"How you mean Anand *sick?*" she asked now, thinning her eyes to razor blades. "You never tell me that. So you starting to hide things from me?"

"No, no," he said hurriedly, not wanting her to step even one fungal toenail down the path of thinking him ungrateful. In the past, he'd erred into letting that happen and had suffered the consequences: a banishment from her bed and a *tabanca* so intense its grief had disoriented him as if he was being ripped from her womb itself.

"Is only yesterday he start-up with a lil fever-and-thing. I never get chance to mention it last night before we…"

"So that's why you couldn't—"

"Nah, is not that—" he interrupted, his machismo smarting. But, mid-denial, he perceived that a greater danger lay in Miss Jackie seeing his slack penis for what it truly meant: he'd been thinking about another woman last night. He'd been thinking about Salma. Up the hill, alone with the child, needing him.

"Well, yeah, is that. I worried 'bout my son," he said. "Thirteen months. Is the first time he get sick. I don't know what to do. I don't know if Salma even self know what to do."

Clucking her tongue the way she did when petting her granddaughter, Miss Jackie pulled Shiva into her arms and smothered him between those sagacious breasts. "Oh Gawd, luvva, don't worry. Ent you know Jackie raise two healthy chirren? And look: I does see 'bout Denyse now-and-all. You think I would ever let something happen to your boy, Shiva? All Salma have to do is step out in the gallery and bawl, "Miss Jackie!" I go handle she. I promise: you could go to work with your conscience clean like holy water. I here for them."

She released him and stood, signaling the conversation was over. "I have a hot piss," she said, "and watch the time… almost four o'clock. You better go or you might miss your ride. Allyuh still paving down Moruga-side this week?"

"Yeah, we reach Bois Jeune Gens area," Shiva said distractedly, as he trailed her from bedroom to bathroom. Part of him wanted to grab her arm and insist on the extra cash so he could march up the hill and plunk the money down in front of Salma, so he could be that kind of take-care-of-everything man in his wife's eyes. But another part of him was relieved to not have to be that man—because there was someone more capable in charge: Miss Jackie.

"Not long again though: the road finishing at Grand Chemin beach. Then, I feel I might ask for—" He'd intended to say, "a transfer closer to home," but Miss Jackie interjected from her lavatory throne.

"Well, I warning you again, Mister Man: don't eat or drink nothing from them Moruga people, eh. They love obeah too bad! And the magic down there real, real strong—is Shango spells mix-up with Catholic and Hindu prayers and all kinda Venezuelan simmy-dimmy. You hearing me?"

"Yeah," he said hurriedly, then headed for the front door.

Every week, she repeated this same caution. So he hadn't told her that last Friday, while digging up some roadside land, the crew had found shards of pottery and colored glass, bits of bone, tiny teeth, plenty conch shells, and square nails like the ones from Jesus' hands. The foreman had guessed, "ancient settlement," but the local workers—two strapping fellas sent by the Moruga Councillor's office—had bleached from black to grey and scampered out the hole. They'd claimed that the property belonged to Mother Cornhusk, a now-deceased but once powerful obeah-woman, and that "spiritual wickedness" still lingered in the soil.

Shiva, with the other men, had ridiculed those country-niggas over Friday evening beers. But look: by Saturday morning, Anand was sick for the first time ever; and by last night, Shiva's prick wasn't working. He wondered now, while unlocking the burglar-proof gate at Miss Jackie's front door, if he should've taken those Moruga fellas to heart.

The gate's metal hinges creaked ominously.

"Aye, boy!" Miss Jackie called. "See if you get two piece of *bois bande* bark while you down there. I go boil it and make tea for you, when you come home. All your man problems go solve. Moruga bush-medicine could raise anything, even the deadest dead."

Shiva did not hurry up the hill. He walked deliberately, pressing his full weight into every step, feeling the dew dampen his hair, listening to the complaining pebbles and the querulous crickets, the gloating frogs. This dark Monday-morning trek had grown so tedious lately, his feet becoming heavier each week. And his mind seemed to be tripping over itself, less and less able to make what used to be a smooth transition between the women in his life.

Two years ago, it was Miss Jackie and Lall who'd decided, "Is time for you to marrid and breed, Shiva." And they'd agreed that the bride should *not* be a Town girl—like Shiva's wastrel mother—but a quiet decent country girl, who would always know her place. Miss Jackie had, on his behalf, even prayed a novena to The Holy Spouse, St. Joseph. She'd already covered five days of the nine when his crew had started work down south, in Barrackpore Village, and he'd met thirteen-year-old Salma and her sister who was older by two years. He'd almost chosen *that* one, because she was squat, dark and ugly, with desperation wafting from her like fumes from a dung patty. *She* would never horn him with another man. *She* would always be grateful to him. But Miss Jackie had said, "Take the smaller one, so we could train she up to be everything you like. Ent you say she fair skin, too? With pretty-eye? Better yet! Allyuh go make nice, nice chirren." Three weeks later, he and Salma were married, and ten months afterward, Anand was born with mid-tone skin and normal eyes—but still a cute lil fella. Lall had held him up to the heavens and declared, "*Meh fuss* grandchild. This generation go be gold."

Shiva arrived at the house and set one foot on the front stairs he and Lall had built to dress-up the place for his new bride, make it look less like a lean-to shack. But he now found himself hating the fucking steps and unwilling to climb them. Sick child, sick penis, sick to his stomach is how he felt. He walked around to the back of the house, where the land sloped toward the forest. He sat on one of the buckets they used for storing water, and just stared into the wall of black which he knew was the tree line.

Overhead, the floorboards sighed. Salma was moving in the kitchen, probably making his breakfast, as a well-trained wife should. Yes, she did all the right things, but from the outset, from their wedding night, she'd made him doubt himself and his decision to get married as Lall and Miss Jackie had insisted.

He'd never forgotten that horrific August night in the middle of the rainy season. A tropical storm, with raindrops the size of gravel, had been pelting the galvanized tin roof. The wind had been trying to outdo by lifting the tin sheets and banging them against each other. Despite this, Shiva had heard Salma's winces and whimpers, he'd felt her holding her breath and bracing, her body refusing to admit him. "Relax, just relax," he'd kept saying to the girl, pleading really, for her to make this easier on him. He'd known Lall was probably listening—maybe even peeping at the door—waiting for him to prove himself a man in his own house for once, instead of "the toy-prick" of "old-quenk Jackie." But Shiva hadn't been sure how to overcome this young-girl's naked inexperience and distaste.

He'd tried kissing her. Over and over, again and again, and she'd twisted and clawed until, finally, he'd caught her; and although she'd opened her mouth then, her jaw hung and her lips and tongue had remained slack and ignorant. Her spit had drained all down his chin and hers, as if she didn't want it anymore, or couldn't bear to claim and swallow what he'd contributed. That had hurt his feelings with a force he hadn't expected. And he would've given up then—her virginity, which they'd made him pay three thousand dollars and "become a Muslim" for, had no longer seemed worth the effort. But how would he face Lall and Miss Jackie the next morning?

So he'd persisted, enduring squall after squall of rejection, his pelvis chasing hers to the rat-bitten edge of the bare sponge he'd spread on the floor. And every time she cowered—*No, No, No!*—he was forced to think of how she'd bawled, "Mammy, Mammy!"a nd held on to the gate when it was time to leave her parents' house in Barrackpore, and how she'd fought and flailed until her lipstick had stamped red stains all over her white wedding dress.

"No, no, no!" Soon, he couldn't bear the word anymore. That's when he'd raised himself onto one palm, smashed the other against her temple, and rammed into her. A loud booing wind had raged through the gaps of the rickety house, sucking everything—even he and Salma, it seemed—up toward the roof for a terrifying instant, and then her flesh had snapped, stinging them both and releasing them back to ground. Her yelp dissolved into a gurgle, then coughing and sputtering like she would drown.

He couldn't finish. So he pulled away from her and stood, listening to his own panting, aware that, in the semi-dark, devoid of edges, he must've resembled a *lagahoo* or some other man-monster. And he'd known what she was thinking, too. This couldn't be the same Shiva who'd called her "sundar larki"and plied her with presents? The same Shiva who'd said he loved her and would make her happy and give her a good home "up in Town"? The same Shiva who'd made her—no, her whole family—trust him?

He'd felt so ashamed. But then she'd gone from whimpering to full-on crying, a sound so sickening that he'd shouted, "Stop it, girl! You's my *wife.* Stop this shit, right now!" only to loathe himself even more for how much he sounded like Lall: *Stop crying, boy! You's a lil bitch or what? I didn't hit you that hard.*

You better stop before I really give you something to bawl for. So Shiva had left Salma then and went to the bathroom, to rid himself of the slipperiness and the slime he'd felt coating his body, head to toe, like a new unwelcome skin. As he bathed, he kept assuring himself that he had not meant to hurt the girl, he would never have hurt her if she'd only gone along, the way he was going along. "She look for it, she look for it," he kept chanting, reminding himself that Miss Jackie had said he wasn't to blame if somebody provoked him to violence.

When he returned to the sponge, Salma was still lying like a broken doll, limbs splayed. A spirit-lash of compassion knocked Shiva to his knees, frantic to gather her up.

"Come, babes," he'd whispered. "Lemme help you. I leave half-bucket of water and the Dettol in there for you."

She had walked with her legs wide apart, rocking from side to side, obviously scorning herself in the place where he'd just been. And when he'd flicked on the bathroom bulb, she'd turned away, hiding the half of herself he'd just possessed. He'd felt an urge to grab her and take the rest of her, just for punishment, or maybe just to get this marriage business over with: teach her everything that a wife should know, in one wet bloody night—everything he'd learned from Miss Jackie.

But Salma started screaming, begging him to turn off the light, shrieking like some forest creature maimed in a trap. And although it was the kind of sound that probably made Lall proud, twenty-six-year-old Shiva became, on his wedding night, a scampering fugitive from his own thirteen-year-old wife. He'd fled straight to the sanctuary of Miss Jackie's open thighs.

Something was moving in the undergrowth ahead. Shiva stood cautiously, craned his neck, but saw nothing. Perhaps a *manicou* or *agouti* looking to feed on garbage. Still, it had spooked him. He decided it was time to tote his bucket of water upstairs and get ready for work.

As he retraced the path to the front door, he steeled himself for what awaited inside: the innocence of his wife. Lately, as she'd begun filling out her clothes and her maternal role, she'd seemed less and less like a useless girl. And he'd begun to admire all she did for his son: how tenderly she cradled his neck while bathing his helpless twitchy body, how her eyes came alive every single time the child awoke from a nap, how she endured his endless, endless cries. It was a devotion Shiva had never received from his own mother.

Recently, too, he'd begun to hope that Salma's view of him would also evolve. Perhaps become more… forgiving… of their wedding night, of his dependence on Miss Jackie, of every damn thing. But Salma's grey eyes were always blank whenever he walked through the door, they never projected anything other than resignation.

This morning, when he set down the bucket by the front door, her stare was wide and glassy. She was sitting on the couch, looking shrunken and haggard in a long white nightie; her hair hung black and stringy, and she didn't answer when he said good morning.

"How Anand?" he asked, heartbeat quickening.

"He groan with fever whole night," she replied, shaking her head. "But I keep sapping him with the Limacol and rubbing him with the Vicks. He sleeping now."

"Good," Shiva said, hurrying toward the bedroom door. "That mean he getting better. I go peep at him while I—"

"No. Look I bring your things out here, so you don't have to go in the room."

"Okay." Shiva changed direction toward the pile of clothes on the couch next to her. As he reached for them, she grabbed his wrist. "Suppose something happen. I feel you should stay home this week. Stay close to we, nah?"

When he straightened, her hand fell away. "How I go stay, girl? I still daily-paid with them people. But hear what: I done talk to Miss Jackie. She say just call she, night or day, if you need help or anything. I leave extra money there, in case you have to go doctor or buy medicine or—"

"Why you couldn't leave it here?" Salma glared up at him, her eyes now slitted and snake-like compared to a moment ago. It surprised him to see this much emotion on her face, and to find that he couldn't exactly name what he saw—*was it rage or scorn?*—but he knew for sure that it terrified him. Just as that thing in the bush outside—whatever it was—had done.

"But wait," he growled with excessive bravado. "Who the fuck you feel you talking to, lil girl? I not asking you, Salma. I *telling* you: call Jackie if Anand not better by lunchtime today. If you play proud and let my son dead on your hand, I go come back here and pitch your cunt right off this mountain. Watch and see."

That was this morning, but Shiva has since been humbled.

He is now lying, injured, under the canopy of a van's tray where his co-workers have brought him. The padded upholstery of the fold-down bench is softer on his back than the raw gravel and cracked earth where he'd collapsed. Around him is the familiar smell of dust, caked grease, unwashed coveralls, sweaty shoes, and someone's lunch spoiling in the heat. It is darker in here, than outside in the blazing three o'clock sun. Later, at the hospital, he will hear words like *photophobia* and *blepharospasm*, but for now all Shiva can mumble is that he's having trouble opening his bleeding eyes and when he does—even by a millimeter—he cannot bear the naked light. And this headache, it is getting worse and worse; he can no longer pinpoint its epicenter, he thinks his skull might soon explode. All he can do is groan, grip his grubby coverall, and try to endure what must be, he knows deep in his heart, Godfrey's revenge.

If he could open his eyes and turn his head to the right, if it weren't being held in the vice-grip of one of his co-workers, he knows he would see the other bench where duffel bags and knapsacks are sitting, spaced out at intervals, almost like an audience of small people watching him suffer.

From that direction, somebody, it sounds like Kalloo, is saying, "... hold he head better... prop him up some more, nah." Then, Shiva hears the rustling of plastic, the rattle of small things colliding, the *shhhh* of boxes being dragged. Someone is searching beneath the benches, digging through the safety gear that the crew has almost never used during his two years with them. Traffic cones stacked together but lying on their side, split and warped boxes containing reflectors, caution tape, hard hats, plastic glasses and sheet metal signs—*Stop and Go, Men at Work, Danger*—but with many of the letters peeled away.

"Look, put on this for him. But careful, eh... be *careful.*"

The blood trails are drying on the side of Shiva's face. He feels some scrape off as the bandana is lifted and a pair of welding glasses is wiggled onto his temples. The mere agitation makes pain whirl through his body, then return to his head with a hurricane's vengeance.

"How long again? Call back and see how far they is, nah?" Kalloo asks. The CB radio crackles inside the cab, while outside there is a clatter of real voices. But Shiva cannot follow what is being said anymore. He's using all his energy to think through the pain, he is wondering how he will get news to Bagatelle, and what would happen if he dies here. Miss Jackie will be fine without him, she's a big, hardback woman, but Salma and Anand are both so small, they need him. He's sorry he didn't peep at Anand this morning, he's sorry for how he spoke to Salma, he's sorry for how he's treated her from the very start—bleeding her dry of hope, while pretending not to notice the wound—he wishes he could tell her so right now.

The nearest pay phone is about a mile away, outside the rumshop in Grand Chemin. Two hours ago, on his lunch break, it had been so easy for him to hitch a ride there, on the open back of a passing truck. And he'd been so happy when Miss Jackie had answered her house phone and said she'd just returned from the doctor with Salma and Anand. The child had been diagnosed with bronchitis, he'd gotten an injection to bring down the fever, and Miss Jackie had filled his prescription. "Your boy go be fine by the time you reach back Friday," she'd said.

Shiva had celebrated by slipping into the rumshop and, despite the warnings of the toothless and raisin-faced proprietor ("This here is no joke, son. This here might make a Town-fella like you see 'round corner"), he'd bought himself a shot of real Moruga *babash*, poured from an antique-look-ing black bottle. But he hadn't thrown it back like an expert; he'd dragged a three-legged stool to the doorway of the bar and sat there savoring how each mini-sip assaulted his senses: the fumes burned his nose, while the kiss was cool to his lips, but then it raged hellfire going down to his heart. He'd felt alive and grateful for every salt-crusted thing his gaze fell upon. Then he'd let his attention stroll away from the fishing village squalor toward the rolling murmur of the ocean. He'd admired the Catholic church rising from the shore like a giant ornate sandcastle, the statue of St.

Peter, patron saint of fishermen, leaning dejectedly over beached rubbish, and between the two structures, the gemstone blue waters of the Columbus Channel.

Then, the wiry shopkeeper had appeared at the other post of the doorway, smoking something that smelled of secret rituals, of hemp, frank-incense, myrrh and blood combined. "Pretty, eh?" the old man had said, veiled in smoke. "And if you walk down closer and squint your eye good, you go see Venezuela. Why you don't go? Take a walk, nah, Town-boy?"

All Shiva could see of the man's face was the flint in his yellow-marbled eyes. In that instant, he knew this was an actual *obeah*-man, who could see and tally every blot on his soul, and who knew that he hadn't set foot near the ocean in thirteen years, for fear of *who* might wash ashore. And he'd suddenly realized that his Moruga co-workers and Miss Jackie had been right all along: spiritual wickedness was everywhere in this place… maybe even in this drink…

Kalloo's voice interrupts. "You awright, Shiva? Ambulance almost here, boy."

"Hold on, *padnah*. Just hold on," another voice says.

"You hearing we? Move your finger-them if you hearing we." Kalloo, again.

But Shiva is too tired, too weak and too far away to answer anybody right now…

His spirit is back in the bar again and he's reliving the proprietor's sneer as he'd pitched the remainder of the drink away and left; reliving every moment of the long walk back from the bar to the job site. Yes, he is there again, listening to his stomach rumble because, in his earlier eagerness to reach the pay phone, he hadn't eaten the lunch packed by Salma. He hears a baby wailing nearby and, in the same moment, notices a little wooden building whose signs—*Bermudez, Kiss, Orchard, Solo*—tell him it is a parlor, the same kind of village shop where he'd met Salma. He climbs the warped steps and smiles at the handwritten scrawl on a square of nailed cardboard: HOT ROTI EVRY DAY. Inside, the place smells not of curry but of stagnant water and dead flowers, but he orders anyway, from the frail orhni-wrapped Indian woman behind the counter: a gizzard roti and two cream-sodas. He is in a hurry to leave, though, because of the crying. Another woman sits in a hammock to his right, cradling the wailing infant who is frantically churning its legs beneath a grey fleece blanket. "He must'e feeling hot," Shiva calls to the woman, over the baby's cat-like bawling. She doesn't respond and he cannot tell if she's heard; her long black disheveled hair hides her face and the child's. Louder, he says, "Too hot, too hot!" But it is no longer the woman to whom he's speaking… Rather, it is himself, minutes later, as he flings the half-eaten, pepper-laced roti into the tall roadside grass. He walks a couple more yards and comes within eyeshot of the job site but, over those last few paces, cramps have overtaken his belly, twining his insides around some invisible finger, forcing him to run into the trees of Mother Cornhusk's land where he will have privacy. He barely has time to peel down his coverall and stoop before water gushes from his ass. He feels lightheaded with relief, but the foul liquid keeps coming, keeps him trapped there in a vulnerable, half-nakedness. In the silence of the overgrown banana and cocoa trees, Shiva realizes that the crying sound has never left him—in fact, it is nearer than ever now, and standing in front of him is its source: the same baby from the parlor. Same grey blanket dragging at its side but its face is hidden now under a wide, low-brimmed straw hat. A soiled diaper hangs at its crotch and its chubby legs are—*Good Lord!*—turned backward in the wrong way. From the coverall pocket Shiva pulls a cream soda and opens the cap with trembling fingers; he angles the bottle away from himself, aiming arches of clear sparkling liquid toward the crying child. Shiva screams with every flick of the bottle, "I baptize you in the name of the Father... of the Son... of the Holy Spirit," because everybody knows that's what you must do when you meet a *douen* in the forest. Then the ghoulish child switches from crying to singing in a sad immature falsetto:

Dodo piti popo[1]
Piti popo pa vle dodo
Zambi a ke mange li
Sukugnan ke suce san

Shiva recognises the old patois song because Miss Jackie sings it for her grandbaby. He knows these lullabies are how *douens* lure hapless children into the trees, so he imagines Anand toddling in the backyard toward the frowning Bagatelle forest, Anand tottering towards an innocent death. "No!" Shiva stands, naked, coverall bunched at his boots, penis engorged with fear. "You not taking my son! Punish me, don't touch my son!" But then the *douen's* voice changes to that of a man saying, "Ok, you ready?"... Shiva finds himself holding a wheelbarrow with jittering hands as he watches Kalloo aim a jackhammer against the concrete culvert on Mother Cornhusk's land. His mouth is

---

[1]A Trinidadian French patois lullaby, which threatens monsters will come for the child who refuses to sleep. It may be translated as:

Sleep, little baby,
The little baby doesn't want to sleep.
The jumbie will eat him
The soucouyant will suck his blood.

dry and he cannot get the singing out of his head—*Zambi a ke mange li, Sukugnan ke suce san*—until the moment Kalloo revs the jackhammer; then, only then, the lullaby is overruled. So Shiva moves closer to the machinery, closer to the hole and to the noise. He doesn't hear his co-workers call, "Watch out!" but, when the flying shard of concrete punctures his right eye, he hears his own blood-curdling wail…

Shiva spasms and jerks as the ambulance siren is switched off. The filthy van wobbles as paramedics enter, bringing hospital smells: latex, antiseptic, peroxide. He hears their strange voices calling his name from a distance, "Mr Gopaul, Mr Gopaul… Shiva." He can only grunt because his head is a broken calabash leaking, leaking. But he feels certain that what happened in the bush between him and the *douen* was a fair trade: he's been injured in place of his son—his innocent little son, the apple of Salma's eye. And it feels right to finally be a take-care-of-everything man to her, and it feels just to finally be requited for his many, many sins—against Godfrey, against Salma, against everybody.

Cool fingers touch his cheek, they search him, they hold his hand, and a kindly female voice asks, "One-to-ten Shiva, how much pain?"

But Shiva's fever-addled brain decides it's Salma, speaking with the love he's craved for so long, and he thinks that now *she* is the one offering him a trade: pain, for forgiveness and the chance to treat her better. So he smiles and his heart almost ruptures with joy as he accepts in a loud, garbled groan.

"Bring more, girl. Bring a hundred, even. You bring, I go take."

SUNDAR LARKI[2]

2000, El Socorro Village, Trinidad, West Indies

Yesterday, while she'd watched Kwame cooking dinner, his muscled dark torso sweat-slick and undulating like the surface of the Pitch Lake itself, Salma had whisked herself into a kind of madness where she thought she could have everything she wanted in life. So she'd run into the bathroom, called her sister and pleaded, "Just cover for me a lil while longer, nah?"

But Yasmeen, in her typical big-sister style, had lectured, "Look, pull your ass home, eh. It bad enough you hornin your husband and involvin me in this chupidness. But now you takin things too far. You have three chirren, or you forget?"

Salma had returned to her senses then, hating herself for this whole sweet, sticky weekend away from Anand, Nadya and Abby. She'd loathed herself so much that she'd made tender-loving Kwame hurt her last night. Really hurt her. She'd been lying on her stomach while he tongued his way up the varicose vein snaking from her calf to the inside of her thigh. Suddenly, that wasn't enough. She'd reached around, pulled him higher and demanded that he bite her shoulder as he entered her—

---

[2]"Sundar larki" is a term commonly used in traditional Indo-Trinidadian culture to mean "a beautiful girl." It is the Trinidad Bhojpuri cognate of the Standard Hindi "Sundar ladki." The difference in spelling is because some phonetical sounds used in Hindi are difficult to transcribe into Standard English, or to replicate with an English-speaking tongue.

"Now! Now!" And when *that* wasn't enough, she'd ordered him to seize her hair at the scalp and pull, while jamming his palm into the small of her back, unfurling and unnaturally arching her spine until—at last!—she became a flaring cobra. She'd cried out, almost fainting from the pain—well, not the pain itself, but the relief of feeling nothing but that pain, in place of all her motherly shame. And when Kwame had kissed her mouth afterward, she, overcome with gratitude, had gnawed his tongue; and he'd gnawed hers back until they drew each other's blood for the first time.

But now, it was morning, and sunlight streaking through his dusty glass louvres made their naked bodies appear as two-toned as she felt in her heart. Kwame wriggled forward, gliding his hand over her stretch-marked tummy, then down between her legs. "Girl, you can't leave me so, after you get on like let-go-beast last night. Just one more day, nah? I really need for you to stay," he said.

"How I could do that?" she said, her voice sharper than intended. In part, she was embarrassed by his mention of her behavior last night, but mostly she resented how he'd classified his trifling desire to bull her again as a "need." When she had *real* life-and-death needs. What about what *she* needed? Did she need him bearing down on her now? Forcing her to apportion guilt between him and the children, the same way she shared one sandwich between three mouths whenever money was tight and her husband, Shiva, hadn't sold enough at market.

"I have to go and organize them chirren for the first day of school," she said in a faraway voice.

"But they father there. He could handle them."

"Their father?" Salma grunted. Shiva? A half-blind drunkard, thirteen years her senior, who was more loving to his crops than to his children, who interacted with them only to teach and beat. Salma had promised her son, twelve-year-old Anand, a big reward if he'd take care of Nadya and little Abby himself, keeping them out of their father's way this weekend. Ten whole dollars, she'd promised. She'd stooped that low. Yasmeen was right: she was a bad mother, a "selfish bitch in heat," and now it was time to lasso this Let-go-beast Salma, pull her ass back home and become nobody again.

"The man manage for these two days. What's one more?" Kwame asked, and the sureness of his tone made Salma's skin flush with annoyance. But then, she remembered, much of Kwame's attitude was her own fault. She'd never told him how hard-won this weekend was, how much planning and collusion had been involved, and how desperate a lie she'd told Shiva (*"Yaz beg me to come Barrackpore to help them for Eid ul-Adha holiday."*) It was a cardboard lie which needed Yasmeen to continue propping it, and last night, she'd flat-out declined. In truth, Yaz would never have agreed in the first place, had she known that Salma's outside-man was "a negro."

Yes, Salma had been keeping dark secrets from everybody. She'd probably kept way too many from Kwame over their year of "friending" and two weekend trysts. She'd never told him that Shiva might kill her ass if he found out she was horning—worse yet, with somebody like Kwame. In fact, he'd threatened to kill her for less: when the old Indian man in Central Market had smiled at her too long and she'd smiled back; when she'd put too much garlic in the tomato *choka*; when she'd asked him point-blank if he was still screwing Miss Jackie, the older negro-lady down the hill. It wouldn't take much for Shiva to turn her into Trinidad's latest front page sad-story.

And yet, she'd come to Kwame's apartment. Twice. She'd

come and never told him these things. Partly because she liked to pretend Shiva didn't exist when she was with Kwame, and partly because the boy was so hungry for her—young engineer like him, he could've had any free-and-single, educated girl, but he'd wanted *her*, the office cleaner with three children. She'd wanted his desire to remain just so: pure and pity-free. She'd come feeling only that she deserved this pleasure and was justified in taking it, because one day Shiva *would* kill her and she would die without ever having lived in her body... and that seemed to her the greater sin. But, oh God, the children. She couldn't get greedy and take stupid risks—Yasmeen had reminded her—not with the children still so small, they needed their Mammy.

So what Salma needed right now, was for Kwame to help her leave this apartment—even though she longed to stay, even though he was heading out tomorrow for a rig in the Gulf and they wouldn't see each other for two weeks, even though she had no idea when she'd be able to arrange another weekend like this. She needed to leave with the assurance that he'd continue to make do with whatever she could spare of herself, whenever she could *safely* spare it.

"Look, I done tell you: we could have we fun and thing, but I have my responsibilities," she chided him now.

A small space opened between their damp bodies, the fan's air replacing his breath on her spine.

"So where your 'responsibilities' was since Friday?" he dared, her shoulder still aching from the imprint of his teeth.

"You know what?" She sat up and wheeled on him. "You damn right. I was wrong to come and, in future, Mr. Gentleman, I will never make the same mistake."

She stomped her nude self all the way into the bathroom, locked the door, turned on the shower, made fists in her own hair and pulled. She cried in that heaving but noiseless way that had become second-nature at home, so the children wouldn't hear. Now, though, silent crying seemed more difficult. Especially when she *wanted* Kwame to barge in and say something like, "I sorry. I know this hard for you. Don't worry 'bout me. I go be here whenever you need, nah." Just as he'd done in their first real conversation, when he'd been the only person in the office to notice her swollen lip, and he'd sought her out in the cleaning supply closet—her little hideaway—where he found her sitting on a bucket sobbing, and he'd knelt on the floor amongst all her brooms and mops and gallons to share the same bleach stink air and to listen to her story. That was the time she'd answered-back Shiva and he'd dunked her head into a barrel of water and held it there. She'd come up gasping, her lungs, eyes, nose, burning, greedy, and grateful for air. These weekends with Kwame—two weekends out of her whole suffocating life—had felt the same; they were air. And he could restore that feeling right now—if he stopped asking her to be a bad mother, to risk more than she could.

But, as Salma soaped and lathered and tried to rid herself of Kwame's musk, she couldn't help wondering how different life might've been had she been a bad daughter, the type everybody called "force-ripe"and "own-way." She might"ve fared better. *That* type of thirteen-year-old girl might've uttered a *steups* and walked right out of Tanty Nazroon's shop, when the curly-haired stranger in coveralls and rubber boots had aimed his chin at her and called her beautiful.

"Hello, *sundar larki*," Shiva had said. "You look just like your Mammy."

Both she and Tanty Nazroon had blushed—as much at his mistake as at the compliment. Then Tanty had pushed his two dollars change across the cracked laminate counter and turned to admire Salma. "Nah, this is my sister daughter," she'd said proudly.

"What you name?" he'd asked, and Tanty Nazroon had urged, "answer the nice Mister."

"I name Salma," she'd complied with a shy mumble. But a "bad" thirteen-year-old might've followed her own mind and stayed silent. At twenty-six years old now, she could see plainly that had been her mistake. She'd demonstrated to Shiva that day, and over the next few weeks of that fateful July, that she was wife material: a "good" little Indian girl who'd always obey her elders: her Mammy, her Pa, her Tanty, her big-sister Yasmeen, and even him.

Somewhere along the way, though, she'd changed. She no longer wanted to be good; she ached to be happy.

Kwame flitted around her, droning apologies, while she dressed and packed her bag.

"Look, I sorry. I not used to this… sharing thing. I never deal with no marrid woman before. It does mess with my head, nah. You slaving behind that asshole when—"

"When what?" Salma heaved her canvas tote marked *Brightstar Contracting*—the company where they worked—onto her shoulder.

"When *I* should be your man. Your *real* man. Why you don't just leave him?"

Her arms fell so limply at her sides that the tote slid off and landed at her feet with a dejected thump. In a whole year of friending, Kwame had never spoken like this—commitment talk, leave-your-husband talk—and she'd never let herself hope for it.

"Yeah, I saying it with my whole chest. Leave the damn fool. This is love, girl."

He laced his arms around her waist and drew her close, looking into her eyes in a way that made her realize she'd never seen him nervous until now. A soft hope stroked her heart but, almost instantly, she clamped shut, just like the Ti-Marie plants her children loved to play with and prod.

"Leave him and go where?" she said, in that weary tone she often used when one of the children called, "Mammy," too many times. Where could she possibly hide from Shiva? And did Kwame actually think she could just saunter off and go pay a rent and mind three children on a cleaner's salary? He laughed and threw his head so far back she saw straight up his nostrils. *He* could laugh, yes, because he'd never heard all the times Shiva had threatened her and all the times he'd mocked her: *Go where? Back by your mother-and-them to shame them? For the whole village to laugh at you? Go where? Nobody go want you with that string-band of chirren behind you!*

"Come *here,* with *me,*" Kwame said, with a winning smile that told her he wasn't nervous after all, and more than that, he expected her to be grateful to him and happy for this offer. That's what he was searching for on her face now, she guessed. But her mind went immediately to her "string-band of chirren." Did Kwame's offer extend to them too?

"Well, what you waiting for? Say, yes, nah girl? Today, today we could go and collect your things. I sure is not much. Just some clothes, ent?"

Salma's anger revved, like a noise that had always been there in the background, like the sound of Shiva's old weedwhacker whenever he moved from the garden's depths to the roadside grass. She tried to tear herself from Kwame, but couldn't, and they ended up struggling, pulling and tugging with arched backs, bounding from wall to wall like one organism with two shells.

Then she burst into tears, wailing so loudly that he kept asking, "What the ass wrong with you? What you getting on so for?" And, every time he said it, Salma cried harder because it became more and more apparent how little he understood her situation.

Finally, Kwame pinned her against the fridge. "I love you, Salma. That's what I trying to tell you, girl! Why the hell you can't understand that?"

The only "love" she was certain of was what she felt for her children. They'd been scooped from her flesh, she belonged to them, and they to her.

So, she shut her eyes and set Kwame a final test. "Then tell me bring the chirren and come, nah?" She needed him to prove Shiva a liar, to whisper something that would drown out the thirteen years of reproach roaring in her head. She needed to know that Kwame loved *all* of her—not just the Let-go-Beast Salma who'd ridden him like a *saapin* all weekend—but Mammy Salma as well, who packed lunch kits and wiped tears and shitty little asses. For a love like that, she'd be prepared to risk her life.

Kwame released her. "Ok, go," he said. "Go see 'bout your precious chirren and the man who try to drown you and thing. That's the life you like, eh? You like man to beat you up, ent? Well, gone from here!"

She grabbed her bag and ran to the front door, half-blinded by tears and hating herself for having dared to believe—even for a second—that Kwame's love might be big enough.

He followed and caught her in the gallery, prised open her fist. "Wait… at least take this for taxi money, nah."

She fled down the stairs with only the vaguest sense of dollars sloughing from her, like fish scales. She flagged the first taxi to come along, and got in without so much as a look-back.

Only then did she notice the two, red, dollar-notes, softening in her sweaty grip.

Two dollars. That's how it had started with Shiva, as well. He'd pushed the change from Tanty Nazroon back across the counter. "This is for the *larki*," he'd said, indicating Salma. And from her seat on the crates, she'd blinked down at the money, sensing she should refuse it. But he'd insisted, "Take it nah, girl," and Tanty Nazroon had nodded encouragingly, so Salma had jumped down and claimed the cash. Then she'd done a "big-woman" thing—crumpled the bills and shoved them deep into the too-big brassiere she'd inherited from Yasmeen—knowing instinctively that something about her life had just changed.

Later, over the course of these thirteen unlucky years of marriage, she'd come to understand that she'd been the object of a too-cheap shop transaction. And that's exactly why she hadn't wanted to accept taxi-fare from Kwame today, to accept chicken feed, compared to what he could've given, if he'd really loved her.

Unfair exchange is robbery, her Mammy and Pa had always said. And yet, look, they'd still given her away and exchanged her whole life, for only the three thousand dowry Shiva had paid. Of course, they'd also made him take *shahada*—accept Islam—so an Imam could perform the marriage quick, quick. But while it had cost Shiva nothing to lie to God, it had cost Salma everything every blasted day since then. She was tired of paying these debts that other people had thrust upon her. Paying, paying, paying, and getting cheated in return.

As the car pulled into The Croisée, she paid the two dollars and boarded a maxi-taxi heading to Port of Spain. Her phone rang. She felt its vibration through the bag on her knees. But confined as she was in the back seat, between other passengers, she got to the device a second too late. It was Yasmeen who'd called. Salma jammed her thumb and switched off the phone. She was not in the mood for another lecture about her responsibilities, when she knew them all too well.

The last time she'd made this exact walk, her body still warm from Kwame, she'd glided along this same Port of Spain pavement, not noticing the sleeping vagrants and not even wrinkling her nose at the smell of human excrement and unwashed flesh. Instead, she'd marveled at how pretty the place looked with the six a.m. sun dancing across the stained glass of the Cathedral and onto the Promenade's trees, and at how the retreating chill of night and the oncoming warmth of day combined to harden her nipples and make her wish to return to Kwame's bed.

Now, however, her body throbbed with left-over hurt, and she saw nothing but tired, despondent people. She felt crowded as shoulders and elbows scraped her, but she made no effort to avoid collision. She simply kept walking in a straight line, just the same way her father had taught her to do if she ever got lost in the Barrackpore forest. She passed a nuts vendor who interrupted his own chant—"Salt-and-fresh, salt-and-fresh!"—to heckle her, "Baby, fix yuh face, nah?" but she scowled deeper. A Jehovah Witness standing under Republic Bank shoved a magazine at her and said, "Smile, God loves you." But she walked by without taking the book, as she'd usually do. She was sick of hearing that the meek would inherit the earth. To hell with the whole earth, all she wanted to have was one man—just *one*—who would love her.

She was about to cry again, so she distracted her eyes, hitching them to the person walking immediately ahead. From his back pocket, the fringed end of a rag waved as he walked, its fabric so white that it glowed blue. The thing was either brand new or this man had a good woman who scrubbed her knuckles raw with blue soap on a jookin board. Did he even care? What a shame that, any minute now, he was going to pull it out and wipe his greasy face, soiling some poor woman's sacrifice.

Like Kwame.

Kwame had spoiled everything. He had corrupted the one thing she'd had to look forward to and draw comfort from: her times with him. She could never go back. Not now that he'd proven Shiva right: what a fool she'd been to think that she—a stupid lil coolie girl, a woman with three children—could ever set her own terms with a man.

Even Pa had once said similar. That morning when she'd gone to him before dawn while he was seated at the dining table, drinking his coffee before heading out to the field. Twisting a finger in her cotton nightie, she'd stood at eye-level with him and said, "Pa, I don't want to marrid Shiva. Yasmeen like him. So, why you don't marrid she to him?"

"But he don't want Yaz. He want you, Sally."

"But I not ready, Pa. I want to go back to school. I feel I go do better this time."

Pa had shaken his head and wrapped his hand, with halting tenderness, around the arm of the yellow enamel mug. Salma had stood there, wishing it could be her skinny yellow arm. She'd wanted him to cradle and baby her like he used to, a few guava seasons ago, before she'd gotten breast swells and underarm hair, before he'd abruptly abandoned her to Mammy and Tanty Nazroon and their endless lessons on how to *balay* and *sakay* and clean and wash for a future husband.

"School is for bright chirren, Sally. Otherwise, is just wastin time. So, I send you to wuk in Nazroon shop, look, only couple weeks and this Shiva come sniffing behind you. More will come, and more will come, until *braps!* you make a mistake and let some chupid fella use you. Nobody go want you then, you go remain on my hand, get over-ripe and rotten. I can't let that happen. It better you marrid now. This Shiva say he go carry you in Town, where it have plenty white people and rich people and thing, where you could live free as a big-woman in your own place."

My God, Shiva had lied so well!

Salma reached the Diego Martin maxi-taxi stand. She climbed into one of the empty mini-buses idling there. It would take a while to fill up, but the wait would give her time to collect herself and practice her story—one last rehearsal—to make sure it matched what she'd said to Shiva and the children during calls over the weekend: *It was a real big bull. Uncle Kazim and the other brothers in the mosque kill it. I spend whole weekend helping Aunty Yasmeen cook for visitors. Kazim drop me by the bus place early this morning. I didn't bring none of the beef 'cause it woulda thaw out and drip blood all over the place.*

This would be *her* last lie, Salma swore to herself. By the time Kwame returned from the rig, there would be nothing but vapors left between them. She would no longer encourage him, and she sure as hell wouldn't listen to him talk about "Love."

She hopped from the maxi and began trudging the dead end street to the base of the mountain, craning her neck because, at a particular angle, she'd glimpse the house. Over the years, Shiva had replaced plywood walls and roofing sheets blown off during rainy season, but the structure had remained substantially the same: a wooden box on stilts, teetering on the side of a bushy hill. They did not own the land. Like all the other squatters, Shiva had simply cleared a space and, with pine lumber he'd credited from Chang's Hardware on the Main Road, he'd fashioned a marital home out of the smaller box in which he'd grown up.

But Salma had never gotten the chance to be a big-woman in her own house, the way Pa had predicted. Still, she reminded herself now as she drew closer, there'd been some good days up there, in that box. That was where her children had been born and where they were now sleeping. She experienced a pulse of joy at the thought of seeing them, inhaling their smell: Abby like baby oil, the other two like Lifebuoy soap—except, in Anand's case, there was the musky promise of teenaged boyhood. She *had* missed them this weekend. Despite all the ramping with Kwame, she hadn't stopped thinking about her children.

She came to the foot of the mountain, where the village standpipe stood. Its brassy head had once been attached to a length of PVC which would often break and cause a fountain that all the squatter-children enjoyed. But recently, some Good Samaritan had encased the raw plumbing in a concrete tower, and made a level platform underneath, so buckets could stand without tipping. Tomorrow, at this hour, Salma would be jostling other parents to fill water for the children to bathe before school. But today, she used the concrete as a bench, to rest her aching back and gather courage for that steep unpaved trek to her "home."

If only Kwame had said, "Bring the chirren." If only he'd loved her that much, she would've loved him back for the rest of her life. She would've gone straight to the police station on the Main Road and asked them to come back here with her, and all she would've taken was Anand, Nadya, and Abby. Shiva could've kept everything else.

And how long before he woulda find you? she chided herself.

How long before he would've shown up on her job brandishing a two-by-four as he'd done the last time she'd worked late? How long before he would've shown up at the children's school?

A flock of wild parrots squawked overhead, taunting her with their lofty green freedom, splattering her with sadness. It wasn't the same old hurt she'd carried since thirteen years old; this was fresh and unexpected. If only she had somewhere to go with her children, someone to protect them from Shiva. Not even Kwame could ever do that, she had to concede, and maybe he'd been right not to offer to. Maybe she was wrong to be so mad at him? Maybe...

She drew her phone from the bag, switched it on and saw no missed calls from him.

But five from Yasmeen? She dialed and then aborted the call. If she spoke to Yaz right now, she would find herself asking a question for which she already had the answer. And Yaz would say: *No! You can't come here, girl. What Kazim will say if I encourage you to leave your husband?*

Within a few months of Salma's marriage to Shiva, the same Imam had found Kazim Hosein to marry Yaz, and it seemed that the tension between the sisters—because Shiva had chosen Salma over Yaz—had begun to dissipate. They did, in fact, grow closer during their first simultaneous pregnancies. And closer still after Shiva's accident: somebody on the road crew had been using a jackhammer and something had pitched up and hit Shiva, taking half the vision in that right eye. Government didn't want him no more, so he'd gone from sulking at home to drinking at the rumshop down the road. He wore an eye-patch—put it on every day, like a uniform, before picking his way down the mountain—and people sympathetic to his injury bought him drinks. Anand had been about a year old then, Salma had needed milk and Pampers, she'd tried to talk sense into Shiva one day. "Get a next work, or go plant garden and sell," she'd said. And that was when everything had changed for the worse. Instead of the few slaps she was accustomed to receiving—the normal way she'd seen Pa fix-up Mammy—Shiva had beaten her that day like she wasn't a real flesh-and-blood person, like she was a demon he was trying to slay; beaten her till her face had doubled in size. And it became a hobby for him after that. And after every beating, Yasmeen had counseled, "Girl, that's how all them man is. Kazim does well cut my ass, too, when he drink he rum." And in that way, the sisters, though distant, became each other's confidantes. Chatting every day, detailing the joys of motherhood, along with the horrors of wifehood, but somehow Salma continued to sense a vein of resentment beneath the surface of their sisterly love. She heard it throbbing like background music every time Yazmeen said: *Count your blessings, at least you get to live up in Town.* Salma was glad Yaz had never come to visit, had never seen how she really lived here, among these ketch-ass negro people on a mountain outside the city. These people who'd always known about Shiva's relationship with Miss Jackie, who'd watched him lead Salma straight up the mountain as a teenaged bride, who'd seen him pen her in, who'd heard her cries and bleating… but had chosen never to intervene in "coolie-people business."

The front room—combined living room and kitchen—was empty. The children's bedroom door was closed—they must still be asleep. The door to the smaller bedroom, the one she shared with Shiva, was open. Salma walked bravely toward it, not knowing what to expect. For good luck, she touched her glass-case of ceramic figurines and religious ornaments, and—*phew!*—

he was not in the bedroom. Probably in the garden.

She unpacked her clothes and put on an old house dress. Then she tiptoed into the children's room, stood over the king-sized mattress—something her boss had been ready to throw away—and studied the children. How Anand and Nadya formed two sides of a capital "H"while the steamroller, little Abby, formed the bridge in between. She recalled what her father-in-law, Lall, had said about them before he died: *This generation go be gold.* Well, to Salma, they were worth more than gold; more than Kwame or any blasted man's love. Their happiness was fair exchange for hers.

She closed the ill-fitting door carefully, to reduce its dragging, and crossed to the kitchen. From the lower part of the rust-freckled fridge, she got eggs, but had to fight the freezer door, which was iced shut. She used a sharpened screwdriver to dislodge a pack of chicken feet to thaw for lunch. She was supposed to defrost the fridge this weekend. She would do that today, she decided. Along with ironing school uniforms and making some cheese paste for the children to take tomorrow. Since last week, she'd covered their books with brown paper. And she'd left instructions for Anand to pack everybody's schoolbag and scrub everybody's school shoes. He'd complained, "But Mammy, my toe squeezing in these," but Salma had known it was just a trick to get new shoes. She chuckled now, remembering the conversation.

"What have you so happy, girl?" Shiva's voice came from behind.

She wheeled to see him sitting in the doorway, removing wet boots, garden coverall peeled down to his waist, muddy cutlass on the floor.

"I ain't hear you come up the steps, nah. I not-too-long reach. The boil egg almost done. You want Milo tea? Or coffee?" She talked fast and moved even faster, trying to look dutiful: grabbing the small pot, filling it with water from the plastic barrel next to the sink, taking it to the stove.

"Coffee," Shiva replied.

While the water boiled, she peeled eggshells. There was silence, except for the sound of metal on metal, him using a file to scrape mud from the cutlass blade, as he usually did after a damp morning in the garden.

Back to normal. She was in his box, as if the whole weekend hadn't happened. This was her lot—she'd just have to accept it—but at least she'd had those few times with Kwame.

"So where you was?" Shiva asked.

"How you mean? Barrackpore, with Yasmeen-them for Eid—"

"I say: where the fuck you was?" He raised his voice. "I call there this morning, to tell you pass in the bank machine and take out forty dollars for me. The daughter answer. She say she ain't see you whole weekend. She say you was never there."

Salma felt her face reddening, her pulse quickening. She tried to recall whether there'd been a missed call from Shiva on her phone. But there had been so many from Yasmeen—her sister had been trying to warn her, she now understood.

She kept her back to Shiva as her quivering hand raked eggshells into the trash.

"That lil girl over-dotish," she managed to say, her voice steady only because she knew she had a trump card in Yasmeen. Yes, they'd had some pulling-and-tugging ever since they were small, but no matter what they were sisters and, knowing the danger Shiva posed, Yasmeen would never put Salma at risk. "Let we ring Yaz now, now. She go clear up everything for you."

"I done talk to she," Shiva said. "She lie like wind… till she tie up she-own-self… and then she confess it: you was never there."

Once upon a time, some years ago, Salma had been toting a full bucket of water up the hill, carefully, losing only a little now-and-then as some splashed over the brim. But then the handle had snapped and Salma had screamed at the sudden release of weight and at the horror of watching all her effort and everything precious plummeting down the side of the mountain. Strangely, that moment came to mind now, as she turned slowly to face Shiva. She started to say his name, but in one lunge, he crossed the kitchen and grabbed her neck.

"W'happen? Dog bite you?" he asked, poking her shoulder.

Kwame's teeth marks. They'd been so far from her mind—like something from another life—she hadn't thought to wear sleeves.

With his free hand, Shiva ripped down her housedress as if it were made of Anand's kite paper. "And w'happen here?" he asked, pointing to her breast, "*Soucouyant* suck you?"

He released her neck then, and sure enough, on the pale flesh beside her nipple, there was a purplish bruise.

He slapped her. She stumbled backward, but the sink caught her.

"You feel I stupid! You feel I dotish! Since you get that office wuk, you feel you better than me. Which one-ah-them you fuckin? Eh? Who it is? Is a nigger man, nah? Or is the boss, the white fella?"

Normally, Salma would just stand there and take the loud cussing, or curl up like a *congoree* on the floor and take the heel pounding, wishing to die. But normally she was innocent; today she was guilty, and it made her determined that Shiva should not take the rest of her life, leaving her children motherless, without a bloody-good, ring-down battle for her soul.

She dashed to the stove, reaching for the pot of hot water, but then her arm fell away, like a broken stem, and hung at her side. She glanced down to see why it had disobeyed her. When she looked up, the cutlass was coming at her again. In her mind, she raised the same arm to block, but in real life nothing happened, so she shut her eyes.

The children's door grated open, and Anand shouted, "No, Daddy, no!"

Salma cried, "Go, son!" willing him to remember what she'd drilled into his head, like schoolwork, so many times: *If I ever tell you go, leave everything, take your sisters, run by Miss Jackie and tell she call police, you hear?*

But Anand didn't move, he just stood there screaming, "Somebody come! Daddy killin Mammy! Allyuh come!"

Shiva turned away from her then and moved toward the boy, pointing the cutlass. "Hush your mouth, boy! Your mudder is a old 'ho! She look for this! Is she who make me—"

With her good hand, Salma retrieved the screwdriver atop the fridge, jammed the tip into her husband, and kept pushing until he cried out. Only then did she withdraw, satisfied that she'd hurt him as deeply as any woman could, almost as deep as his waste ah time mother had. She wanted to stab again but, suddenly, she was so very tired. She heard him thundering down the front steps while everything around her—the entire kitchen—began to dissolve into tiny yellow dots, like the chicken feed she and Yasmeen once fed to their fluffy little common-fowl pets: stroking, loving, fattening them while knowing full well that, soon enough, Pa would take them away, to be plucked and gutted. But that would not happen to my daughters, Salma decided, as she sank to the floor. If Allah saved her life today, she'd never ask her girls to be "good"and she'd never marry them off—*they* would have to choose when to leave *her*, for she would never, ever leave them.

In fact, she swore, as her eyes closed, she would teach Nadya and Abby to be "bad," to fight for their happiness like their lives depended on it, like no one was coming to save them.

Because in the end, no one was.

TERRE BRULÉE

Boy-chirren different. A daughter will always be yours, but boy-child come like guava: brace yourself, it might have worm. My son, Shiva, was like that; something was eating him from the inside, till he rotten through-and-through.

But it have good boys. Like this one here, my nephew, Sheldon. We in the gallery, smoking, like how we does every Friday. Me in a plastic chair, Sheldon lolling-off on the banister with one hand on the clothesline spanning the gap between this concrete house and the old family house—the wooden one—where he does live with my favorite-sister and she string-band of chirren. Sheldon is the onliest one get me out my room this last month, since Shiva dead. You see, I always had a soft-spot for this boy. Me, with my whoring, Sheldon, with he dreadlocks and he black-man father who breed and leave—we is the two outcast in this family. And from small, this boy spirit always match mines more than my own son, Shiva.

Oh Shiva, Shiva! I been crying forty days. And tonight, even though Sheldon and all of St. James so excited for Small Hosay parade, I can't celebrate because one thought steady beating me like drum: *Lord, forgive me for Shiva!*

So when Sheldon take a drag on he *ganja* post, then ask, "Is how big people could just starve a lil child, ent, Aunty Pinkie?" I mistake it for accusation.

"Catch your-damn-self, boy. I never starve nobody."

But he was talking 'bout the Hosay story: 'bout Ali-Asgar,

The Prophet great-grandson, and how the infidel-them kill the child during the Battle of Karbala. The story why Muslims does make small *tadjahs*—baby-size Taj Mahal-looking tombs—and parade them like funeral, through the streets. I did learn that story back when I was a girl in Muslim-school, but Sheldon—poor soul—he only now finding out.

"Cease and settle, Aunty. I not accusing you," he say, sounding real hurt. I pull on my cigarette, soften my tone, and say, "I know," hoping he don't notice how my eye-them full of water like icetray in a bruk-down freezer. "I just saying: my child, Shiva, never starve. I wasn't perfect. Me and he father used to war, so I wasn't there all the time, but I always make sure that lil boy never starve for nothing." That part true: I used to make grocery, pack cardboard box, and tote that bugger up the mountain—me, one—to go feed my son.

But it have other parts I can't tell Sheldon: like when I did get lay-off from the Chinee laundry, and I couldn't even pick-up a Mister or two to tide me over ('cause I did went with a Vincy sailor-man and catch a bad case of the runnings), so to buy groceries I had-was to pawn my most prize possession, the gold *bera* bracelet my grandfather make with he own hand and give my father, who then give me. It safe now, under my bed, but to buy it back, I had-was to sex the *bowsie*-back Mister in the pawn shop. Shiva was worth it to me, though.

Suddenly, the sound of a *tassa* drum ripple through the night air, like the rifle fire we does hear whenever gang war break out in the valley. You see, St. James come like a big amphitheater—the sea in front, the mountains behind—so every noise does bounce and come back louder. More drums go be starting-up soon enough. Nobody eh sleeping tonight. But for me, that normal, because I eh sleep in a month. If Shiva was here, he woulda point he finger and say: *Yes, Mammy, no rest for the wicked!*

But he not here. He dead as Ali-Asgar; onliest difference is: my Shiva eh bury yet. And that's what bothering me this whole month: How to send my son to rest in peace? When I-self wasn't at peace with my son. I wasn't on good terms with Shiva, neither he wife; I did stop going by them long time—must be five years now. We was living like strangers.

"Aunty, everybody else in that Karbala desert was big people who coulda fend for theyself. But them soldiers watch a baby and just murder it? When Jameel tell me that story, I cry, you know."

"You *must* cry," I say, and in the darkness, under this low-watt green bulb, I take a chance and let my own tears run wild from cheek to jaw, like *carailli* vine on a rusting fence. "Lord, was murder, in truth."

Forgive me for the man Shiva grow to be! A man who chop he wife dead in front their chirren, then drink poison and murder he-self, all because she wanted to leave him. Since it happen, I eh leave this house. To come out and go anywhere, I woulda have to walk down the hill, past all my neighbors; I woulda have to walk wondering if they done put two-and-two together and realize the latest murder-man in the news is *my* son. Wonder if they calling me *La Diablesse*—a devil-woman who does breed beast—or if they still watching me as just a innocent ex-*jammette*. And even if I get past *my* neighbors, then I woulda have to walk past the cemetery where, rumor have it, all Shiva neighbors done chip-in and bury he wife. And even-self I get past the cemetery, then, to turn left is to face Forensics where Shiva still lying down, waiting for me to claim him. To turn right is to face the crematorium where he always say he did want to go ("No worm must eat me, Mammy. Just burn my ass.")

So forty days I asking myself: *How to come out from inside of here?*

I so shame.

Sometimes, the shame does be so deep in my belly, it does bend me over and have me on the floor, twitching up like fits. Yes, we wasn't on good terms, me and Shiva, but a mother does feel guilty for everything bad in she chirren life, whether they do it or receive it, she does feel is *she* fault.

Sheldon say, "I wish I could go back in time and fight for the lil boy. You know wha' I mean, Aunty?"

And, instantly, I wonder if is Allah sending message in code: *Pinkie, if you don't fight whatever it is keeping you from your boy-child; if you don't go down there and claim him, who go do it? Time ticking.*

Is true. I used to brush a old-police from CID, so I know them fridge-and-them in Forensics barely working. I know Government can't keep Shiva long, maybe one more week, then is plywood box and pauper funeral. Rotten and stinking. No headstone, no name.

I bolt from the chair, lean over the banister and retch... but only water coming up. Belly too empty.

"W'happen Aunty?" Sheldon rubbing my back and I coldsweating. "Must be gas. Look, sip the sweet-drink," he say.

I wipe my mouth on my duster sleeve and take the cup. Sheldon know I does only drink old-time glass-bottle Cokes—not the horse-piss they selling in plastic bottle—so he does buy six every week and bring for me. More than Shiva ever do. I always used to feel that boy had me in he craw, and he father used to *chook* thing in he brain against me. And is he father whey force my son to marrid that country-bookie girl, who come to Town, get bright and make Shiva run me like dog from their yard.

Still, I sorry. Every woman have a right to go. Why he *kill* the girl?

The Cokes burn slow, going down, till a different question pop-in my head. "But, Shel, how you end up by Jameel, for him to tell you the Hosay story?"

He was delivering fabric, he say, for Jameel-and-them to make their flags and big *tadjahs* for Hosay. "Them was now knocking the wood-frames together. I make a joke and say if it have Small Hosay and Big Hosay parade, it should have 'Medium Hosay' for half-breed like me to party. But the man get irate, *oui!* Call me ignorant and make me listen the whole history."

A grunt drop out my mouth. I agree with Jameel: young people ignorant bad. But is who make them to be so… ent is old people? That's the question I can't escape: What *I* ever do to make Shiva so ignorant till he want to kill? And I keep coming back to one answer: is not me, is he father have him so. Yes, I coulda bring Shiva to live with me here, but I don't see how that woulda work. A boy should never watch he mother making fares. A boy should never know. That's why I did always keep my two worlds separate. It easier for people to love half-pound, rather than the whole weight of you.

"Then, Jameel invite me to build with them," Sheldon still explaining. "If you see how them men does sacrifice—so much nights building *tadjah* and tuning drum in fire—all for their God. Tonight, I go be pushing a small *tadjah* that I build. Come and watch me, nah, Aunty? It go help you."

I study him hard. I start to wonder if he know 'bout Shiva, if somebody tell him that was he own family on the front page of every papers. Me eh think anybody inside here know—nobody say boo to me—except my favorite-sister, she did knock quiet

quiet on the door one day and say, "Pinkie, girl, I sorry." And she wouldn't run she mouth. She know I never like all the *marish* and the *parish* in my private affairs.

I refuse Sheldon invitation. Silence fall. I puff my cigarette, he puff he joint. We exhale the same: aiming the smoke from the house. We know how to stay outta people way. That's what I used to do when I was young: when my sister-them cuss and kick me here, I used to go there by Shiva and he father; and when he father cuss and kick me there, I used to come back here, by my sister-them. Bob-and-weave, is so I live.

Prrrrrrat-ta-ta-ta-taat! Somewhere down the hill, another *tassa* drum roll.

Sheldon say, "Them-fellas warming up."

"I hear," I say, and my mind follow the drum echo. I thinking 'bout what did happen after Shiva last daughter born. Three months straight, that baby *screel* out she lungs. I did keep telling Shiva wife, "This child born with a *caul*, she seeing spirit. Let me carry she by a pundit to get *jharay*." And one day, I did pick up the child to go but the wife start bawling for Shiva. He run from the garden, grab the child, and say, "You playing best-grand- mother? *You?* The worst mother ever? Go! Nobody want you here!"

Them is the last words my son ever tell me.

How I could barge in Forensics, saying, "I name Mother. I want my son"? He didn't want me in life, why he go want me in death? I know my place.

"So, you turning Muslim now?" I say, trying to swing the conversation, and my own thoughts, back towards Sheldon and the *tadjah* he so proud of.

"Nah, Aunty. I-and-I would never betray Jah. But when I listen Jameel, my heart start gnashing. I had-was to do something with the downful vibes. I had-was to either break something or build something, you overstand? So I build that pretty pretty baby tomb, and it make me feel better."

I nod, again and again, because I know that same feeling: sadness that trying to claw through your chest, restlessness *chooking* you to do something but you not sure what or how.

Sheldon slide off the banister and stand up. He biting he lip and watching me sheepish as he say, "I hadda leave now to help them-fellas. But... you go come tonight? It go do you plenty good, Aunty."

Poor heart, like he sense in he spirit: Aunty Pinkie have plenty plenty things she need to bury. He sense I need a funeral more than anybody else in St. James tonight.

"I go come, Shel," I say, without fully believing it, but I know that deep down I *wants* to come out from here; and I know if I could even-self crawl out tonight, maybe tomorrow I could stand up in broad daylight.

I drag the grip from under my bed—old-style grip: cardboard and vinyl, with metal corners—Pa used to call it he "valise." Inside, have all my important business. Me eh open it long time, but tonight, I searching for something—not sure what, I go know when I see it—but I just feeling that the way out this house tonight is not through the front door or back door, is through the past.

The latch spring open. I lift the lid sl-o-o-w like opening a crypt, like I expecting a evil *jumbie.* But nothing happen. Scatter 'round, it have some mildew-white envelopes with a setta fading studio pictures: Ma in she best frock, Pa in he one suit, me and my sisters in we *dan-dan* when we was small, even Baba Khan, my grandfather who did come off the last Indian ship, watch him in he *dhoti* and jacket.

Now, look the envelope with only pictures of me—pictures nobody ever see, except me and the man whey take them. When Pa did carry me in Town for the first time, was to pay rent by we landlord, old Mr. Stone, and I was twelve years. And when Mr. Stone call me in the back, I did went because Pa say, "Go, *beti*." And that day, and every month after that, Mr. Stone used to make me lie down on he office couch and, starting from my head, the man used to sniff me straight down to in-between my toe-them. In all the years, till he dead, Mr. Stone never touch me no other way, he never feel me up, he never sex me. He only used to smell me and then pose me and take picture with he big black camera. That's all. Until I did get to like it—being worship by this old white man, with he red jiggly face and he trembling hand so prune-up as if whole day he jookin 'clothes in tub instead of counting cash behind desk. But I couldn't show the man that I like it. He did steady telling me, "Don't be afraid," because is frighten self he did want me—"shy and demure," he used to say—just how he meet me.

But now, I come so old, things change: nowadays, I does frighten to feel exposed.

Inside a long manila folder, I find the Deed paper for this property: 33 Terre Brulée Road. From Mr. Edward Stone to me, Pinkie Khan. This coulda be Shiva own. I never tell he wotless father 'bout this, and I never tell *he* neither. I did hold back because I didn't want no man—not even my son—to love me for land. But now, I eh know what go happen when I dead, it go be one setta *commess*: somebody go find this paper and then they go hadda find Shiva chirren—the boy and two girls. I sure the wife family take them. Wherever they is, though, I staying far. Ent that's what Shiva wanted? I's over sixty years now, I can't fight-up again for chirren love. I go make-do with Sheldon alone.

My hand fall on a plastic bag. As I loose the knot, a smell hit me. Baby powder. I pull out a vest with blue piping and press it to my nose. I did put this on Shiva to bring him home after he born. I dip again and find the plastic ID-band the nurse-them had on him. Watch how small it is, nah! Hard to believe a man hand does start off so small and then grow so big it could damage a body. This was the first time my child name ever get use in this world. I read it out now, "Shiva Gopaul,"and the sound cause that trembling again, deep in the ravine between my chest and my belly, as if my *butchette* drop or I take-in with *nara* strain.

I *shub* the ID-band in my duster pocket, not sure why, but I feeling like I have to carry it with me tonight to that parade.

And now, a next bracelet on my mind. I shifting things until I glimpse the old "Y de Lima & Co" box. *Oui-papa!* In one blink, I see all the man I ever truly love parading through my mind in Indian-file: Shiva, Pa, Mr. Stone and Baba Khan. He was the best jeweler in Coolie Town; De Lima used to send for him whenever they had big-shot clients who want "exquisite" things. That's how this *bera* get make.

I take it out the box and heft it—so heavy, the gold bright, the rod thick like my little-finger and glittering with *carailli* cut diamond pattern, then each head is a globe swirling upward to a point, like the dome of a *tadjah* or even the great Taj Mahal. What a bracelet! I remember the store did order it for a client who never pay, so Baba Khan keep it because is the first one he make with this design and he didn't know if he would ever make something so perfect again. He did give Pa and Pa give me. And when I did make Shiva, I hold the same lil plastic ID-band, and promise he newborn ears that, when he come a big man, I woulda give him this *bera* instead. But one day, one day *congotay!*— that day never come.

I drop the *bera* in my next duster pocket—it going parade too! And I have no time to ask myself why, because a fresh setta hurt start collecting in my chest, like somebody turn on a stand-pipe full blast. I open my mouth to cry out, but my throat have a pressure valve that lock-off, while my eye-rim overflowing. Then—*Bam, Bam, Bam!*—somebody pound the door.

"Aunty Pinkie! Sheldon say you walking with we to watch Hosay! You ready?"

With the sheet hem, I wipe my face. I hurry to close the grip. Stop crying now, I need my energy to walk out this house and do something with this *bera* and this ID-band—I not sure what the hell yet—but I know I go feel better afterwards.

Is midnight and we heading downhill: down Terre Brulée Road, down Bournes Road. Them chirren—my niece-and-nephew-and-them—talking a setta shit 'bout Sheldon.

I hearing them, eh, but I not listening. I feeling so strange since I leave the house. Is like everything around me—things I seeing my whole life—looking so weird like I watching them for the first time. Is like St. James grow big, big over the forty days I was inside. Every lamppost taller, every streetlight higher. Till the night come like a roof over a mansion for giants, and I's a midget on this pavement. I so lost, me eh even notice when we pass the cemetery.

One of my nephew say, "Sheldon not stupid. This hadda have profit in it for him."

A next one say, "Must be some Muslim girl he tracking…"

Steups! This modern generation believe in scheme and con. They can't believe somebody could just have a good heart and decide to sacrifice for somebody else. Hear them talking big, as if they wise, but they don't even know where the roof over they head come from. Is *me.* It come from me. Pa did always tell me, "If Stone ever ask what you want, say you want to own where your navel-string bury. He ha 'plenty land, he could gi' you this one easy." So I was ready when the opportunity did come, when Mr. Stone take-in sick and send for me one last time. I was seventeen when I ask for the land and them pictures; he give me without a fight. I over-cry when that man dead a few months after; I did studying *Who go love-off on me so again?* Then I did meet Shiva father by the laundry and, to this day, I feel I woulda never put myself with *he*, if I wasn't still grieving Mr. Stone; and I woulda never ever stay, if I didn't get pregnant with Shiva. I didn't want the child, until he come out and I watch he and he watch me, and I feel this is the one man who go be worth any sacrifice, even my own soul.

We reach we usual spot: the traffic-light opposite Luckput Street. Small crowd, just like any other Small Hosay. Is only die-hards on these first few nights of Muhurram month. Most people only interested in tomorrow night, Big Hosay, with all the big *tadjah* that almost touching the telephone wire. You see, most people could only understand BIG things. But, simple as you see me here, dumb and stupid with no education, I know it not good to scorn small things. Small things carry plenty goodness, press down like seed. You never know what hiding inside a small thing. I know, though—I been small all my life.

Suddenly, in the nearish distance, I hear *tassa*: small drums rolling (*prrrraat-ta-ta-ta-taat…*), and cymbals chiming (*ching-cha, ching-cha, ching, ching…*).

In one pocket, I grab Shiva ID-band; in the next pocket, I slip on the *bera*. I feeling like I in-between baby-Shiva and man-Shiva, holding on to both same time.

"They coming." Somebody say it, then everybody repeat, "they coming… they coming…" and people start angling to see down the road, and the night start to change, and the air start to crackle like fire.

"Who in front?" I ask my niece. "Jameel Yard supposed to be first. That's the order from since I small."

"Me eh know, Aunty. I only seeing the *tassa* boys."

"Look behind. Check the flag-them on the *kathiya* platform. What color flag you seeing most? Purple?"

"Yeah, I think so."

"That's Jameel Yard. Sheldon with them. He coming."

My heart pick up a pace. Breeze twirling my dress, I's a lil girl again: standing up beside Baba Khan watching Firepass ritual, hearing the drums and feeling excited and scared same time, because I know God about to pass and touch some people and it have a chance I could be one, and I want that but I don't want it same time, cause I don't know what He go want me do in return. "Pick a drum," Baba Khan used to tell me, "and listen it good. It go talk one of these days and tell you what God want."

"They coming!"

The drummers near enough for me to feel the *dhol*—the big bass make from tree trunk and goat skin—vibrating through my body. My heart start to pump in time—*dhung-dunk, dhung-dunk*—and my lungs turn harmonium. Ever since I small, I did always like this feeling, this oneness with something powerful. For me, big drum was always the closest thing to God—although, it never really say nothing to me.

But tonight, I pick the small drum. Or rather, I feel when the small drum pick me. It happen just now: the moment them *tassa* boys change their rhythm from the slowness of the "Marching Hand" to the fastness of the "War Hand" that supposed to make everybody think of the Battle in Karbala. The drum say, "Pinkie! Is war! Is war!"

Well, I shock, *oui!* I born and bred in St. James, I see countless Hosay and a good few Firepass, but a drum never talk my private business before. Yes, is *war* self I been fighting this last month, war between the love I still have for my boy-child—the eight-pounds baby I did born from between my two *nashy* leg—and the disgust I feeling for the man he turn out to be. War, between this feeling that I coulda do something different as a mother, and this knowing that you does make chirren but you don't make their mind. Is war! I start to shake. Everybody shaking, because *tassa* playing and their body want to dance, but I shaking different. I shaking from a war that want to fling me down in the road—just how it had me fling-down on my bedroom floor whole month—and *pappyshow* me for everybody to see my vulgar shame.

I falling but—*quick!*—I drop everything in my pocket and grab my niece on one side and my nephew on the next.

"You ok, Aunty?"

No time to answer. The *tassa* boys reach alongside: every man have a cloth round he neck holding he drum, and he forehead frown and he lip press, and he two drumstick lashing the goatskin like he killing the poor animal again. And every roll getting longer—*prrrraat, prrrrrraaat*—like the drum begging now, "Pinkieeee, doh fall down! Time to stand-up for your childddd!"

I glimpse the *kathiya* now—the silky flags fluttering and mirroring streetlight. Then the drum-hand change again, it slow down lil bit, just as the *kathiya* reach where I could see it in full: a square platform surrounded by flag poles but, in the middle, a small *tadjah* resembling a wedding cake, when is really a tomb. The white walls, the domes shaped like the ends of the *bera* in my pocket, the crescent moon and shimmering star. Yes, is just cardboard and paint, glue and paper, but it looking like it build from magic and love.

"Sheldon!" somebody call.

And is true, he right there, behind the *kathiya*, wheeling it forward. He have-on the same black track-pants and T-shirt from when I did see him earlier. He right: is a funeral. All of we shoulda be wearing-on black.

"Dougla-Gong!" somebody say and Sheldon wave. Then he spot me and… *voosh!*… he dash over.

"Aunty Pinkie, you really come!" He hug me tight and lift me off the ground. And that's when the drum talk again: *Let go the child, so you could bury the man.*

I whisper in Sheldon ears-hole. "Go with the *tadjah* by the sea later."

He put me down and say, "Ok," but he eye-them groping my face like they trying to find the door in a wall.

"Take this," I say, and I fold Shiva ID-band into Sheldon palm. "Chook it inside the tomb before allyuh push it out to sea."

"Ok," he say again, but this time he eye steady, so I know he understand. "I go do that for you, Aunty. I promise."

He run back to the *kathiya*. It passing us now but he glancing back at me and smiling. The *tassa* hand change again, get even slower. I recognize this rhythm and remember the name from Muslim-school: *The Hands of Sorrow.*

They does beat this rhythm to symbolize the Battle done.

Well, I lean on the traffic-light, and right here on the Western Main Road, I spread open my heart and surrender. The sadness ease out wet and gentle, like when you peeing down yourself in a dream. And the dream I seeing is the future—what Sheldon go do by the sea later. I don't need to be there to see it, I could stay right here, because I done see it happen so much times in the past. He and some next fella go jump-out the pick-up truck, but leave-on the low-beam to shine a path to the water. Sheldon go hold one side of the base and the next fella go hold the 'nother side, and they go lift the *tadjah* out the tray and walk, in the light, down to the shore. Then he go say, "Wait, *bai*," and they go rest it down so he could pull off he sneakers and hoist he track-pants as high as it could go. Then, they go walk into the sea with the *tadjah*. They go walk careful, careful, feeling with they foot. They go walk as far as the beam from the van could stretch, and when water hit them high enough, they go float the *tadjah* and push it 'way into the Gulf. And it go make the water ripple for a minute and, in the van light, it go look like is God zipping open the black sea. But wet cardboard and paper don't take long to sink. Blink twice, it go disappear: a watersoak tomb for two innocent lil baby: Ali-Asgar, The Prophet great-grandson, and Shiva Gopaul, Pinkie Khan onliest son.

"Look the next Yard coming!" somebody say, and is so I remember where I is. Yes, it still have six more tombs to parade, but I done get-through with the first one.

Now is time to bury the man. But not everything could clean off in water, some things does take fire. So Baba Khan did say, a time when we was watching Firepass and I did ask him why so much people does walk them red-hot coals. Shiva did always insist he want to cremate. Maybe he did know a secret that the rest of we didn't know. Maybe he did understand that he had something inside him that needed to burn 'way for he soul to come pure gold.

I will go for him tomorrow. But I have two stops to make first: one by the crematorium to find out the price, and one to pawn the *bera* to pay that price.

And this time I don't want it back.

This time, it go belong to my son.

Thou hast made me endless, such is thy pleasure.
Rabindranath Tagore, Gitanjali

There is no death, only a change of worlds.
Chief Seattle, 1854 speech

NOW

2008-2017

STAR-GIRL

2008, Barrackpore Village, Trinidad, West Indies

Once upon a time, if you'd asked who my best friend was, I would've said I had two: a girl-bestie, Brianna Chinapoo, and a guy-bestie, her older brother, Andre. We were like triplets conjoined at the hip. "Bree" and "Dre" were equally matched, always throwing *picong* at each other in the way siblings do; while I, Nadia, just kind of existed in the middle, quietly happy to be with them and feed off the connection.

But at some point during the year I turned eighteen—maybe it was the looming fact of us all leaving for universities abroad—I sensed a shift in our tripartite relationship. Andre and I were falling in love; it felt incestuous and super-powerful. Brianna seemed oblivious, though, so we found ourselves using her, more and more, as a cover to spend time together safely and platonically, while yet craving the forbidden. I did and did not want to love Andre, because in my experience, it was the people I loved who always got taken away.

Now, as I look back on the moment when he asked what I wanted for my eighteenth birthday, I feel certain I would've spared myself a great deal of pain, if I'd lied to him. Maybe said a new denim jacket, or a G-shock watch—something cool but ultimately forgettable. Instead, I did a crazy, possessed thing that has haunted me ever since: I said I wanted him to help me find my dead mother's family—The Mohammeds. And I wanted to do it on Christmas Day, when families gather under one roof, so it would be easier to locate a scattered tribe. And I wanted to do it on *that* Christmas Day—December 25th, 2008—the last before I was to fly off to study Law. And I wanted to do it with *him*—of course we'd have to take Brianna, but that was fine because whenever we were altogether, I felt thrice as lucky and brave. *And*, finally, I wanted this trip to be *secret* from my adoptive parents, Kenrick and Rosemin Shah, because every time I'd ever asked about the circumstances in which I had become their daughter, and whether there were surviving members of my real family, they'd always said, "We wouldn't touch those people with a ten-foot pole; you shouldn't either."

But I was dying to reach those untouchable people. At eighteen, I was officially a grown-up, but still felt like a child sitting on the floor with a mountain of puzzle pieces dumped in front of me. I wanted to complete the picture of who I was but couldn't… *how?…* without the image on the box. The solution was waiting, I believed, in a place I'd never been: Barrackpore village.

"Babes, I promise: today we finding them," Andre had whispered as we'd piled into the Chinapoo station wagon on Christmas afternoon, with Brianna at the wheel. Then, after zooming out of their driveway, powered by *soca-parang* music and high hopes (*"Yes, we can, like Obama!"*), we'd phased through the clutter of our city, San Fernando, and transited, mile by mile, into the quiet breezy Southern countryside. Over the fields we went, laughing all the way, until we got to Barrackpore, which was empty, flat and green; no tall buildings, no busy streets. We skirted a Recreation Ground, admired the perfectly pressed cricket pitch, and marveled at the chickens and goats roaming the outfield. This place, so quaint to me, was where my mother, Salma Gopaul, née Mohammed, had been born and raised—

that thought alone gave me goosebumps.

I looked around, voraciously noticing every detail, including the slightly sour smell in the air which Andre, well-acquainted with rural sports fields, identified as manure. We had traveled to another galaxy, it seemed, but still the easiest thing to find was a rumshop—a good place to begin our enquiries. Brianna parked and swooped from the car, and I followed. Andre placed himself last, I knew, partly because with his twenty-year-old, football-playing physique, he wanted to act as the chivalrous rear-guard to us ladies. But also, it turned out, because he wanted to hold my elbow, detain me for half-step and whisper, "Those shorts really fit you sweet, girl."

I blushed, then landed a quick, flirty slap—hopefully unnoticed by Brianna—on his delicious mango-shaped bicep.

"Seasons greetings to one and all!" Brianna declared to the only customers, two men who were bent in parentheses over a table, staring at a nip of white rum. No answer.

Up ahead, from the shadows behind the counter, another man materialized. Bald, his small brown head with eyes, nose and mouth clustered in the middle, reminded me of the dry coconut Andre had cracked and grated for his mom to make crab-and-*callaloo* for Christmas lunch. This barman's once-white shirt was unbuttoned until just above his pot belly and, from the way he tugged at the fabric, I figured he didn't clothe his torso often. He'd probably slipped into that rag only moments before, as he'd peered at us strangers, trying to predict our purposes.

He flicked a suspicious glint in my direction and curled his top lip ever so slightly as his gaze traveled to Andre. I took this as evidence of the "country-Indian racism" which Kenrick and Rosemin had warned me against so often. To him, we were probably some kind of ominous constellation: me, a light-skinned *beti*, tethered to two *chinee*-negro "darkies." Our alignment did not augur well, and his frowny-face told me he was either fearful for my safety or was disgustedly viewing me as a "slack" Indian girl who consorted with black boys.

"Merry Christmas," he grumbled, causing the unlit cigarette in his mouth to wag like an accusing finger. "What for allyuh?"

"You have sorrel Shandy?" Brianna asked. When he nodded, she ordered three, and although I preferred the ginger flavor, I didn't object. I was just so grateful and yet guilty that *I* was the reason we were in this blasted village, being scorned by this half-shirted man on Christmas Day.

This was the fifth Christmas I was spending with the Chinapoos. They always picked me up around ten a.m. after I'd returned from Church with Kenrick and Rosemin. And while my adoptive parents approached the rest of the day with the super-holy reverence they thought was expected of Christian converts teaching at a prestigious Presbyterian high school, I got to enjoy the raucous festivities of the born-and-bred Catholic but less self-conscious Chinapoos, who'd become like family to me.

Today, for the entire two-hour drive from San Fernando to Barrackpore, I'd prayed for a similar Christmas reunion with my actual relatives, the Mohammeds—like a Hallmark-meets-Bollywood movie—with hugs and tears and, over in the corner, waving with shy smiles, the brother and sister I'd left behind at the orphanage when I was adopted at ten years old. It's funny, though, how you can believe in prayer and, at the same time, not believe *your* prayers will be answered by God.

So I stood there doubleminded, while the barman searched his standing cooler, and Andre segued into the purpose of our trip. "Hear nah, *bai*, we lookin for some Mohammed-people livin 'round here."

"You hadda come better than that," the barman said, plucking the third bottle from the fridge. He held the drinks expertly, all in one hand, as he shuffied back to us. "You know how much Mohammed it have in Barrackpore... in Trinidad... Dawg?"

"You right, Faddah, you right." Andre nodded as if he hadn't noticed the dismissive tone.

"Old Man Mohammed, we talking 'bout. You *must* know him," Brianna said. This is why it had been a good idea to come with the Chinapoos: combined, they moved like a well-oiled machine and had the subtlety of a big yellow tractor.

"Nah, me eh know 'im." The barman lit his cigarette and took a long drag, expelling smoke dragon-style as he said, "Thirty for the drinks them." I was prepared to give up on him at that point, but Andre leaned even more of himself over the bar, and locked eyes with the fella in that slightly threatening *mano-a-mano* way. "Think again, nah. It important. The man used to raise cattle and sell cucumber and thing. The wife used to sew for people, too."

That was, literally, all the info we had about my mother's family, all I could recall her saying while she was alive, in those years when I had been Nadya with a Muslim "y." Within days of arriving at the Catholic Orphanage, the nice white lady nun had phoned Kenrick and Rosemin and they'd driven from San Fernando to Diego Martin to claim and rebrand me "Nadia" with an "i"—after some famous Russian gymnast Rosemin had admired in her youth. It was like a name-and-family transplant all in one, but you don't just become a new person overnight.

The barman's face gave a crinkle of recognition at something Andre had said.

I spoke up. "And they had two girl children, Salma and Yasmeen." Being in the Chinapoos' orbit had always emboldened me, a girl who longed to assert her will more, but usually felt lesser than everyone else, like some kind of dwarf planet.

"It starting to sound familiar," the barman said, with a slightly warmer tone as he flicked a length of ash into a dirty glass on the counter.

I wondered if he was playing dumb so we'd pass some extra cash to grease his memory. While I was still debating whether to offer and how much, Brianna turned to me and asked, "Nads, girl, what other clues you could give the man?"

In two blinks, I picked through the few remaining shards of memories held in the palm of my mind: my mother in her hammock watching us pitch marbles, me helping her wipe the ceramic figurines she kept in a little glass case nailed to the living room wall; Anand gleefully showing me a new "white man" cut on his shin; Abby in Pampers toddling toward my big sister arms while chugging her "baba" of watered-down milk. After almost a decade, I could no longer summon their faces clearly. But I did know one thing for sure. "Well… Salma was very fair skin, like me," I said, placing my hand on my heart. "Except she had cat eyes… kinda grey, nah."

He squinted.

I swigged a mouthful of Shandy, hoping that the 0.9 percent alcohol would help me swallow whatever he had to say next. I held my breath, and sensed Brianna, beside me, was doing the same. Andre left the counter and assumed a linebacker position near me, his body heat like a solar flare tangling and reorganizing the magnetic field between us. I was momentarily distracted until the barman spoke.

"Yes! Daiz who you resemble, *gyul!* I watchin you since you walk in here and I sayin, 'but I know this face from somewhere. Is that self Allyuh talkin 'bout Uncle Star-Boy."

He snubbed out the cigarette and became a different, friendlier host. "Daiz how we used to call 'im, because from ever since, he did like to dress neat, neat with he clothes always press and hat on he head, like them longtime star-boy on TV, nah. I di 'went Senior Sec with Yasmeen, too. But she di'leave-off school and get marrid, nah. Went to live somewhere up Central side. But I think she down here for the Christmas with she mudder. The old-lady, she real take-on how Uncle Star-Boy gone and leave she a widow just so."

"Don't make joke! Uncle dead?" Brianna said like she'd been intimate with the Mohammed family all along. She hooked her pinkie around mine and milked it. Andre stepped an inch closer, too, as if this news that my grandfather was dead might cause me to faint and fall backward. My stomach did perform a quick flip, but their concern was unwarranted: having never met the man… this grandfather star-boy… it was easy, in that moment, to tell myself that his death was just a footnote in the textbook of my history.

What *did* cause me to return Brianna's squeeze, though, and to ever so slightly lean into Andre's warmth, was the knowledge of who was still alive and within reach: my biological grandmother and, possibly, my aunt, Yasmeen, with whom my mother had chatted so often on the phone (*"Yaz say this… Yaz say that…"*). *Real* blood relatives. I couldn't believe it. A simple two-hour drive was all it had taken—something Kenrick and Rosemin could've done ages ago, so why hadn't they? I knew they loved me; I knew they thought I was safer within our middle-class Christianized life. But maybe their reticence was just plain snobbery, plus a disguised fear of touching the "lower" rungs from which they themselves had climbed? Whatever the reason, I doubted that any harm could possibly have come from letting me at least meet my biological family, letting me have answers for why no Mohammed had rushed to the orphanage to claim me and my siblings, and how my mother had come to be stranded so far from Barrackpore, in the northern mountains of the island, with my father, Shiva Gopaul.

"Yeah, *gyul*, Uncle dead. Couple months," the barman confirmed. "The man went to pull *cassava* and he drop down right dey. Stroke, I hear, but some people saying is… *more*." He stared meaningfully at Brianna, then me, then Andre, daring one of us to inquire into this secret he obviously wanted to tell.

"How you mean 'more?'" Brianna obliged, "You mean, like… *obeah?*"

"Wuss than that, *gyul*. I mean… The Gods. Is *them* whey kill 'im. You see, people does want to use a Hindu god conveniently, as if is any old spirit, or just some small-fry *Kyatolic* saint. But we gods jealousfull, *gyul*. You can't play with them. Watch: Uncle Star-boy was Muslim, but he used to pay the pundit up the road to make Dee Baba puja every croptime. Then, two years in a row, he stop. Pundit say he did warn 'im: *Dee Baba is a powerful incarnation of Lord Shiva. You can't vex Lord Shiva and win!* Well, he never listen, so he had-was to feel. First year… locust come and eat out all he crop. Second year… couple months ago, every-shittin-body in Kunjal Trace see when a no-head man on a black horse ride up and down the road in front Uncle house. Next day self, Uncle dead."

"Where you say the house is again?" Andre moved like a matador to re-direct the barman away from this superstitious gossip toward more useful info.

"Kunjal Trace. It easy to find. Just drive round this bend, pass the sawmill. Then you go reach a junction to turn left or right, but *you* don't turn left or right, *you* continue straight on the piece a bad-road, and then…"

I zoned out, replaying only one line of what the barman had said: *You can't vex Lord Shiva and win!* Funny how well that described the ragged quilt of memories in which my childhood was still swaddled. The details might have become threadbare and worn, but I distinctly remembered the feeling of all of us—Salma, Anand, Abby, and me—creeping through each day under a thick blanket of fear spread by my father, Shiva, Lord and Master of our rickety wooden universe. Nobody ever won against his anger. In fact, all we ever did was lose and, honestly, I could not recall ever thinking of him as "Daddy."

And that's why I wanted to find my brother and sister. I was afraid that the moment I got on a plane to leave Trinidad, I would lose the chance to talk about Shiva, and about the day he'd ruined our lives forever. A day I'd never spoken about with anyone, not the nun, not the social worker, not Kenrick and Rosemin, not even Brianna and Andre. I'd always pretended that I couldn't remember but, in truth, I didn't want to unless I could remember alongside someone else who was remembering too.

Were Anand and Abby here in Barrackpore right now? They weren't on MySpace, hi5 or Facebook—I'd searched and searched without knowing what to look for. Could they be, now, just a couple streets away? Or did I have a better chance believing in Santa Claus?

Brianna slammed the car door. It was only then I realized that she and I had walked out of the rumshop. We were alone, in the back seat. Andre had remained inside to absorb and filtrate the barman's directions.

"You ok?" she asked gently. "You don't really believe spirit kill your grandpa, right?"

"Of course not," I said, chewing at my Purple Reign nail

polish that matched hers. "It's just… this is *real* now, Bree. I reach. I touching my past. But…"

"You frighten, nah?"

"Yes!" I said. "This morning, I walked out that townhouse in Union Hall as an only child, and now I might go back with a brother and sister and a setta new family that Kenrick and Rosemin don't want me to have. I feel I made a mistake not to tell them. I should call, right?" From my denim shorts, I pulled out the little Nokia they'd bought me, thinking of how much they'd actually done for me over the years, the good life they'd given me. "It will look like I was planning behind their back long time now. They might get real vex with me, Bree!"

"Well, you could tell them something *close* to the truth. You could say that you didn't know for sure we was coming here, that we just spring it on you today, as a Christmas present."

"But suppose they stop me from coming back by allyuh? You know spending Christmas by allyuh is the one thing I look forward to every year, and I 'fraid—"

"Nads, who could stop you from doing anything now, girl? You's a big-woman, you's eighteen, you going away to live by yourself in a few weeks. What happen after this is *your* choice. You don't need nobody permission no more."

But the Chinapoos weren't Indian, so there were some things Brianna could never understand about my home life. Every year, permission to spend Christmas with them had been conditioned upon me excelling in end-of-term exams and finishing my household chores to Rosemin's satisaction. And, this year, there'd been the added pressure of keeping them ignorant of my feelings for Andre. They would *never* have let me come if they'd known we'd exchanged I-love-yous and made-out before he left for school in Canada last August, and that since his return this Christmas vacation, the spark between us had been so incandescent we were having trouble controlling it. Kenrick and Rosemin had always made it clear that I was supposed to remain single and chaste until *The One* came along, the one I would marry, that "suitable boy"—which Rosemin had once translated for me as: *a smart Indian boy from a well-off, Presbyterian home.*

And if I wanted to remain a "suitable girl," I could never "make my family shame." Which meant I had to always shine—all A's, choir, quiz team, soon-to-be Law student—and I could never betray any hint of the dark craters that had been deepening inside me since I'd been ten years old. Yet here I was now, drowning in love with a half-negro boy, and about to fraternize with the exact same people Kenrick and Rosemin had forbidden me to know.

I put the Nokia away without calling home.

"It don't make sense to call," I told Brianna, and myself. "Only if these turn out to be the right setta Mohammeds. Then I"ll have something to confess."

Andre entered the car, this time behind the wheel. "I ain't sure is your people, Nads," he said while adjusting the seat to his length.

"But it damn well worth a try. Ent?" Brianna said as she left me in the back and slid herself into the front passenger seat, now assuming the co-pilot role.

"Yeah, we here already." Andre twisted to fasten his seat belt, and his left elbow grazed my bare shin. Nobody takes that long to buckle a seat belt. I could feel him delaying, channelling all of his essence into that ulna, so I directed all of mine into that tibia, and it felt like we were reassuring each other subcutaneously that, no matter what happened next, we would survive it together.

"Make it so, Number One," I said excitedly, as if this whole trip was an episode of *Star Trek* and I was the one in control of the Bridge.

The newish road was way higher than the faded green-and-yellow house with red curtains, which we found teetering on stilts, like an exhausted *mokko-jumbie*. We picked our way down a dirt path littered with leaves from a tall *bois cano* tree overhead, and as we neared the rusting fence, a scrawny canine announced us with the usual pothound braggadociousness. "Hello! Hello!" We tossed our voices above the dog's until an old lady hobbled through the open front door, onto the porch, and silenced the animal with one "Hush!"

A younger, middle-aged woman then joined her and called to us, "Yes! Can I help?"

Was this Yasmeen? She glided down the stairs wearing a red-and-green sequined cardigan that had a good chance of winning an ugly-Christmas sweater competition. She approached the gate with polite curiosity on her face—it looked nothing like my mother's. This lady was too short, too dark, not pretty—but maybe the years hadn't been kind to her, I decided. She didn't seem to notice me, sandwiched as I was between Brianna and Andre, until the very last moment. Then her eyes widened to satellites.

"Compliments of the season," Brianna purred, retaking the woman's attention. "You're Miss Yasmeen, ent? Uncle Star-Boy daughter?"

"Yes. And you is?" Her eyes pinballed from face to face.

"Well, we from San'do and… ahhmm… we hear 'bout your father passing. Is a sad, sad thing, but… ahhmm… we bring Salma daughter." In one motion, Brianna grabbed my arm, then thrust me forward like an offering of the body and the blood. "Look Nadia right here."

Yasmeen made a forward motion but then froze with her limbs at odd angles, becoming a lifesized *murti*—the kind you see towering outside Hindu temples.

I tried to put her at ease with a smile. It wouldn't keep its shape, though, because my stomach was churning like I'd eaten two-day-old curry.

Andre spoke up then, pointing to the porch where the old lady still hovered. "Tell Ma, nah, this is her granddaughter. She come all this way to meet allyuh. Tell her, tell Granny."

Yasmeen's face crumbled then. She made a jerky pivot away from the gate, then tramped back up the stairs. I held both my breath and Andre's hand as my aunty—my real-blood-aunty—crossed the gallery to convey the message to my real-blood-granny. But then, I began to project my longing beyond them and into the house itself, thinking I would soon be up there, in the bosom of it. I imagined the albums that must still be in there, cherishing snapshots of my mother. Was this front window the childhood bedroom she'd mentioned? Had someone fixed the hole in the floor that she and Yaz used to spy on grown-ups? Was the pink chenille spread still on the bed they'd shared as sisters? And who else was inside the house—Anand and Abby?

But a flash of activity on the porch brought me back into my body, still waiting outside, at the fence. The old lady was gesticulating wildly, pointing to the road and flicking her hands, shooing us away, as if we were a cluster of common fowl shitting at her gate. Then, the two women simply stomped back into their cosquelle little house and barricaded the door, which bore the most bedraggled and unwelcoming holiday wreath I'd ever seen.

I kept waiting—lump in my throat, toes scrunched up in my

sneakers—trying to hold on to the soil, to my rightful place in that yard, to hope itself. I stood there with the Chinapoos, we stared like Magi, in expectant silence, for a long time... waiting, waiting... because this couldn't be how the journey ended. We were either supposed to *not* find this lost family, or find them and have a big celebration. We weren't supposed to find them, only for me to be jilted—I hadn't even considered that possibility, and now my mind just couldn't process it. But when the door never reopened and not even a curtain trembled, I had no choice but to turn from the Mohammeds and say to the Chinapoos, "Let's go."

Up the dirt path we crunched as if trying to murder the already fallen leaves.

"You drive again," Brianna sighed, passing the keys to Andre. Then she used her full unhindered mobility to smack the dashboard and dramatize her anger.

"Them stink mudda-ass people! Nadia, you better off without them, you hear me? You don't need them bitches in your life." She clapped her hands together as if dusting crumbs. "What they feel at all? You hungry for family? Nah, Dread! You have *us*, y'understan? *We* is your next family!"

She repeated herself, over and over, swivelling ever so often to confirm that I was paying attention—which I was, vacantly, in the way a just dead corpse pays attention to the ceiling.

At least one of my questions had been answered, though. *Now* I knew why Kenrick and Rosemin had never brought me to Barrackpore. It wasn't for lack of love. It was because they'd wanted to spare me this sensation—for the second time in one short lifetime—of my heart curling inward, like those fallen *bois cano* leaves, into a thing resembling a gnarled fist.

"Aye, see a parlor there? Let's just stop and ask for directions," Andre said.

At Christmas it got dark so early—around five, five-thirty—and none of us wanted to still be in the bowels of Barrackpore, or along one of those lonely stretches between the village and San Fernando, after nightfall. So we approached the roadside shop, but not as the same optimistic people who'd sauntered into the bar earlier.

Inside the parlor, we were greeted by the distinctive soundtrack of an Indian soap opera: theatrical music signaling a slow zoom of the camera, then a rush of belligerent Hindi. I cringed because, after what I'd just experienced at the Mohammed house, it all sounded like mockery. But then, over there on the shop's counter, I glimpsed a shimmer of cheap solace: a little showcase—the same kind in which Salma had housed her ceramics— but this one chock full of Indian delicacies, its glass mottled with potentially delicious grease.

"They have *phulourie!*" Brianna and I said simultaneously.

Our voices prompted the teenaged girl behind the counter to turn from her TV show and become aware of us for the first time.

Jittering like junkies, we asked, "How you selling the *phulourie?*", then debated among ourselves if we should "just buy all and done," then settled on two dozen of the golden split-pea globules "with only slight *tambran* sauce on top," because nobody dared risk a pepper-belly on our long drive back home.

The girl rose to fulfil our order. That's when we spotted an old lady sitting in the corner, stroking a sleeping cat. She was the quintessential village "Tanty": staring at the TV through glasses that resembled the bottom of two Coke bottles, her shrunken frame lost in a *batik* house dress, and her long grey braid draping over her shoulder until it became one with the cat's tail.

"Tanty, you well enjoying your show," Brianna said.

"Yes, darlin," the old lady replied without budging from the screen.

The girl handed us two brown paper bags, we slid her the cash, and only then did we feel it was polite to ask for directions to the Main Road. The girl tried, she really did, but she didn't look old enough to drive and maybe that's why she wasn't making much sense.

With obvious trepidation, she called to the old lady in the corner, "Mama, come help these people, nah. They lost."

"Ah *chut*, man!" the Tanty exclaimed, which made the cat scamper. After several heaves, she raised herself from the plastic chair and shuffied her big-buckle diabetic slippers toward us. "Allyuh couldn't pick a better time to lost than in the middle of my show? Where allyuh heading… San'do, nah?" At the counter, she adjusted her dual telescopes higher on her nose, slowly scanned our faces, then looked me dead in the eye and said, "You."

"Me?" I was off to the side, sharing one bag of *phulourie* with Brianna, while Andre sat atop the lone customer stool, gobbling the other bag.

"Yesssss, *beti*, is you-self I pointin to, ent?"

"Ok?" I made a half-step forward.

"Closer, nah man, let me watch you good." She unlatched and swung open the little gate in the burglar bars between seller and buyer, the one used for passing large packages—flour, rice etc.—over the counter. "Sit down here, child."

Andre vacated the stool and I sat at eye-level with the old lady, wondering why I had been singled out for attention.

"*Bismillah!* You is Salma daughter, ent?"

I was instantly dizzy. The air was too thin. All I could hear was my ear drums throbbing with the velocity of my own blood. I managed to turn my head to look for Andre, but he shrugged as if to say I should answer the old lady in whatever way I felt comfortable, that I was on my own.

But before I could decide, the old lady said, "Don't story, little girl! I know is you!" She smacked my hand as if my silence meant I'd been concocting lies to fool her. "You is the spittin image of my niece Salma...except for the eye-them... she one was grey. I always know she chirren woulda come back here someday. I live to see it. I could go in peace now, *inshallah*."

"Y-you know me?" was all I could get out.

"I's yuh mudder auntie, girl. *Your* great-aunt, Nazroon. And dey's one of yuh pumpkin-vine cousin." She pointed at the girl, who had now claimed the plastic chair and the TV. "Gyul! Slow down that old-noise, so I could chat here with How-She-Name!"

"Nadia," I offered eagerly.

"Ahhhh, yes... Naddd-yaaa..." she said in a way that convinced me she didn't remember me or my name any more than I remembered her—all she knew was that I had Salma's face.

The girl lowered the volume. The ensuing stillness around me suggested that the Chinapoos, too, were transfixed and wondering just as I was: *What the hell happens now?*

Tanty Nazroon spread her chenille-skinned hand over mine, bowed her head and began to mumble. My name a few times, the word "*Bismillah*" a lot—and me being very familiar with the song "Bohemian Rhapsody," I knew what it meant: she was praying to her Muslim god. So, I closed my eyes respectfully, half-expecting that when I reopened them, I'd find myself in the twin bed Kenrick and Rosemin had bought me, and this whole trip would've been just another cruel taunting dream. I'd had many before: where I would sense my mother still alive and waiting just around the next corner, where I could stretch and graze the hem of her garment—always a wedding dress—only to wake up and lose her again, finding only a damp pillowslip.

The kneading of my hand made my eyelids flutter open.

"Child," Tanty Nazroon whispered, "I ask Allah to clean-off all the *nazar* from your mudder and fadder, and to remove every *jinn* and *shaitan* and every bad thing that want to do you mischief. I ask him for only *barakah* and luck in your life, so you go be a star-girl wheresoever you go from here."

I nodded and, out of habit, made the sign of the cross. The Chinapoos behind me whispered a chorus of Catholic Amens. Hearing their voices again made me brave.

"I know *some* things," I said to Tanty, "but not everything. I was hoping maybe you could tell me…"

"Tell you what, Lovely?"

"About that day, nah? The day when—"

"You don't remember?"

"Some," I said, my heart pounding a signal that, for the first time ever, here was somebody who could offer me the strands of her own memory to weave together with my own.

So, I swallowed hard, then explained…

I had awoken to the familiar sound of my father shouting. When it got too loud, Anand hid us in the wardrobe, where the noise was always muted and less scary. But when the usual clamor was surpassed by my mother's incessant screaming, Anand had jumped out and left us with instructions not to move. After a while, there was only silence; then our neighbor, Miss Jackie, came with one of her man-friends. They took me and Abby out of the wardrobe, covered our heads with the sheets we'd been sleeping on earlier, then carried us down the hill to Miss Jackie's house, where Anand was waiting…

There, I paused, feeling short of breath and something akin to the stage fright I'd experienced during my first national history quiz. I knew the words, but they were fighting me. They didn't want to come out and face a room full of people.

So, I used an old trick: I shut my eyes and pretended I was alone in a dark wardrobe…

Anand had been sitting on Miss Jackie's couch, staring. "Shiva kill Mammy," he said and when we started to cry, he'd hugged us and said, "What allyuh crying for? Ent she always tell we this woulda happen? Well, it happen. And I glad he kill-off he-self too, otherwise I woulda have to find 'im and finish it." In a weird way, that had made me and Abby feel better, because it meant this disaster was inevitable and not our fault, there was nothing we could've done to save our mother from a fate she'd long accepted. Then, a WPC had come to talk to us. Miss Jackie begged to keep us, but the woman-police had said there was "a procedure," and then she took us to the orphanage: Anand in the boy section; me and Abby sharing one bed in the girls'section. I was only there for a few days but it felt like years; then Kenrick and Rosemin came and took me…

I could've ended the story there, with those facts, but it felt like a fable missing a moral. Unsatisfying. I knew then that wasn't the true confession, and I finally understood why I had come to Barrackpore. It wasn't Tanty Nazroon's prayers that I needed; no, what I desired from her—my mother's flesh-and-blood—was forgiveness.

Eyes still shut, I forced myself to go on. "I was happy to be the lucky one who got a new family first. But afterwards, I started to feel real bad about it. I still feel bad now. How I just disappeared and left them behind, how I been living so good and comfortable without them... I just feel bad, bad, bad."

An invisible harness unbuckled itself from around my chest and something weighty slipped down the length of my body. Feeling I could breathe freely for the first time in my life, I gasped and opened my eyes.

At first, I couldn't see through the glut of tears, but as they raced down my cheeks and landed on the counter with the pitter-patter of rain, I began to focus.

Tanty Nazroon was crying, too. She gave a snort, blowing her nose with a handful of the napkins stationed nearby. Then she bent below the counter. I heard the rustling of plastic and paper, until she re-emerged and gently pushed a small photo album—the kind that fits one 5 x 7 print per page—across to me. It was opened onto a discolored newspaper clipping:

HOUSEWIFE CHOPPED BY HUSBAND

Salma Mohammed-Gopaul, 26, a housewife, was chopped several times by her husband Shiva Gopaul, 39, at their home in Bagatelle, on Monday morning.

Gopaul, a farmer, then consumed a poisonous substance and ran to the back of the house where he died.

The couple's three children, ages 6, 10 and 12, were asleep when their father attacked their mother, but during the commotion they got up and the 12-year-old alerted neighbors. Mohammed-Gopaul remains in critical condition.

West End police are investigating.

That was it? The ruin of my whole family reduced to a few

journalistic sentences. I read and re-read them, searching for some new glittering insight, while Tanty babbled excuses and justifications for why my mother had died alone ("...we didn't hear 'bout it till long after,") and why the Mohammeds had never tried to find me and my siblings ("...them Kyatolick give 'way allyuh so quick,") and, every few words, she broke off into a wail of "Oh God, Oh God, I sorry..." But my mind was busy dragging and re-dragging an imaginary yellow highlighter over three words: *on Monday morning*. It's weird how you can stash away something so deep that you forget about it, until someone comes along and asks, *Isn't this yours?*

On Monday morning. Yes, my mother had spent that last weekend away from home. The last time I had seen her was on the Friday, when she'd dropped us off at school, kissed us and said she would see us on Monday when she got back from spending the Eid holiday with her family in Barrackpore. She'd returned, yes, but Abby and I, stuffed inside the wardrobe, had never gotten to see her.

Never ever again. I suddenly realized that *we* had lost our mother on Friday, while *Anand* had lost her "on Monday morning." He'd seen her, he'd gotten one more day—or maybe only a few more minutes, but he'd gotten more. He'd been the lucky one. The thought sent me mad with jealousy and a kind of rage I'd never felt before in eighteen years.

I shoved the album across the counter. "I want to see my mother! You must have a picture! Show me!" Someone behind me said *calm down*, someone tried to rub my back—I shoved them away too. Then I stood; the stool fell to one side. "I want to see her!" I slapped the counter again and again. "I want to see my mother!"

Sobbing loudly now, Tanty Nazroon flipped pages in a panic,

then passed the album back to me, "Look they wedding day."

An emaciated, mullet-haired version of my father in a long-sleeved maroon shirt, white soft-pants and white loafers, towered over... *me?* It could have been me, the resemblance was so strong, except *that* me... my mother...was engulfed within a wedding dress way too big for her. I couldn't tell if it was the same one I always saw in my dreams. I couldn't see her grey eyes, either; they were sealed tight to the camera. Neither bride nor groom smiled.

"Is right inside here they di'meet-up," Tanty Nazroon said. "Is me who introduce them, but I di'really like him for Yaz instead. But is *he* whey choose your mudder. He was a nice boy, you know. Yeah, he used to drink he lil rum now-and-then and bruise she up lil bit... just like any other man. Good as any, better than many. But Salma did feel she could have it all—she was always *hoity-toity* from small, sake of them pretty-eye she had. If she did keep she tail home, though, instead of goin'and lock-up for the weekend with she sweet-man, yuh fadder woulda never trip off so."

"She wasn't *here* that weekend? For Eid? What sweet-man?"

"Noooo, that's the story she di'tell allyuh. But you's a big woman now, ent? And you come for truth? Well, take truth in yuh pipe and smoke it. Your fadder had he reasons."

"Reasons?" I scoffed. "You want to talk about reasons, lady? You trying to say *my mother* was to blame?" I was shocked. I'd never viewed my mother as anything other than the perfect, faithful wife. The old lady had to be lying! But it didn't matter what she said anyway, because nothing was going to make me side with my father against my mother. My life, it seemed, had finally circled back to that fight that had remained unfinished in my mind since I was ten years old, hunched inside a cabinet, listening to him advantage her.

"Well, I... I..." Tanty muttered.

"Is *who* put her in that wedding dress? Is *who* send her quite-to-hell up Bagatelle to live with that… that… demon? Is *who?* Tell me? I waiting."

"Child, things was different in them—"

I didn't want to hear her. What I wanted was to no longer feel the shame of an innocent bystander. I wanted to feel what I assumed Anand felt: the pride of a gladiator who'd done all he could to defend the innocent. "So, you want to bump your gum about *reasons?*" I said, "Well let me tell you something: you didn't live with us, lady. None of y'all stinkin Mohammed-people came anywhere near us. So *you* don't know the truth about my mother and father and their reasons. He never needed one. It didn't matter how much man my mother had—none, one, or twenty—Shiva was ALWAYS going to kill my poor mother someday. So just shut your mouth, old lady, and gimme that picture, please."

"Yes! Talk your mind, Nads," Brianna encouraged.

"Nah, ease her up, nah," Andre begged, playing the good cop, I assumed. "She done so decrepit already."

And I did ease her up, because between my shouting and crying, I had exhausted myself and was covered in spit, snot, and tears. I grabbed some napkins. While I sopped my face, Tanty Nazroon bent again and brought up a dog-eared book with a tattered cover which said *Duskfire*. She slid the newspaper article and the photograph from their plastic holsters, and stashed them between the book's browned pages.

"Here," she said, pushing it across, "this was Salma favorite. Take it and go."

It was one of those eighties romance novels, and somehow, that made me cry again, to think of my mother reading it, expecting that kind of happiness from her love life, and getting my father instead. *You can't vex Lord Shiva and win!* I pictured her kissing us goodbye on the Friday before her death. She must've known she was risking everything for that one weekend. She loved us—I knew that for sure—so she would never have done it unless her life had become unbearable; but she must've been so very scared. She must've felt like she was going against everything that everyone expected of her. She must've felt so alone.

I grabbed the book and said, "And just for the record, eh, I want you to know that I don't give my mother wrong for wanting happiness. And if she *did* find it with this 'sweet-man' you talking 'bout, then I happy for her. In fact, I proud."

I stormed off and was almost free of the parlor—my sneakers had just touched the outside steps—when Tanty Nazroon yelled, "Nadia! Wait, child! Wait! It have something you don't know!"

Andre and I walked back to the counter, Brianna remained at the door.

I thought maybe the old lady had some other memento to give me, but all she did was stutter, "The fella was… the fella was…" while her eyes kept darting between me and Andre.

Finally, she shook her head, as if changing her mind about something, then said, "I just want to tell you: *this* fella love you. I could see it in how he watchin you. Don't mind he's a negro, I wouldn't vex if you follow your heart, child, if you love 'im back and get marrid one day."

Rising to my tippy-toes and stretching across the counter to be as disrespectful as possible, I wagged my index finger in her face. "I don't want your permission and I don't need your blessing. I will love who I damn-well want to love, and nobody else going to 'find husband' and 'fix-up marriage' for me. Is my choice, is my *reasons.*"

With Brianna back at the helm, we found our way to the main road, but in complete silence, none of us sure whether this mission had been a success or failure. *Duskftre* remained on the backseat, filling the space next to me, like a whole other person. It was pitch black now, after 6:00, but I recognized the rumshop when we passed it.

About five minutes later, along a bushy stretch with no streetlights, a figure in white came into view, briefly caught by our headlights as we rounded the corner. A little closer, and I saw it was a woman at the side of the road, her long dress billowing in the breeze.

"What the hell she doing out here, by herself, this hour?" Brianna remarked.

"Maybe she need a drop?" Andre said. "Slow down, let me ask—"

The woman ran into the road.

We screamed, Brianna stood on the brakes, the book slid to the floor. But somehow, when I looked again, the woman was on the other side of the road, standing motionless again, as the Christmas wind frolicked with her white dress and her long tresses. We couldn't see her facc.

"She dead? I kill her?" Brianna asked. "Allyuh, tell me quick! She dead or she not dead? I kill her?"

"Shc not dead, girl," Andre said. "Open your eyes. Look her right there."

The woman lifted her hand then, and gave a slow, almost mournful, wave.

"Oh shit, Nads, suppose is a *chooryle?*" Brianna said, a tone of wonder rather than fear in her voice.

Andre, who'd studied Sciences, not Literature, and hadn't

read the same folk stories as me and Brianna, asked, "What the ass is a *choo*—?"

"A ghost," I answered, my voice raspy as I struggled with the sudden constriction of my throat. "An Indian mother who died before knowing her child."

Andre uttered a grunt, and it struck me as more than just disbelieving, it was disdainful. A year later, after he'd brought a Canadian girl home for Christmas and I was forevermore uninvited from the Chinapoo home, I would recall his reaction and wonder if *that* was the moment his love had begun to change into a kind of tolerant pity—or had it happened earlier, in the parlor with Tanty Nazroon.

"No, I serious, Dre, suppose is some ancestor of Nadia, or even Salma?" Brianna said, then turned to me. "Suppose is *you* she come for, Nads. You make her proud just now. Wave, quick. So she could go 'bout her business in peace, at last. Poor thing, she never had nobody else stand up for her."

Without thinking, I said "Bye, Mummy," and gave a shy wave. The woman waved back. Then, kneeling on the seat, I kept waving as we drove away—even though I wasn't sure if I believed it was my mother—until the figure melted into the distance behind us.

Then I turned around and retrieved the book from the floor. I clutched it for the rest of the drive from Barrackpore to San Fernando. I sat mute and frozen in position, like one of Mummy's figurines. As a child, I'd always felt sorry for them, imagining they were real souls stuck in their poses and condemned to be forever on display.

So that night, I made a choice, and I asked no one's permission. I simply waited until I was sure everyone else in the Chinapoo house was asleep, then I went to Andre's room.

I woke him and said only two words, "Break me,"and somehow, he understood.

THE VISITATION

Florida, USA—Tunapuna, Trinidad; 2017

Garth Krüger awakes with a silent prayer of thanks: *Zero four hundred. Alive. No nightmares. Two solid hours. Amen.*

It's Monday, and his first gym client is at six am. He's dog-tired after pulling another all-nighter on the phone with Abby. She's young, so lack of sleep doesn't affect her much, but it's beginning to take a toll on him after these last few weeks. He'd rather die, though, than admit that to her. He' ll always show up for Abby, he' ll do anything for her; one day, he'll even be her man and take care of her. *Maybe.* It's crazy to feel this way about an island-girl he's never met, never even seen in real life, but he's fallen hard for Abby and wants them to be together soon.

Nah, Dude, you' re not ready; she's not ready. You both need more time. Or do we?—he lies in bed, scratching his balls and pondering his options.

Maybe if he was rich, his ugliness—inside and out—wouldn't matter. Here, in Florida, he sees that shit all the time: old buzzards, with bronze bombshells like Abby. Why? Because those rich guys can turn a girl into a Disney princess overnight. Which is what he wants to do for Abby—give her everything her heart desires. She deserves it, she's been through so much, losing her real parents at a young age.

So as bushwacked as he feels this morning, Garth un-asses himself from the bed, ready to target his computer and his

YouTube side hustle: a few online channels peddling ASMR, *tingle-you-to-sleep* videos set in exotic locales—India, China, Ecuador, Trinidad—along with related merch like T-shirts, towels... whatever he can sell. It's a small but growing income stream, and as he yawns and turns on the Keurig to brew a fresh cup of the very same coffee sold on his Ecuadorian channel, Garth whispers, "Don't you worry, Abby. One day, this trickle will become a big-ass river. Bigger than—"

Click! His mind opens a memory of the wide and mighty Euphrates—like a spam link hit by mistake. He sees it all from above, drone footage style—the river's green edges tasselled with date palms; then, himself, as he was back then: whole, "Army Strong" with brothers-in-arms, searching fields and villages, scared shitless of the desert scorpions, spiders, and snipers, but psyched to be doing some good for Lady Liberty. Until she turned out to be as fickle as his ex-wife: a good-time gal who loved him when things were going well, but then took everything and left him broken and lonely in a VA hospital bed. Moved on real quick, she did.

And now, after all his sacrifice for America, he's living under a Commander-In-Chief who mocks people with disabilities, people like *him*. A Commander-in-Chief who might as well be the Grand Wizard of the KKK—*heck, they love him in this part of Florida!* Garth would never bring Abby here. With her brown skin and long jet hair, she looks too much like the *haji* girls he'd seen in Iraq, she'd be a surefire target in these parts— maybe anywhere in America right now.

"Gotta leave *this* shithole," he says to his image in the microwave door as he churns vanilla protein powder into a steaming mug. He laughs at his own political joke, but his pulse is racing as it tends to whenever he feels trapped. He shuts his eyes and tries to focus on the rhythmic tinkling of the spoon and the incense-like aroma of the rising vapor—his meditation teacher at the VA would be proud.

A loud *thump* against the living room wall. Next door, Rustam and his stripper girlfriend are either fighting or make-up fucking again. Garth shakes his head in disgust but takes a big gulp of tongue-scalding coffee and actually smiles through the burn. He's thinking that not too long ago, a noise as sudden as that would've set him off. *Last year, man. Last year.*

Last year was a complete shitshow. His mind went Elvis on him: forty nights of sitting up in the recliner, not knowing if he was awake or asleep, staring into the darkness, sweating like a rapist, Glock on his lap, listening to the *rat-a-tat-tat* of (real or imagined?) gunfire, waiting for somebody to burst through the door. Forty days, wandering from the gym, stalking through the adjoining mall, glaring at people, daring someone to bump into him. Until that final night when the gym manager found him on the floor of the locker room, cradling a gun, a bottle of Wild Turkey and a blister pack of sleeping pills, just bawling his eyes out. It had had to come to that, for him to say yes to therapy, for him to go looking for online support groups, for him to join and leave three of them, until the one where he met Abby four months ago.

Four months! You've only known her for four months!

He crosses the apartment's small spare living room—TV, glass coffee table, oversized recliner—interesting only because of the kitschy souvenirs he's collected on his travels since "retirement" from the Army. Behold: three mother-goddesses, each dedicated to protecting a different YouTube channel. There, on that shelf, a hand-painted plate from Ecuador showing Jesus's Mom all gussied up as "Maria Santísima del Buen Suceso de la

Purificacion," And there, below it, from China, a fake-ivory statue of Guan Yin cradling *her* male baby. And there, from India, a small *murti* of Kali Mai wearing the skulls of her enemies. She's his favorite—probably because she's so strong and in-your-face, mocking everybody with her outstretched tongue. So different to his own Mom. She was always half-hidden behind his big, brash Army Dad; and always so sad, too—as if she'd wanted more from life than to be a dutiful, carpooling Army wife, holding down the fort for everyone else's sake. She'd been to war in her own way, Garth had realized that far too late. He'd taken her for granted like everyone else, until his accident, but by then, the cancer she'd hidden for years had claimed her. Ok, they are definitely screwing next door. That chick's an expert at fake, PornHub groaning. Garth tries to block it out as he waits for the computer to boot up, but the groaning gets louder, the thumping more frenetic.

What would Abby sound like in bed? He wouldn't want her to pretend, like this girl. He'd want to *really* please her. The thought almost has him reaching for his dick, but he flips the kill switch because he wants to keep his thoughts of Abby pure and guilt free, just like her. He reaches across the desk instead, snatches up the souvenir—a kind of talisman—he keeps closest these days. This copper wire sculpture he'd bought on a business trip some months ago, before he'd met Abby online: two *panmen* beating steel drums above a heavy base that says, "Sweet TnT." What a coincidence that, after buying it, the first girl he connected with turned out to live in Trinidad and Tobago!

Well, she lives in *Trinidad*; she's never been to Tobago. He asked her last night, because he's been secretly toying with a notion: maybe they can go together, for the first time, if he makes a second business trip to TnT. It's a real possibility, given the clusterfuck happening with that channel—he has an online ad contract from the spanking new government cocoa company, but now they' re threatening to bail because his Trini YouTube star, Mrs. Hosein, aka "The Nara Guru," is on strike and not making videos. Honestly, he's close-to-black on patience with that old woman. Might have to bite the bullet and just fire her, then head down to TnT and pull off a rescue mission: recruit some new talent, win back the hearts and minds of the client and the viewers.

Is that before or after you tell Abby about your face?

When are you gonna stop hiding behind ten-year-old pictures?

When are you gonna show her the real you?

A wounded animal cry comes from next door. Then, finally, silence. Ten minutes instead of six—a new long-and-meritorious-service record for Rustam.

Garth sets the *panmen* aside and gets to work. He opens Dropbox, where all his videographers should have uploaded new footage overnight. The cursor hovers over the "Trinidad" folder, but he doesn't click. He's afraid to click. If there's nothing in there, he *will* have to fly down. He *will* have to step under the same sun as Abby, breathe the same air. How can he, though, and not try to meet her? And how can he meet her, without showing himself and all his brokenness? What if it's too much for her? He's never given a raccoon's ass when people stare, avert their eyes, or avoid him, but Abby is not just "people," she is his future. She's his last hope for love. *You sure as hell ain't getting no younger—or prettier.*

Blech! His mouth suddenly tastes bad, like he's been French-kissing a revolver. Maybe the protein powder was off. He goes to the bathroom, shoves a finger down his throat, dry retches in the sink, tries to empty himself but... nothing. Maybe brush his teeth? Maybe that'll neutralize this acidic tang. In the mirror, as the toothbrush makes his cheek vibrate, he traces a finger along his jawline, trying to appraise it from Abby's eyes. But he can't see anything to love—or even like—in this face. All he can see are the skin grafts, their tone-on-tone geometric patchwork, like aerial photos of some war-ravaged country.

He scoffs. A scattershot of toothpaste hits the mirror just as the smartwatch on his wrist beeps. Instinctively, he glances down for the time. But it's the date that zooms toward him and shatters his clear-glass vision of where this day—09-04-2017—was headed.

Holy Shit! Today is his Tenth Alive Day Anniversary. Ten years ago, to the motherfuckin day, he died in a Humvee in Iraq—*Tango Uniform*, he was gone!—and then came back to life in an Apache helo over the desert. IED explosion. He never saw the 600 pounds of bomb.

Ten years. How could he have forgotten? Or maybe he didn't forget. Maybe something inside of him has known, for weeks now, that this ten-year anniversary was ahead. Like a silent transceiver encased in his hard chest, maybe this knowledge is the thing that's been directing and accelerating him toward Abby. He's spent the last four weeks needing to talk to her every night, texting her all day, feeling his heart collide with hers in a way that hasn't happened since he was a teenager playing footsie with the cheerleader who became his wife… ex-wife.

Ten years. A mile-marker. There are no mile-markers in the desert, hardly any roads, you learn to navigate by your GPS and by your gut. He should've trusted his gut that godforsaken day on the road to Tikrit: *The air is too still. Is the woman in the white burqa waving hello or warning us to stop? I should stop, I should—*

The memory of that day unsheathes itself and slices so

deep that Garth grows dizzy, drops the toothbrush, and doubles over the sink. Behind his clenched eyes, he sees the tea-spilled sunset and warm shadows that had made his fateful day seem but a liquid seeping away. One minute, he'd been staring at the roadside woman, and the very next minute he was staring at a demon reflected in his platoon sergeant's sunglasses: a blackened skeleton, blood leaking out of every hole in its charred face. He hadn't known it was his own face until his ear had popped and he'd heard himself screaming. Then he'd heard the men in the helo screaming over him ("You' re gonna be ok! We got you! You're gonna be ok!") but their eyes, their faces, were saying something different. But at least he was *alive!* How he'd cried with joy to know he was alive! He *is* alive—more alive than he'd felt on that day—because of Abby. To stay this way, he must move beyond his reconnaissance of her, his endless feeling out of who she is and if she can love him. It's time to do what he would've done in battle: disperse the screenline around his heart, advance, take the risk—like the good First Team soldier he's always been.

Dude, if you don't make a move now, you' ll lose her. You' ll become a fucking cadaver again. Is that what you want?

Garth rises, staggers at first, but then runs back to the computer. He clicks into the Trinidad folder.

Nothing there.

It's fate. It's a message: *Go to Abby.*

He sprints to the bedroom and grabs his phone. *I want to see you…* he types, then deletes. Feels like a lie. Yes, he wants to see Abby, but he *has* seen her profile picture, she looks fine, she's beautiful. What he really wants is for Abby to see *him.*

"Too dangerous!" he says, slamming the heel of his palm against his dented forehead, assaulting the too-taut, shiny skin borrowed from somewhere else on his body.

He stalks back to the living room, thinking of the last time a woman he loved saw him, all blowed-up and broken; she'd high-tailed it from the hospital and filed for divorce.

"Abby's gonna run," he predicts while standing in front of the knick-knack shelf and the tribunal of goddesses, with his heart revving like an M-16 on rapid-fire mode. He can barely hear his own thoughts as he paces and pleads both sides of the case aloud.

"Adopted, fucked-up childhood, daddy and mommy issues, depression… she's so loaded down already, she might be looking for something breezy and light, with someone less…"

Less what, Garth?

"But then again, she's the one who said, 'No video calls unless we fall in love.' Maybe she *is* looking for something deeper than skin. We have that… I feel it… she feels it too… but—"

The panmen topple from his desk, landing with a merry tinkle that distracts Garth long enough for his careening mind to steady itself and alight upon a solid conclusion. "Fuck it, it's my Alive Day," he says as he stoops to retrieve the *pannists* from the carpet, convinced that their sudden fall is no accident, but rather an act of the goddesses. A man is supposed to celebrate his Alive Day—some of the guys in therapy group, they do that *every* year—but he's never done that (he doesn't count the fifth anniversary Vegas binge with two Russian prostitutes supplied by Rustam.) He's never *truly* celebrated, like in his heart. But he will today, with Abby, if she'll let him. It's time to ask her to take that next step: to meet. He's scared but excited, adrenaline-pumped, in a way he hasn't been in a long time. He can't think of a luckier day to start trusting his gut again.

Two thousand miles away, in Trinidad, the sun and the metal door-grate have risen on a new Monday at Seepaul's Household Emporium, where the good people of the town of Tunapuna can purchase plastic flowers, ceramic knick-knacks, and home haberdashery—buckets, bins, and hampers of every size, color and perforation. Not to mention brass *puja* supplies for Hindus, and religious candles in skinny glass vessels for Catholics. Those are a bestseller, of course, given the store's location in the valley below Mount St. Benedict, Trinidad's Vatican. Gods and goddesses are good business here for Abby's adoptive parents, Ramesh and Leela.

Behind the cash register, Abby reclines now in Daddy's rickety swivel chair, cocks up her feet on the laminate counter, and does a deep dive into her Samsung smartphone. Satesh, the store boy, is in the back sorting rubber slippers received yesterday from China. There is no one here to see Abby's face pulling tight like a drawstring bag (aisle one, middle shelf) as she reads the latest message from her online boyfriend, Retired Staff Sergeant Garth Krüger.

I' m coming to Trinidad next week on business. Can we meet?

What the hell this man thinking! Her fingers lunge out of WhatsApp and barge into Instagram, seeking the insight of her online spiritual guru, Kayte (@immacukayte_guidance).

"There will be a full moon tonight," Kayte predicts in her lead caption, declaring it, "the biggest and brightest permission slip ever."

Permission for what? What is Garth really asking—or not asking? Abby stares off into space, weighing and tallying his words until they total only one possibility: he wants to break up with her. He's probably found some old picture of her somewhere, on some old site (the internet is forever), and he's figured out that her current profile pic—the one he's been relying on these past four months—has been lightened by so many filtering apps that it is pretty much not her. She is not that beige Bollywood *beti* with silky-straight black tresses and a peony-pink pout. She is a frizzy haired *madrassi* with two-toned lips—upper almost as black as her face, lower as purple as an unhealed bruise—and skin impermeable to the lotions and potions Mummy has applied over the years. She is the Indian woman Google delivers when you search for *Dalit*, for Untouchable.

The only truth in the picture is in her grey eyes. Her one redeeming feature according to her parents ("Don't mind you so dark, them cat-eye did make you the nicest child in that whole orphanage.") So, on Mummy's advice, Abby had made Garth agree that they could only turn on the cameras if they made it to six months, and only if they each fell in love "with the other's soul." Is he suddenly in love with her soul? They've been chatting more and more lately—a lot about "kindred spirits" and "twinned souls"—but neither has uttered the L-word.

Nah. It's not love, it's lies coming home to roost. He's found out how black she is, and he's either feeling deceived or turned off—or both. That must be it. He's just asking to meet because he knows she won't, and he'll have a reason to walk away. Which would hurt, but maybe not so much, because hasn't she been expecting it for these whole four months? Hasn't she been waiting for him to get bored? Because, why wouldn't he? He's a handsome, white, *Nort-American-Mister* (as Mummy says) who's traveled the world, and she… well… she's a storekeeper's adopted daughter who's never left the island of Trinidad.

Heart thrashing about in her chest, Abby reverse-pinches the phone screen. *Steups!* Why does the writing on d' Gram have to be so small? Then she scrolls and scrolls through Kayte's advice. Why does Kayte have to talk in circles? Finally, she gets to the point:

The full moon reassures us, the answer is YES!!!

Yes, it's safe to trust yourself!!! Yes, it's ok to say YES today!

Does that mean yes, Garth *is* in love with her? Is that what he meant the other night when he said she's "exotic and gorgeous" and he would marry a girl looking like her "in a heartbeat."

But, of course, he was referring to the fake Abby in the profile picture. Or does Kayte mean she should say yes to the imminent break-up. "Yes," to the life she'd had before Garth slid into her DMs and made her feel… well… interesting? And in a weird way, seen. He's never said it's dumb that she wants to open her own catering business making Indian sweets, that she feels happiest when she's rolling and squeezing and shaping that dough, rubbing sugar, milk powder, and colored sprinkles through her fingertips. He doesn't dismiss her when she says she thinks she's been depressed her whole life, and yet he doesn't chastise when she says she'd never step foot inside a real therapist's office because Trinidad is too small and she would cause her parents too much shame. Garth has never judged her; he has only listened.

"*Papayo!* Watch how you loll-off there," a voice calls from the shop doorway. "Bandit could walk in your father place and you none the wiser."

Abby almost capsizes the chair, herself, and the cash register. She lowers her legs and sits upright, as a proprietor's daughter should. She shelves Garth (for now) because Miss Pussin, Mummy's longtime friend, has entered the store and is glaring at Abby with hand on hip. Astride the other offended hip is a little brown-skinned *dougla* boy—about seven or eight— who Abby has never seen before. The old lady's bulging knuckles look like cashew nuts (snack shelf, near door). She's gripping the child as if he's in danger of falling from a great height.

"Morning, Miss Pussin. What I could help you with today?" Abby asks, distractedly. She makes her way over to the old lady while debating whether to seek a second opinion about Garth from another spiritual influencer. "Kitchen towel? Flowers? We get some nice fake lilies this week."

"No, *Doux-doux*. Today, I looking for drawers."

"Drawers?" Abby thinks of underwear, and is more than a little thankful that it's not something they sell here. She would not want to be standing in front of this doe-eyed boy—who's staring as if her face is an iPad—while Miss Pussin picked out underwear the size of his T-shirt.

"Yeah, them plastic drawers, nah. To pack this child clothes. I see allyuh had them the other day. Sturdy-lite or something so it name."

"Oh. Sterilite. Yes, straight down to the back. Let me show you." While she leads them through the labyrinth of the store, Abby's eyes begin to sting and there's a sudden itch in the back of her throat as if she's been sniffing all the cans of insecticide and Tiger Balm, and drinking all the bottles of pepper sauce, rubbing alcohol, and Kwan Loong oil. A sting like the onset of a cold—only it's not a cold; it's hot, fresh tears. She tries the "mindful breath" tactic they rave about in the online support group where she met Garth. And while she waits for her vagus nerve to relax and the bad feelings to abate, she listens to Miss Pussin rambling on about the boy ("Is my grandson. My son take him back from that negro girl, that *jammette* child-mother. She used to leave this poor baby home alone to go meet she next man. But I praying on she head.") By the time she arrives at the plastics, Abby's face is nothing but a thin wall full of holes, barely restraining her lifetime of dammed grief. "Here," she says, hoarsely, slapping the drawer-stack a little too hard, "and we have these cheaper ones, too."

The boy is staring still, unrelenting, no smile, just a petrified glare. It reminds Abby of how she felt at his age whenever she encountered this very same Miss Pussin. Ancient, with teeth like Stonehenge, the old lady is reputedly a *soucouyant*, a monster who sheds her skin at night and bursts into flames so she can slide under doors to suck children's blood. Mummy says she can't remember a time when Miss Pussin was young, and that she and Daddy had befriended the old lady and always given her discounts because it's best to keep soucouyants on your side—they are like influencers within the black arts community, Abby supposes.

"You like living with Granny?" she asks, hoping the transfixed child will blush and lower his eyes, or peer upward with love at Miss Pussin—do something, anything, other than stare at her trembling face—because Abby suspects she knows why he's staring. People always stare when they first meet her.

"Mikey, where your manners? Tell Miss Abby good morning, please."

The boy's good morning is less greeting and more recitation of a two word poem. Then he swallows hard and says, "Miss Abby, excuse, how you so black and your eye-them so white, white? You's a blind person? Or you does see good? I 'fraid blind people."

Now he clings to his grandmother's skirt, buries his face and starts to cry, as if Abby is the monster after all. "Ah *chut!* This boy, eh! I sorry girl, he don't mean nothing by it. He just don't know better. That *jagabat* child-mother had him growing wild, wild in Valencia, with no broughtupcy, till he come like a orphan now. He does bawl for every lil thing. Ent *you* know how it is?"

Miss Pussin gives Abby's forearm a knowing rub which

burns like Ben Gay: *This boy is damaged goods, just like you.*

"No, it's ok,"Abby replies, her voice high and strained. She tousles the boy's curls and explains, "I' m not blind, Mikey. I does see normal, like you. Is just that God color your eyes black and he color mines grey. That's all." She offers her hand for a fist bump, receives Mikey's timid response, then says, "Allyuh, excuse me a minute, eh," then leaves the old lady there, knocking the hard plastic, pulling, pushing and inspecting the three-draw unit.

"Satesh, deal with Miss Pussin, please…and remember her discount," she calls out, lunging past the storeroom, stifling beneath this shrink-wrap of professionalism.

Over the bathroom sink, she gulps for air and tries to swallow her feelings, but it's no use; she's too sad for too many reasons. So she just grips the stained porcelain and waits while the pain escapes her in a million tears that slither down into the drain.

She wishes she had a better explanation to give Mikey, one that didn't involve God. Children aren't stupid: they know adults palm off everything on God when they can't be bothered to look for real answers. What's the *real* answer for why her eyes don't match her skin? She's always wished for some tangible reason: her father had grey eyes or she got it from her mother's side, some explanation that would make her seem the natural consequence of something, rather than an aberration and a freak. But Abby doesn't have the answers she needs. So, God. That same silent God who'd watched when, at six years old, she'd climbed into the Seepaul's Mazda toting her small garbage bag of belongings and a lifetime non-refundable supply of sadness, but strangely, no memories of her life before the orphanage, no photos of her real parents. Did she have any siblings? If she did, their names and faces must've dry-rotted somewhere in the backroom of her mind.

Garth has said he' ll help find her real family one day. He's good at both techie-stuff and at spying—that's the kind of work he did in the Army. "Time to put it to good use," he's said. Garth, sweet Garth. He's even helped her find a different side of herself. The past four months have been the only time she's ever felt free of that hazy longing which has haunted her whole life and kept her always on the verge of crying. Always being chastised by Mummy: *You too thin-skinned!... Don't give me no crocodile tears... Depressed, my ass! Is Satan chooking you. You just have to pray harder.* Everything for Mummy is pray harder, pray harder—but prayers have never really worked for Abby. Mummy has hauled her up to the Mount and lit candles and made her say countless decades of the rosary, but that didn't work. Sent her so many times to the pundit next door to get a good *jharay* for spiritual cleansing, but that didn't work. And oh, how Abby used to beg and beg God to heal her of the loneliness, the hopelessness, the blank spaces that the Seepaul's love have never been able to fill. But God seemed deaf... until Garth. Only *he* has made her happy.

From the first text in the morning, to his last whisper of "Good night," Garth's tenderness has garlanded each day of her last four months. Sure, the clock was ticking, but six months felt like such a long time away, and she never honestly expected they would make it to that horizon. She's just been grateful for each day of gliding aimlessly, into unfamiliar waters, with him. And now that her moment of reckoning has arrived, Abby realizes that she cannot go back to a life without Garth. She *has* fallen in love with his soul.

"She was on the phone extra late last night," Ramesh says to his wife, Leela, as he enters the kitchen before dawn.

"I know. And is not even Friday. Them does only stay so long on Fridays," Leela replies. She gets up from the table and turns on the stove below the kettle.

"Is either something going very right, or something going very wrong with them," Ramesh says.

"Is true. I so frighten for them, eh. Come, boy, let we pray on they head."

The Seepauls are a deeply religious couple; they worship together every morning. To the half-performed Hinduism of their childhoods, they have engrafted a vigorous Catholicism. With double the symbolism, incense and shiny brass receptacles, they believe they've afforded themselves access to the widest cross-section of deities. So they kneel now before the little altar in their kitchen, where they regularly interchange *murtis* and statues of saints, where they light candles to St. Michael and to Hanuman, to St. Peter and to Lakshmi, to St. Anthony and to Vishnu.

As today is a Monday, they must recite the Joyful Mysteries of the rosary. In tandem, they make the Sign of the Cross, say the Nicene Creed, speed through the introduction—the first three little beads and the *Glory Be*—then, Ramesh takes the lead. He reads from their little *Living With Our Lady* guidebook. "The first Joyful Mystery, The Annunciation: Angel Gabriel tells Mary she will conceive the child, Jesus."

Then they alternate. Ramesh says the "*Hail Mary full of grace*" bit, Leela answers with the "*Holy Mary Mother of God*" bit, over and over again. It's normal for them to become so entranced by the rhythm and repetition that they see things, behind their closed eyes, things that only God could show them.

This morning, worried as she is about Abby, what Leela sees is her former self, as she was in her twenties, spinning and dancing wildly, wet from head to feet, vibrating during *Kali* worship at a nearby temple, begging for a baby; and then she sees herself as she was in her early-thirties, kneeling within a polished wooden pew on the Mount, fingering these same red glass rosary beads and pleading with Mary to make her a mother too; and then, there she is, still childless in her late-thirties and on pilgrimage with Ramesh to the black Madonna statue in Siparia Village. See them reciting with the Catholic contingent, "*La Divina Pastora, pray for us*," then chanting alongside the Hindu devotees, "*Om Om Soparee Mai*"—and see the phone ring a few days afterward, the Catholic orphanage calling with news of a miracle: a beautiful little Indian girl who could be theirs. Abby.

For almost two decades, the Seepauls' hearts have been inflamed with love for Abby and yet pierced by a sword of worry, because she seems eternally unhappy despite the life they' ve given her, eternally lonely... until she met Garth.

Oh Mother, Mata, Mai, strengthen their love and save them, Leela repeats in her mind as she rolls bead after bead. Then suddenly, the decade is over and Ramesh is saying, "As it was in the beginning, is now, and ever shall be, world without end."

"Amen," says Leela.

Then they rise and approach the cluttered altar. She lights a candle to St. Jude, and he burns a piece of camphor while reciting a mantra to Arjuna. In this way, they have double-teamed the immortals in charge of desperate situations, lost causes and recovery of relationships.

"Abby and she Nort-American Mister go be good now," Leela says. "I done feeling it in my spirit."

Later that morning, Abby joins her parents in the kitchen to help make the weekly batch of *kurma* to sell in the store. Leela is rolling and cutting the dough into strips, Abby is deep frying them. Ramesh is at the kitchen table, intermittently watching cricket on the muted TV and pretending to read the newspaper, while eavesdropping on the woman talk. It's his day to work at the Emporium, though; he will be leaving soon, and normally, by the time he slides the store's metal grate, "his girls" would have happily moved on to crafting *ladoo*, fudge and sugar cake.

But today is shaping-up different. Today, there is much discord within the Seepaul home. Abby has just announced that last night, during that marathon telephone conversation with Garth, she agreed that her family will meet him next week, when he comes to Trinidad.

"What possess you?" Mummy asks as she slams the wooden *bilna* onto the dough. She presses and rolls with even more intensity than usual.

Abby says nothing, in the hope that an early capitulation will shorten the victory speech, and that Daddy won't leave her alone just yet with Mummy's wrath. Actually, anger would be ok, she muses, circling her head to relieve the neck-kink from a horrible night's sleep; but what she's always found difficult to handle is Mummy's disappointment. All the fire and brimstone this morning is really just that: a flaming ball of disappointment. It was during one of these very same confection-making sessions that she'd first told Mummy about Garth. With trembling sugar-coated hands, she'd shown his Facebook profile picture: a real manly shot from his Army days. Tight green T-shirt, tanned skin, blonde buzz cut, and surprisingly full lips for a white fella. Together, she and Mummy have admired that one photo at least fifty times since then and, on every occasion, Mummy has credited herself for Garth's auspicious appearance in their lives: *Pundit Sharma did say you born with a caul over your face that your real parents never get lift-off. He say you woulda see lil trouble for a while—might even see spirit, with them cat-eye you have there—but things woulda end-up good with you after all. Praise Jesus! Look it happening now. The prayers and fasting of a good mother does go straight to God.*

"Girl!" A shout yanks Abby back to the present. "You burning the *kurma!* Take them out quick, before they get black. Nobody go want that!"

When the *kurma* is out of jeopardy, Mummy reopens the subject of Garth."I give you *one* simple instruction: just bide your time and make this man love-off on you *before* he see you. When Nort-American people fall in love, they does fall hard and deep like is manhole. They does get *tootool-bay*—I watch enough *Bachelor* to know that. And it wouldn't matter at all then, if you not nice-and-fair like in your profile pic."

"I know—"

"So, he love you yet?"

"I don't know—"

"So how you could say yes to the man meeting all of we next week? Like you take een last night and went mad?"

In truth, Abby can't explain why she let Garth convince her. He was so excited and it made her feel excited, too.

"What to do?" she pleads now. "Go back and tell him allyuh say no?" She looks from Mummy to Daddy, just wanting an instruction. She's ready to do whatever they say because, at this point, she's tired of playing referee between her own heart and head.

"You done say yes, so we hadda meet him. Where in Trinidad you go find a man like that? This Garth is one in a million. But see if you could put it off to a later date, nah?"

"When big fish biting, you have to pull quick," Daddy interjects, without looking up from the newspaper.

"Pull how, Ramesh? We need more time to do something. We don't want she turn the doorknob next week Friday and turn off the man same speed. She hadda look better. Like when the make-up artist did fix we up for Rampersad-daughter wedding. Abby, show Daddy the picture on your phone."

"*A-ya-yai!* Australia putting a *cutarse* on Bangladesh in this test match," Daddy says, signalling he has no interest in seeing the photo. "I want them win. Not because I's a coolie, I go support Bangladesh. Nah, I believe in backing the side with the best caliber. If the white man batting and bowling best, I dey with the white man."

"*Humph*," Mummy grunts. "The man go want to see you every day while he in Trinidad, and when he go back Florida, he go want to start video calling all the time. We need something more lasting than make-up." She stares at the flattened dough for a moment, as if deciphering a Sanskrit scroll. Then she says, "Ramesh, put down that papers and call Miss Pussin right now. Tell she we need the number for she Jamaican cleaner-girl."

"Why?'" Daddy and Abby ask simultaneously.

"Pussin say the girl come like a *sadhu* for skin-problem. Let we try she, nah?"

And two hours later, just as the sugar cake is setting, Sharon arrives. Abby expected a big, jolly, negro woman wearing a head wrap—like the maid from that Jamaican soap opera, *Royal Palm Estate*—but Sharon is a wiry, sexy little thing in a mauve tube top, tight jeans, and a two-toned black and mauve wig. Abby wonders how many headpieces the girl owns, and if she color coordinates her hair to her outfit all the time.

"So *oonu* want bleach?" Sharon asks, looking from mother to daughter and drumming her mauve acrylic nails on the Seepauls' dining table.

Mummy, ear untrained to Jamaican twang, asks, "What you say?" but Abby has listened to enough dance hall music in her life to comprehend immediately.

"Yes, I want to look like this," she says, holding out her phone to Sharon. "*Watch-a!* You favor Barbie there, Miss Abby. And them contacts inna your eye-them jus finish the look and sell it off."

"No, it's not contacts, it's my—"

"Yes, she want to reach that complexion," Mummy confirms. "She have a big date coming up with a posh Nort-American-Mister. And Miss Pussin say is *you* did help Rampersad-daughter, and it work out nice, because the Tiwarie-boy from Valsayn propose to she quick, quick. So we need your help, Sharon."

"That ah no problem, ma'am. *Oonu* coolie people skin nuh tough, like we nayga skin, so it easy fi come."

"You sure, girl? You sure you could bleach this one? We trying all kinda thing since she thirteen—Nadinola, Fair and Lovely, Vicco Turmeric—and nothing ever work."

"*Cho!* Dem tings nah go work, ma'am. Dat ah old time sum'n. The new-model sum'n guarantee fi work. Besides, Miss Abby no need bleachings, she just need fi tone-in and pep up, couple shades, so the man can see her more clearly. Eee?"

"Exactly!" declares Mummy, clapping her knees in delight.

"Trust me, Ma'am, mi do understand. In this world, yuh nah gwaan when yuh black, nobody nah really see yuh. Them see yuh how *them* want fi see yuh, not how *you* want dem see."

"Yes, oh my God, yes." Now it's Abby's turn to be impressed with Sharon—she's wise, and has an air about her like she's witnessed every trick in the book of life and survived to tell the story—like a ghetto-*Kayte*, maybe. "I really, really like this fella,"Abby admits. "I want to feel more brave with him—just like how I was feeling in this picture. Like all the parts of me is a matching set, not some odds-and-ends from a jumble sale. You get what I trying to say?"

Sharon nods and leans in. "See mi here: mi look black and rusty now, but every time, 'bout a two month before mi go back ah Jamaica, mi start tone-in. Mek mi family-them look pon mi and feel mi ah live high-life ah Trinidad. Mek everybody respect mi when mi touchdown inna mi yard. You sayin you want this man respect you, Miss Abby? Mi can mek him do that, easy. How much time we have? One month?"

"No, less than two weeks,"Mummy replies. "They meeting next-week-Friday."

"Lahhhd, dis ah one emergency case then! Good thing mi walk with mi sum'n them," Sharon says, as if Miss Pussin hadn't already explained the dire timeline to her.

From her knapsack, Miss Pussin pulls several bottles and packets. "You mix this Idole cream with one Omik gel, one paw-paw gel and one tambrin gel. And like how you nuh have whole heapa time, add one teaspoon ah curry. Then you tip likkle baby oil inna the mix. Rub down your skin every night before you go sleep. Ah daytime, wear your long-sleeve and hat and cloak-up nice from the sun. If you start tonight, four, five days and you will see a big difference."

"So how much for all this?" Mummy asks, as if she hasn't been forewarned of Sharon's price by Miss Pussin.

"Hundred US dollar."

"Why so much!" Mummy exclaims in the fake horror voice she uses to haggle with the store's suppliers.

"Ma'am, you cyah get this ah Trinidad. Mi get this from the best Chinee shop ah Jamaica. And mi pay lotta money fi people come carry it here inna them suitcase. So the price just reflect the shippin-an-anglin, ma'am. *Oonu* have business-place, *oonu* must know good ting nuh cheap, and cheap ting nuh good. Seen?"

Friday night arrives, four days after Garth's proposition to Abby, but seven days before the date set for his momentous visit.

With a solid week of texting under their belts, the star-crossed lovers typically spend Fridays in a state of positive chemical imbalance, each anticipating an extra-long WhatsApp phone call around nine pm.

But tonight, they're both dreading that call.

Garth's insomnia has come back this week. Every night, he's watched the ASMR videos on his YouTube channels, desperate to relax. Every night he's meditated. But he just can't sleep and now, four nights in, he's scared.

Texts have become fewer, more sporadic and hurried from Abby, which has caused Garth to slip into emotional-Kevlar mode, matching her curt tone. He's had no way of knowing that Abby's change in mood is because she's been suffering as well. After applying Sharon's potion, she's gone to bed every night feeling like a congealed ball of grease and smelling even worse—curry, peroxide, and artificial papaya combined. She's been uncomfortable 24/7, sweating and scorning herself under the thick hoodies, sunglasses, and big, floppy West Indies cricket hat—mauve, just like Sharon—plucked from Daddy's closet.

Ignorant of these things, Garth doesn't even realize that his curt replies are only making the poor girl agonize even more over her responses, making them even slower to come. All he knows is that his connection with Abby has been buffering… buffering… buffering, all week.

Eighteen Hundred Hours. Have I made a mistake?

Garth checks his phone for the millionth time today. The needle has been all over his mood. One minute, he's grumpy and snappy with gym clients ("Move your ass and stop being a baby!"); the next minute, he's quiet and sullen, hiding out in the locker room, which is where he is now, trying to catch some shut eye.

So little sleep. His mind, the same mind that was flooded with hope on Monday, now feels like a sandy ditch—the kind of place where the Ali Babas used to hide out, with their handheld devices, waiting to blow shit up. Every word from Abby has felt loaded, like something that might detonate if he responds wrong. And what's made the week even more of a torture is that he can't be sure if the whiff of death he's detecting in their communication is coming from his own sick mind. Should he distrust himself, or Abby? He's not sure how to talk with her tonight; he's downright terrified she'll ambush him with "goodbye." Was asking to meet her and her family so wrong?

The phone beeps, his heart soars, he fumbles, opens the message app but—no, it's not her. It's the last client for the day, canceling his session. Garth leaves the locker room, clocks out and enters the dead air of his car's capsule, wishing he could stay in there, hermetically sealed and safe, forever. For the next ten minutes, the car seems to drive him home, through all the usual back streets, avoiding as much traffic and as many big intersections as possible. He parks and walks to the elevators feeling like he's walking against a wind while pulling something heavy behind him. He slumps against a wall as he enters the apartment—then suddenly, every hair on his arm stands at attention. He draws the Glock, tiptoes across to the bathroom… nobody… then he's about to kick in the hall closet when he stops himself.

"Get a grip, man! You know there's no one here."

He holsters the weapon. He balls up his fists and presses them into his eye sockets, the way he used to whenever a *shamal* would rush across the peninsula, picking up dust between the Tigris and Euphrates, spraying his face and leaving him disoriented, teary and almost without breath.

Maybe it's working, Abby guesses, as she inspects the patches on her skin. Home from the store, she's had dinner, showered, and is now on her tiptoes at the bathroom mirror. They'd started as a yellowish constellation, as if she'd developed a mild case of *lota*, the skin fungus everybody gets as a child. But the patches have expanded over the week, becoming planets floating within the dark firmament of her face. Maybe they will connect soon, click together like a solved puzzle. "Four, five days and your skin *gwine* start come with that chrome-out, air-condition look," Sharon had predicted. So maybe this is progress?

Maybe then, by the time she sees Garth, she will be the beautiful, bronzy color of under-fried *kurma*. So, she should be happy, right?

But no, she's been on edge more than ever. Kayte says it's because Mercury is retrograde in Libra right now, she says Abby should expect "tech glitches, disappearing texts, scrapped travel plans, and blood pressure-escalating misunderstandings with loved-ones…"

And sure enough, the week has lived up to that. So much

tension—the bad kind—in her texting with Garth, she almost expects him to say he's not coming anymore; she almost wishes he would say that.

And, for some strange reason, she's had no patience for Mummy's matchmaking advice this week. They've been at loggerheads every day, and tonight, during dinner, when Mummy said, "Cheer up, daughter. Nobody saying you hadda bleach for the rest of your life. Only till the man put ring on your finger,"Abby wanted to scream.

How can she explain to Mummy that this lightening isn't having the effect she'd expected? It isn't seeping below her skin, stimulating her hope follicles or growing her confidence, like she'd intended. If anything, she feels more a fraud than ever now, and is suddenly aware that if Garth cannot love her at her blackest, he can never *truly* love her. And why is Mummy so eager for Garth to be her husband, when nobody's even met him? Nobody knows him! He could be a serial killer looking for his next victim. What has he done to bypass all the tests her parents have set for every other boy? Just be white?

When she'd said that while they were washing dishes, Mummy's response had been, "Daughter, if I did have a white fella in love with me when I was young, I woulda never marrid Ramesh. Don't get me wrong: I love your father, eh. But I woulda try anything to keep the white man— whether I did love him or not. Because then, I woulda never have to sacrifice and ketch my ass to mind shop, and save, and cut-and-contrive, and bruise my knees in prayer to get my own house. I woulda had a gentler life. Is that-self I want you have, the thing what I never had."

And that had upset Abby because it had confirmed what she'd begun to suspect since the moment she told her parents about Garth. *His* feelings were more valuable than hers. And she'd come face to face with what felt like an old fright dressed in new clothes: the helplessness of having to wait for some kind stranger to show up, look her over and find her worthy of their bountiful affection. Relationships have always been someone else's prerogative, never hers.

A blast of ringtone startles her. She sprints from the bathroom to her bedroom to answer and… *Oh God, it's him, a whole hour early!*

Answer or decline, green button or red button?

She slides her thumb across the screen and says a cautious, "Hello."

But Garth's words come at her, gung-ho. "Hey there, look, I know I'm early and I'm sorry but I just had to… you know… it's been kinda weird between us this week?

"You find so? I didn't notice," she says. She climbs onto the shaggy bedspread and sits sideways on her knees. In the dressing-table mirror she looks like Jasmine on Aladdin's magic carpet. "Just kinda busy, nah. Stock-taking and things in the store. Plus, we had an order for two dozen bags of gluten-free *kurma* so… You ok? You sound—"

"Yeah, no, I'm great." Garth's voice goes from prince to frog in her ear, then silence.

"You still there?" she asks.

"I'm here," he replies. "Look, I know we don't talk too much about my past, the Army, it's heavy stuff. But tonight, can I tell you a story? I just feel like it's something you should hear… before I visit."

Visit, visit… Does she actually want him to visit? She knows that's what *he* wants, that's what Mummy and Daddy want, but what would *she* want, if it were up to her alone?

"I like stories," she says, trying to sound lighthearted.

"So, my accident. What I never told you is…" Garth starts and stutters a few times. She can sense his courage faltering but she doesn't want the conversation to spin backwards in her direction. She wants to hear *his* confessions tonight, so she doesn't have to think about her own.

"It's ok," she encourages, "tell me anything. I can handle it." Then she wriggles beneath the bedspread, lies back, closes her eyes to better hear his voice.

"So…" he tries again. "It happened on the road, this big intersection near Baghdad. We couldn't turn left or right, there was stuff, wreckage, kinda piled up everywhere. Thought I'd navigate around but the Truck Commander gave the order to go north, so I did. Then there was this woman, came outta nowhere, just appeared beside the roadside ditch, her long white *haji* clothes just flapping in the wind. She starts waving her arms at us. I felt for sure she was warning us not to drive on, but I did anyway. That's when the blast happened. It was my fault. Everyone else in the truck died because of me."

Abby's eyes open, her body stiffens. A worse revelation is coming, she sixth senses it. She's always known there was a blast, that he'd been in a coma for a bit and had multiple surgeries, suffered with survivors'guilt—but she's known these things the way you know a triangle moving way up in the sky is a flock of birds. They seem to have come down now, and perched themselves on the rail of her bed, where she's staring, afraid to even breathe.

"When I came back stateside, I couldn't handle traffic, especially at big crossroads, where you're gridlocked in and you're trapped. Sometimes I'd be fine, but most times I'd sweat and kinda freeze up, even think about ramming the cars ahead of me. Man, this shit went on for years and years. But then, last year, my therapist did this thing called 'exposure therapy.' Drove me to this big, multi-lane motherfucker, parked our asses right there alongside. And my heart, I tell you, it was racing. I was dizzy as hell; I was ready to get out and just run. But she made me stay right there. 'Stay in the stress,' she said. And I did, and it kinda peaked and then flattened out. Now, I don't freak out so much anymore. I'm doing a lot better."

"That's great," Abby says from the shallows of her mind. The rest of her has floated out of depth, wondering why he's telling her this. What is he building to? "You're so brave."

"Nah. Not brave."

"Why you say that?" She steels herself. *Here it comes.*

"Last year," he sighs so heavily the line goes all garbled, "before the therapy, I tried to kill myself, Abby. Jammed that pistol into my mouth, right up to my tonsils, ready to squeeze that trigger and eat all the bullets."

She shuts her eyes, shakes and shakes her head to dislodge the image, and although she knows the story ends well—he's alive—she groans, "Oh my God," the words rising up her insides and spewing forth like some kind of spontaneous prayer from her spirit. She can't imagine this man, who makes her laugh every day, who's been so encouraging, so tender and attentive, being that defeated by his loneliness and sorrow. It makes hers seem so small. She longs to reach through the phone and hold him.

"But then—it's gonna sound weird, but I swear this is true—I had a vision, Abby. It was night, almost closing time. I was naked on the floor of a shower stall, chugging whiskey and trying to decide between bullets or pills. Then right there on the foggy glass, I saw my mom. Her hair was long again, like before the cancer, and she said, 'Son, don't do it. Help is near.' So I cried and cried, but I didn't do it, I obeyed, cause I figured I'd failed her so many times while she was alive, it's the least I could do to make amends."

I wish I could see my mom. Abby thinks not of Leela but of the mother she's lost, the one who, she's dared to believe, would've found her beautiful just so.

A flash beneath the bedroom door. *Maybe Daddy turned on the corridor bulb?* But no! Abby gasps as, hovering across the bedroom ceiling, in a vision of shadow and light, a woman appears. At first, Abby wonders if this is Miss Pussin finally revealing herself in soucouyant form. But then she notices the dark face and long hair are framed by a luminous wedding dress and veil… *La Divina Pastora*! It *has* to be her. There's something long in her hand, something shaped like… a brushing cutlass?… no, a shepherdess staff. Abby looks for sheep but there are none, just a little boy standing beside. *Is that Garth? Mikey? Some other lost boy?*

Abby can't look away, can't even blink. The only thing she can think to do is recite the Rosary. Which one, which one? She decides on the Second Joyful Mystery, The Visitation. Her lips move soundlessly while Garth is rambling on the line—something about scars on his face and skin grafts—but then he stops. The silence is a beat too long. Has he asked her a question?

"Sorry, what?" she says, her eyes still on the Shepherdess, her heart crackling like melting ice.

Garth replies, "I said, 'I think we should turn on the cameras, tonight, *before* I visit.'"

"I—"

"I know, I know. It terrifies me too, darlin. You're so beautiful, a total knockout. What would *you* want with *me?* You might take one look and… *scram!* But, Abby Seepaul, you're the best thing to ever happen to me. And I'm at a crossroads here. I need to show myself to you. My gut is saying I need to do it *now.* So I can make my way through with a clear head next week, and have a chance at earning your precious, precious love. Or maybe you'll want me to back away and stop wasting your time. I gotta know either way, baby. I gotta know what you want."

Garth is The One, La Divina whispers into Abby's heart. In her excitement, the girl flicks the bedside lamp and in the explosion of new light, the Shepherdess dissolves. But the divine permission has already been granted. Abby's never felt more at peace, she has never had more faith. She knows now that she and Garth have always been threading a course toward each other, because her Divine Mother—a dark-skinned Madonna—has always been their guide. She senses now that she and Garth are two souls standing at the eternal river where they were always meant to meet, just as they are. Their journeys, however perilous, have perfected in them the courage to drown.

"Let's do it now,"Abby says, her face streaming.

"You sure? It's ok, I'm not trying to pressure you if—"

She swipes the blue video button. "Look me here. I'm ready."

He swipes too. Then, with the milky eyes of the reborn, Abby and Garth slowly take each other in.

GOAT-MOUTH

Piarco Airport, Trinidad, 2017

When Anand saw movement at the airport exit, he lifted the name sign to his beefy chest and—hard luck!—it was a false alarm. Only a security guard ambled out, jiggling his pants waist, eyeballing the crowd, simulating importance. *Steups!* Typical useless rent-a-cop. Oh how Anand hated them. He lowered the sign and tapped it against the hard line of his quads, careful though, not to bend the thing—8 x 10 paper stapled to a box flap—it had already caused him way too much trouble for one day.

His boots ticked clockwise as he turned away from the doors. Everyone in the arrivals area seemed to have the same impatient expression etched onto their faces. But, as an Executive Protection Specialist, Anand was accustomed to long waits. He didn't even mind them so much anymore because he used the time to study the people around him, imagining their lives and writing their stories in his head. Sometimes, even sneaking quick snapshots and videos to show Denyse. But he couldn't do that today because, this morning, he and Denyse had fought about the sign.

He'd had to ask her to rewrite it *twice* for stupid mistakes: firstly, she'd added an "e" that wasn't supposed to be there, then she'd put three dots over the u in "Krüger."

"Is like you deliberately trying to fuck up this job today," he'd said. "You damn well know these foreigners funny 'bout they name. Look, fix it."

"Well, if you have to get-on so hoggish, write the damn thing yourself," she'd replied.

But they'd both known the sign was just convenient repackaging of a deeper hostility: she had ordered him *not* to take today's armed escort job, and he had chosen to defy her.

"The man is *what?* American spy? Boy, just pass on this job and tell D-Boss you go take the next one in line, nah. Years ago, I did watch a horror 'bout a man name Krueger. Look... my pores raising. Trust me: anybody who name so, they bringin trouble in your life. And I can't handle no unnecessary drama with you."

Yet Anand had left for the airport at 5:15, had watched the big white bird from Florida slide into Trinidad's orange Sahara-dusted sunrise and, almost two hours later, he was still waiting for the client, Mr. Krüger. And still fuming about Denyse, too: how she purposely hadn't replied to his goodbye, when she knew how deeply that would affect him. She knew her "goodbye"was always his "good luck" for the day, and that without it he felt naked and exposed to the elements. She could be a real bitch sometimes, yes!

Anand's mother would never have dared order his father to do or not do something. And if she'd tried, his father would've knocked her teeth out. Anand had never hit Denyse, although sometimes he'd wanted to so bad, but more than anything he wanted to be a different man from his father, a different kind of husband. Did Denyse even realize how lucky she was? Sometimes he reminded her, and her response was always, "Monkey know which tree to climb!" as if all credit should go to her and not him. "Allyuh Indian man could advantage them mooksie lil coolie girls. Not a strong black empress like me. The day you put God out your thoughts and raise your hand for me, Anand, I will happily make a jail. Trust and believe."

She had a cutting tongue. Sometimes he wondered why he stayed. But Denyse was the girl of his childhood, his first puppy dog crush, granddaughter of Miss Jackie from down the hill. Coming from the same place as he, she'd known who he was without him having to explain the tragedies that had befallen his family—and she'd loved him anyway. Enough, after he'd aged out of the orphanage, to let him into her home where they'd taken care of Miss Jackie until death; and into her heart, even after all the hardship she'd been through with other men (first boyfriend used to beat her, next one was a druggie who paid his coke debts with her body). Bagatelle Village had scarred them both at a young age and had made them protective of each other.

So maybe she was just being protective this morning? Anand tried to reason with himself. And didn't she have a right to be? She was the one who always had to shake him awake and cradle him whenever he got too stressed out and the crying in his sleep resumed. She was the one who, for days afterward, would live with his silence and watch him half-killing himself in the rusty little home gym he'd accumulated under the house; and she was the one who, for nights afterward, would have to wonder when it was safe to reach across the blanket and make love to him again.

He knew he wasn't an easy man to live with. And look, she'd still done the damn sign.

Anand decided to rack his resentment and forgive Denyse. He'd carry something nice for her later, he pledged—maybe a Jack Daniels steak from TGI Fridays—bought with the US dollar tips he was sure to collect today from this client.

Travelers were flowing through the customs pipeline now,

spilling into the arrivals area, many in jeans and T-shirts, a few with surfboards, a handful with briefcases.

Which one was this mysterious Krüger-man?

"Keep things low-key," D-Boss had said in the call last night. "The man is some kinda ex-Special-Forces but now he say he 'in high-tech' and he have a meeting with the Trade Minister. Well I say: he's a fuckin spy for the US! Them Yankees feel we stupid or what? So, just pick the man up, drive wherever he tell you, do whatever he tell you, then drop him back in the airport tomorrow. No long-talkin."

"Low key" meant the usual protocol for dealing with foreign dignitaries didn't apply: there was no necktie choking Anand today. It was Friday and he could dress like it, in slacks and a simple white shirt-jack, the billowy side-split tunic hiding a pistol on his hip. He pressed his abs now against the holster's cold belt clip, assuring himself that he too could've had a career as an intelligence big dog like Krüger—Spy... Special Forces... even frickin Police Commissioner—in another, fairer life. He had the brains for it.

But an Indian "strong-man" is all people saw in him. Weightlifting had been an obsession since his orphanage days. He'd figured if his arms looked big enough, he'd never have to actually use them against anyone, as his father had done all the time. And sure, it had worked: nobody called him "Pie" or "Coolie Boy" anymore, like when he was growing up. But very few people took the time to realize that he was *smart.* He was a fella with five O Level passes. A fella who, at eighteen, had gone straight from the orphanage dorm to the police barracks after acing the entrance exam. The other recruits—mostly negroes—had been jealous of him from the outset, and they'd hazed him, and he'd ignored them until the day they'd tried to "pants" him in front of some female trainees, to prove "how small them coolie-man is," so he'd used his arms then, smashing one fella's face and cracking the ribs of another fella named Tony.

Those guys were allowed to stay in The Service, though Anand had been kicked out. He saw them, now and again, strutting around in their crisp, shiny-buttoned uniforms. Meanwhile, he'd had to settle for the second rate career of "Executive Protection Specialist"—a species of rent-a-cop. All he did was chauffeur people and tote around this semi-automatic that he'd never even used. Nothing had ever happened in this job to render him even semi-important to anybody. Drop them off, pick them up, run errands. Almost thirty years old, he was a strongman messenger-boy—a far cry from being some kind of hero like this Mr Krüger.

Where was the frickin man anyway?

Anand held the sign higher, his gaze combing the froth of white faces until it snagged on something big. There, in the shadows just inside the doorway: a tall man in a long-sleeved shirt, dark suit jacket draped over his arm. The man's silhouette spliced a remembered fear through Anand: he had the exact build and profile of Brother Matt, the Canadian monk who'd run the vocational school at the orphanage. Odd-looking in the same way: too tall but slightly bow-shouldered like he was carrying an invisible rucksack, and baldheaded, too. The suitcase at his side seemed miniature as he towered over it, obstructing the flow of innocent passengers.

The man turned and stepped through the doorway into the full blast of the morning's light. His face was like a cracked phone screen—its surface all in shards—as he blinked through various name signs, until he arrived at Anand's. He gave a lightning nod that seemed to overload some circuit, causing a glitch of a smile. Then he reverted to blank and aimed himself toward Anand, whose own skin had turned *quaily-quaily* at the recollection of Denyse's warning: *This client bringing trouble.*

"Oh *shiiit,*" he wheezed through the gritted teeth of a pretend smile. Had she put goat-mouth on this job? Why did this man look so damaged? And how, despite his unique face, could he still look so much like that sonofabitch Brother Matt?

"Hey, nice *guayabera,*" Krüger said, pointing down at Anand's shirt- ack. "Lotta these threads in Florida. Cubans."

There was no smile, though, to accompany the words; so Anand wondered if he'd worn the wrong attire for today's role of American Espionage Assistant.

But, then again, could this man even make a smile? Up close, his face appeared too smooth and tight in places, too rough and ridged in others, and his bottom lip was off to the right, slightly misaligned to the top one. His skin was a camouflage of pinks and corals, so much like a Hollywood-made-up burn victim that Anand knew at once the man *was* a burn victim and was way too noticeable to be on active spy duty.

He felt a moment's pity for Mr. Krüger. But could not get past the fact that, even this close, the eerie parallels to Brother Matt continued: the sandpit voice and North American accent, the bluish-grey gravel for eyes.

Anand had tried his whole adult life not to become his father AND not to think about Brother Matt. Yet here he was, thumbing his ear at a memory of the monk bending over the miter saw, feigning instruction while bristling his brown moustache against the silky skin of Anand's twelve-year-old ear: *Back room. Now.*

"So you're Garth Krüger, right?" Anand said, a little too loudly, as he tried to switch gears in his head.

The man scowled. "Dude, who else would I be?"

While the American waited curbside, Anand slammed the car door, gunned the air conditioning, and dialed Denyse. It didn't matter what had transpired between them earlier, she was his best friend—his only friend—and he needed to tell her the horrible news.

"Girl, if you see this man," he said.

"W'happen? Tell me fast. I now walking in work."

"Like he get burn in war or something, so his face have a kinda horror movie finish—"

"Why you didn't take a video? You does be sending me video of all kinda stupidness, but you eh send this?"

It was true. He'd formed a habit of recording short clips of all the odd people, places, and things he encountered. He'd also written countless short scripts, and harbored hopes of making a movie one day because, as he often told Denyse: *Something good have to come from this shitty work.* Yet he hadn't once thought of filming Krüger, the most cinematic man he'd ever met.

"When I see him, I just freeze girl. Is not that the face frightening; I could live with it. The problem is who this man resemble, girl?"

"Who?"

"Outta all the frickin people in the whole frickin world, you know the man talkin and movin just like Brother Matt?"

"Yuh lie! Brother Matt? The Duttiness from the orphanage? The priest?"

"Yes, girl. It have me feelin... *ahow.*" What was the right word? Confused? Disoriented? If Anand was honest, he would say "scared," but he didn't want to hear himself say that word.

"You see? If you did listen to me, this woulda never happen. You woulda done drop me to work and—"

"I can't talk long. He waiting," Anand cut Denyse off mid-sentence. Slowly, he dragged his palm from hairline to chin, as if that could vacuum the anxiety from his head.

"Well just be careful, ok, babes." Her tone had softened. "The past is the past. You done pelt that in the picker-bush behind you long time. Today, you is to focus on the road in front, and have little as possible to do with that Krüger-man."

Anand agreed, then hung up feeling more confident. She'd said "bye, babes," this time, so he was fully clothed in the armor of her love.

He paid the parking attendant, then navigated a thornbush of jutting vehicles, to find Krüger waiting at the curb with oceanic patches of sweat on his shirt. In the time it took Anand to pop his suitcase into the trunk and return to the cockpit, Krüger had already installed himself in the front passenger seat, adjusted it all the way back, stretched the seatbelt across his bulky frame, and commandeered the air conditioning vents. But clients were supposed to sit behind—that was the rule: money in the back, muscle in the front—and Anand did not like breaking rules, he preferred to stay on the side of Right. Besides, he didn't want a stranger, particularly this grim stranger, clogging his personal space.

He took his time adjusting the floor mat and the rearview mirror, while aligning his next words. "Sir, you sure you don't want to relax back there?"

"No,"Krüger said. "Old Army habit. Like to see where I"m going. Let's go."

Anand squared his jaw. He was just about to swerve from the pavement when his phone rang.

"Aye, you find James Bond?" D-Boss whispered.

"Of course, sir," Anand replied with exaggerated professionalism.

D-Boss caught his tone. "W'happen? Something happen, *nah?*"

"Not really. Just… different." Anand noticed, in his side vision, Krüger's face growing twitchier by the second. He considered driving off while still talking on the phone, but that might vex the man even more. Foreigners were funny about things like that.

"He right there, nah?"

"Yes, we now leaving the airport."

"Remember, Uncle Sam is watching you, eh. Just keep it low-key."

D-Boss hung up and Anand left the curb. "Where to first, sir?" he asked Krüger.

"Trade Minister's Office," Krüger said, sliding a little spiral-bound notebook from his trousers and plucking a pen from his shirt pocket. Although he *clickety-clicked* nervously on the pen, he had a drill sergeant's tone as he read, "Meeting at zero nine hundred hours. You"ll wait, it shouldn't be too long. Then, the Hilton Hotel. I'll stay there, get myself oriented, but you'll proceed South to McBean Village to pick up Mrs. Hosein, bring her to the hotel for a lunch meeting at eleven-thirty, then take her back home afterward."

Krüger paused, swiped a scarred hand over his patchy skull, then continued.

"I'm gonna try to keep that one as short as possible, but you know how it is when you're firing someone, especially someone old enough to be your mom—gotta let them down easy, listen to them cry for a bit. Isn't that right?"

"Yes, sir. Respect the elderly," Anand said, although he'd never been in the position to fire anybody.

"Then, dinner appointment in Tunapuna town set for nineteen-thirty hours sharp. Don't wanna be late for that, no way, not by a second. I'll be meeting someone very important... well, not exactly meeting... seeing them in person... and they'll be seeing me... for the first time. So, it's..."

Krüger suddenly seemed so tongue-tied that Anand understood he could only be talking about a woman. Probably some kind of blind online dating thing—plenty Trini-girls just looking for a white man and a visa stamp. But the young lady in Tunapuna was about to have the shock of her life when she lay eyes on this gash-faced Romeo. His invisibility had been his superpower. *Humph!* Anand endured a spasm of sympathy for Krüger. He himself had felt invisible for so long in this job, and had thought that was a bad thing; it now came as a shock to realize that being *seen* could have a downside.

Krüger snapped the notebook shut. "Anyway, hectic day ahead. Think you can handle it, big man?" he asked.

"Yes, sir," Anand replied, but in truth he was skeptical about the timeline. These foreigners, from these fancy efficient countries, never understood that to set a tight schedule in Trinidad was to goat-mouth your whole day. Anything could happen here, if you tempted fate enough.

"So how much you benching, dude? Like, one-fifty?" Krüger asked. Anand felt the man's laser gaze scanning his body, the same way Brother Matt used to look at him. As every muscle in him resisted the memory, he found himself squeezing the steering wheel. The last thing he wanted was a pissing contest with Krüger about who did more in the gym. But he did want a hefty tip at the end of the day, so he answered, "Yeah, around one-fifty, how 'bout you?" and braced himself for the hard work of befriending a man who resembled an enemy.

From the airport to Piarco roundabout—clear. From the roundabout to the highway intersection—clear. From there to

Curepe Junction—clear. But then, gridlock. The Curepe traffic lights were working, cycling through their colors, but only a few cars at a time were able to cross the intersection. It took Anand half an hour to do so and by then, it was 8:00, his hands had grown sweaty and ahead of him three westbound lanes of chrome and metal glinted still in the sun, like the tines of a silver pitchfork.

Krüger, who'd fallen silent after ten minutes of traffic, now sat staring out the side window, jigging his leg with a force that vibrated the whole vehicle.

Anand slipped his phone out, tapped the messaging app and scrolled to Denyse's name. He intended to sneak a quick video of this Everest-of-a-man quaking next to him, but before he could find the camera button, Krüger swung to face him and asked, "Is this crap normal?" His eyes seemed wider and more blue than grey now, like ice topped by a watery sheen.

"It will clear up soon, sir," Anand replied, re-pocketing the phone. "Probably somebody changing a tire. We call it 'macco traffic,' but you might know it as 'rubbernecking,' right?"

No answer from Krüger.

8:10 came. The car in front of them rolled forward. Anand eased off the brake. Krüger, who was now dripping with sweat despite having every vent trained on him, said, "Take the shoulder."

"What? I mean… I can't do that, sir. That's a big, big charge from police."

"Look at the time. It's an emergency."

"Sir, I can't just—"

"That's an order, boy! Take the fucking shoulder!" Krüger slammed his palm against the dashboard. A big white hand, the kind that had once pulled Anand's lice-ridden hair, smacked his underfed cheek, punched his cardboard chest, forced him to kneel. When he blinked back to the present, he found the car was already on the shoulder, as if Krüger's clout had steered it there. He had obeyed and now he cursed himself, yet maintained a tentative crawl, loose gravel gurgling under the car's wheels.

"Faster," Krüger said. "You're almost as slow as the traffic. I need you to get me out of this gridlock now."

A quick glance in the rearview mirror showed Anand he was heading a convoy of lawbreakers. This happened all the time on the roads: drivers waited for one fool to take a risk on the shoulder, then they followed. He had never followed—he'd always preferred to keep on the side of Right. But now, look at him: like Josey Wales, the outlaw, setting the pace. And somehow, this knowledge made him press harder on the pedal, just as Krüger wanted. He needed to end this criminal interlude and get back to himself as soon as possible. He longed to turbo-boost like Knight Rider over all the traffic, get Krüger to the Minister and out of the car, call D-Boss and say, "Yo, send another driver to handle this man. I done."

Valsayn Junction materialized, shiny and mirage-like up ahead. Anticipation sloshed like diesel in Anand's belly. He began planning for that four-way intersection. He couldn't just dart across—too dangerous. No, he would make a quick U, follow this shoulder onto the left side exit, then swing through the gas station and re-enter the highway on the other side of the lights, where the road seemed—at least from this distance—to be free and beckoning.

"Stop!" Krüger yelled, grabbing the wheel with his big white hand. Anand shoved it away and, through its blurry retreat, glimpsed a police woman as she jumped backwards out of his path. He braked, knowing it would trigger a domino effect along the convoy. He prayed, hoping every lawbreaker behind him would be able to stop, and yet expecting to be rear-ended into the middle of the crossroads. Mercifully, the vehicle traveled further than expected, screeching past the triplet of westbound lanes, to jut into the open intersection.

G-forces slammed Anand back into his seat. His heart, though, galloped on. He saw, with acute adrenaline-fueled vision, the entire cross-section of the highway and the cause of all the traffic: a twisted red car, a halo of broken glass on the road, a leaning lamppost. Police were clearing the accident scene; they spidered everywhere while a tow-truck angled to claim the wreck. No ambulance, though. Anand guessed the injured were few and had already been taken.

"Fuck!" he said, as a cluster of constables stared in his direction. But Krüger mumbled, "Don't worry. I'll handle this."

The woman police, a squat cuboid of anger, appeared at Anand's door, banging on the glass. "DP and insurance. One time, one time. Don't stick," she said, ticketbook already in hand, as he lowered the window.

"I real sorry offi—"

"I don't want to hear. Just pass the papers."

Over Krüger's mountainous knees, Anand retrieved the vehicle's insurance from the glove compartment. Then, from his trouser pocket, he fished his wallet, and presented his permit.

"So, *Anand Gopaul* of Bagatelle, you trying to kill people this hour of the morning, eh?"

She'd stressed his name, Anand guessed, because Indians were so rare in Bagatelle—she probably thought the permit was fake or something.

"*Eh?*" she repeated, daring him to answer her rhetorical question.

"No, officer, is just that this—"

"I know, I know: where you going more important than my life, ent? You playin hero on the road? Well, take some charge in your waist: 'Driving on the shoulder' and 'careless driving' and maybe even…"

While she wrote, two male officers approached with inquiring faces. One was called back to the tow truck, but the other came to stand behind the woman-police.

"So, Strongman, you's the Pied Piper," the male officer, a tall redman, said, flaring his arm to indicate the trail of shoulder-drivers behind Anand.

"You didn't see he nearly bounce me down?" the woman-police asked.

"Serious? Well, now-self we keepin him to inspect this whole vehicle from top to bottom—I sure we could find at least ten different charge," the male officer said.

The other male officer now arrived and asked, "What really goin' on here?" A young-faced Indian, he and Anand held eyes long enough to exchange code, and he telegraphed—at least it seemed so to Anand—a willingness to block the two negroes and their plan of railroading Anand. Growing up in Bagatelle, he'd always thought himself as black, equal and poor as his negro neighbors, but he'd come to understand, over time, that black people didn't see him the same way. Not even after he'd married Denyse, the blackest girl he knew. No, negro people still thought that *he* thought he was higher than them—with his softer curls, narrower nose and lighter-brown skin—so they seized every chance to mortar-and-pestle him. This young-police had probably endured the same kinda shit, every damn day, in the Police Service. They were blood brothers, in a way, so Anand decided to trust him.

"Who's your senior officer? I wanna talk to him," Krüger demanded.

The woman-police bent and peered into the car, as if the voice had come from within a sarcophagus. Anand noticed her slight recoil at the sight of Krüger's mummified face.

"Sir," she said, pointing her pen at Krüger, "I am speaking with the driver. Please—"

"And I want to speak to the *man* in charge."

"Sir, I am warning you," the woman-police tried again, but Krüger was already out of the vehicle. He left the door wide and, with surprising speed for such a big man, made it halfway around the front bumper by the time Anand could say, "Wait, wait..."

All three officers startled. They yelled simultaneously conflicting warnings—*Stay there! Step away! Don't move! Go back inside!*—then the first male officer drew his baton to barricade Krüger at the fender.

Cornered now, Krüger bombed spit balls at the officers as he raged. Expanding in every direction, growing higher and wider, he swung his long arms, gesturing at the police cars in the crossroads. He shouted about being a US citizen, about his rights, about the chain of command, and—*Geez-ah-nages!*—it was a sight to behold. Valsayn Junction had never experienced anything like this: a white man—not local white but *real* white—the size of an ostrich, in shirt and tie and shiny shoes, stomping the dusty shoulder and screaming at three police officers. And yet, not one officer made a move to touch Krüger. Instead they pleaded, "Sir, sir, excuse me sir..." like Jehovah Witnesses.

But Anand had seen this all before—how white-hot fury

could reduce some people to stupid lumps of coal—and he found himself celebrating, just as he had whenever Brother Matt raged at all the other boys except him, and whenever his father, Shiva, had cussed at the neighbors' children instead of him. He was safe; he was not the object of that scorching ire.

The woman-police rapped the door. "What he saying? What happen to the man?"

Anand took a long moment to appreciate her frantic eyes and to revel in her desperation. Since being kicked out of Barracks, he had, like a spurned lover, avoided interaction with police. They had disappointed him too many times: he'd grown up watching police shows and wanting to be a hero like them, but then he'd learned that their jeep passed through Bagatelle every day because they ran the drug block, and then he'd learned how they'd ignored his mother every time she'd tried to report Shiva, and they'd never bothered to come when her bawling for help had caused neighbors to phone the hotline; no, they didn't come until Shiva had pulled a cutlass and chopped her in the kitchen while Anand and his sisters hid in the wardrobe; no, not until Shiva had swallowed *paraquat,* collapsed and was frothing in the grass—then the police had come, and all they'd done was call the Catholic orphanage, that hell-hole. Anand had once thought himself smart and strong enough to become Commissioner and change "the system," but they'd kicked him out and wide—like a badly-taken penalty.

And look at them now: the mudder-asses needed *him* to save these piss-in-tail constables who'd made trouble with a big shot, foreign, white man. "Just get your boss," Anand said, hopping from the car. He shouldered past everyone, put himself between Krüger and the officers, spread his arms—becoming a human bridge—and rattled off his lines, as much to the potential camera phone videographers in traffic as to the officers, "I am an Executive Protection Specialist, an Estate Constable under the Supplemental Police Act. This man is a dignitary in my charge. Please get your most senior officer. We have an international emergency. Let's work together, folks."

The male officers hollered for their Sergeant, then everyone waited, frozen in defensive poses. Traffic, although uncorked by removal of the wreck, slouched at molasses-pace as people craned their necks to observe the *commess.* Being seen like this, in this posture of influence, gave Anand a thrill he'd never known. Then his ears picked up the crunch of police boots on gravel, coming closer and closer. He held his breath and, with the anticipation of a fisherman reeling in something heavy, braced to see what he'd caught.

"Don't make joke! Is Anand Gopaul, *oui.*"

Anand turned to see Buss-Ribs Tony. A barrage of cusswords fired off in his head, but he uttered nothing more than, "Aye, Tony, is you again?" As he said it, though, Anand realized things would be different in this encounter: he and Tony were no longer on equal terms, as they had been as teenagers in the Barracks, and Anand didn't have to feign that they were equal men, as he had done every time he'd encountered Tony in uniform. He had the advantage today, by more than a nose, because he was on the side of the American.

He cleared his throat and rattled off, in the same professional voice he'd used earlier, his job title, employer's name, passenger's name, their destination, and then, after punctuating the monologue with a deep breath, he requested a police escort to get his client to the Minister before "zero nine hundred hours."

"After this?" Sergeant Tony scoffed. "Watch: a whole string-band behind you. Jesus died for his followers, you have to go down for yours, Gopaul. They watching."

The woman-police chuckled on cue, which annoyed Anand. But he reminded himself she was a nobody.

"Look, Tony... *ahhhmm...* Sarge, I can't talk for these other drivers.But, in my case, it was a matter of national importance."

"National imp—Boy, you nearly kill my officer. You feel I didn't see? And I ain't hear no apology yet. Who you feel you is, boy?"

The Indian officer shook his head and walked away then, toward the other offending cars. This hurt Anand deeply, that his blood brother should abandon their cause when he sensed himself on the verge of a major victory.

"Well, Tony," he began, feeling like an All Fours player clutching King, Queen, and Ace while his opponent held bare Jack, "you seem to feel I's any normal citizen you could just bully and torture with that chargebook. Maybe that's true on any other day. But today different, *boss*. Today, if you touch me, you touch this US Special Forces man here." Anand's eyes flitted toward Krüger. The American winked and gave that lightning rod smile—it was there and then gone—but it was enough to embolden Anand to finish with an ultimatum. "You feel is marbles he come to pitch with the Minister? So make up your mind: escort or no escort. Talk fast, we late."

Sergeant Tony's stare was an unblinking strobe that might have glowered for several more hours if Krüger hadn't interrupted with, "Ugh! All this talk, already." From his trouser, he withdrew a toad-thick wallet.

Anand stood there, slack-jawed, wondering if Krüger was actually about to pass a bribe, *frankomen* with no shame, in front of everybody. Then, suddenly, flap-flapping in Anand's face like an exotic green butterfly, was a US money bill.

Krüger shoved it into Anand's shirt-jack pocket and said, "Here. Stay, pay the ticket. Just come get me at the Minister's afterward." Then, addressing Tony, he continued, "Officer, would you please drive me to the Minister's office? I'm sure she and the US Embassy would welcome hearing of your courtesy to a Purple Heart."

Sergeant Tony's plaster-of-paris face cracked into a broad grin. Anand saw and heard it… or was that his own pride splintering? Why had he sacrificed himself for Krüger? Why had he obeyed this bully again? Just like he'd kept obeying Brother Matt in the back room of the carpentry shop. For a whole year, just going along, his body taking hurt after hurt, penance for his sin of hiding in the wardrobe and not defending his mother. For a whole year, surrendering, until a revelation came that his pain couldn't bring Salma back, that he was orphaned and needed to fight for *his* life, the way he should've fought for hers. In the end, one black eye was all it had taken, and the Canadian monk had left him alone then, for a younger, weaker boy.

Tony shouted an order—"Let's go!"—waved for another officer to join him, then headed toward the police car. Krüger disappeared for a second, then returned with his suit jacket on his arm, and his cellphone at his ear. "Luggage," he mouthed at Anand, who hadn't moved.

"*No,*" Anand said, making a missile of the word and aiming it upward, as if hoping to further damage Krüger's face. "This hundred," he continued, slapping his chest the way he did after going heavy in the gym, "it can't even cover the ticket. What I supposed to tell D-Boss? Look, I wake up since before daylight to come for you… I make my wife chook-up inside a hot, smelly maxi-taxi because of you… This is not enough. I want more."

"My apologies, Minister," Krüger said into the phone, as he

turned his back on Anand and set course for the trunk.

Stalking behind, Anand's whole body revved with an urge to seize the fucker's elbow and spin him around. But he redirected the impulse, reaching under the shirt-jack to fondle the grip of his weapon.

At the tail lights, Krüger pocketed the phone and repeated his demand, "Luggage, dude. C'mon, I gotta get outta here."

In that instant, Anand was overcome—almost to tears—by a murderous clarity. He knew exactly what would satisfy him for all his trouble today, and it wasn't money. What he wanted was to draw the weapon, to point it at this cocksure bully and watch terror widen his eyes, to watch his ugly face tremble, to see him fumble and doubt himself, to hear him beg for mercy. A fist fight would not be enough. Some fights could never be fair, no matter how big you grew your muscles, no matter how hard you punched. A gun was needed. If only there'd been a gun in that wardrobe at home when he was twelve years old, if only there'd been a gun in the orphanage workshop when—

With a flick of his thumb, Anand unlatched the weapon.

But his phone came alive, pulsing just below the holster. Instinctively, his hand rushed to his pocket, and, yes, there was Denyse's name and face beckoning to him, rendering him dizzy with a feeling of being caught in between worlds.

He declined the call. Then, with unfocused eyes and prickly skin, he stared up at Krüger, marvelling at how close he'd come to killing—as his father had killed—for no cause other than a punctured ego.

Krüger must've read something on Anand's face. He reached out and gently splayed his palm over the trunk's lid.

"Look, man," he said in a shaky voice, "I'm dealing with a lot here. This is a super important day for me and I… I… don't respond well to situations like… these." He tapped his skull. "So, I'm sorry. Really sorry. It's my fault, I know that. Please, I… I just need a good guy on my side today. Can you help me out, dude?" His blue eyes were now marbled with red. Anand had never really stared into another man's eyes for this long before, but now, in Krüger's, he saw a fear that was bigger than his own. He studied the shark-like way it circled with every blink. And he wondered if all men were as frightened of themselves as he and Krüger. He felt sure that if he'd ever had the chance to look Shiva in the eyes, man to man, this same carnivorous fear is all he would have seen.

He lifted the lid, hauled out the suitcase, and offered it to Krüger. "See you at zero-nine-thirty," he said, then added, "Sir."

"Garth," the American said, accepting the bag. Then he pulled a few more bills from his wallet and enfolded them, via handshake, into Anand's palm. Each man tried to out squeeze the other's grip, but in the end they parted with equivalent smiles.

Anand returned to the driver's seat. While awaiting his fate with the police, he counted the cash, then took out his phone again and texted Denyse: *Not to worry, babes. Everything good. Steak tonight.*

THE GOSPEL ACCORDING TO BOISEY

I

In the beginning was the Wood, and the Wood was within the Garden of Light which, in the brilliance of morning, was often strolled by God, through whom all things were made; without whom nothing was made that has been made; and in whose image man and woman were made. In the midst of the Garden, among all the trees that were pleasant to the sight and good for food, loomed the Beau Mortel, a tree handsome but deadly, and upon which mankind was forbidden to climb.

Now the serpent was more subtle than any creature of the Garden and one day, from a forked branch atop the Beau Mortel, he spoke unto a certain man, saying, "Are you not bored here, in this exceedingly dull place? Climb up and I will show you what is possible. You shall see all the kingdoms of the world to come, and the neon glory of them."And as the man's foot touched the Beau Mortel, the green pods upon its branches withered and split open. And as the man climbed, the tree shook, and from its pods tumbled an exceedingly great number of tiny red-and-black seeds, which were immediately dispersed by a great gust, and fell upon the nearest regions of the Earth. And then Bitterness took root in the world, and dark spirits sprouted from it. But fear not, the Garden of Light persists, amidst darkness, and the darkness has not overgrown it.

For the Wood can be made flesh, to walk upon and reclaim the Earth. There is a new "man"who is sent, from time to time, by God. He is known to the forest and proclaimed in the wilderness as *His Imperial Majesty, Papa Bois, Guardian of Wild Animals and*

Custodian of Trees, The Wood Incarnate. But to the world, today, on the occasion of this story, he is a servant: a work-stooped black man of seventy-three, clothed in a waiter's uniform with trousers expertly pressed, shod in *brogans* whose heels have been worn to nubs, and wearing a nametag pin which reads, "Boisey John." And so, mankind has not recognized him. Nevertheless, he has been sent as a witness to testify concerning the salvation of certain lost souls, so that through him all you others might believe.

Behold he comes, bearing a plastic tray of clean cutlery and a wily smile. Now *this* is the testimony of that Boisey John.

II

Immediately, the servant departed the kitchen and approached the Sky Deck of The Trinidad Hilton, an open-air patio which boasted a view of the canopy of trees below, of the Queens Park Savannah, of the City of Port of Spain all the way to the Gulf of Paria, and of the shoreline of the island's mountainous western peninsula. It was the kind of place that, lit up at night, would be perfect for a romantic dinner, but by day was so grey and ugly that it usually remained empty.

Truly, it was a good place to deliver bad news.

Or to perform miraculous works. The trees knew this.

A white man and an Indian woman were seated on the patio. They had just eaten lunch. On the low glass-topped table between them, half-finished plates and drinking glasses remained.

Far below them, a certain mahogany—a French Creole *bois* planted in 1882—wept its pods over the perimeter pathway of the Savannah and exuded a sigh, saying, "If one could shed tears, one would. After decades of waiting, she is here, within our grasp. Today is an auspicious day."

A few pods were then carried on the wind, lifted high and deposited upon the tree canopy of the Hilton, affixing themselves to a swaying bamboo patch. The rambunctious Bamboo replied to the mahogany, "Auspicious? You mean 'suspicious?'"

Along his walk from the kitchen, Boisey had been listening to the banter of the trees, but as he drew closer to the Sky Deck, he resolved to concentrate upon the raised voices of the two guests. He insinuated himself into the waiter's station behind them, and feigned busyness by wrapping silverware in cloth napkins as he observed the odd couple and awaited further instructions from the bushes.

Garth Krüger, broad-shouldered, bald, his face covered in patchy burn scars but softened by sad eyes, wore slacks and a dress shirt with sleeves rolled to his elbows. Though seated among the slouchy cushions of a woven patio chair, his carriage was so erect that anyone looking would suspect him of being a soldier. But not everyone would notice what Boisey noticed: the nervous jiggling of Garth's leg. He took a long sip of sparkling water with lemon, then set it down slowly before speaking in his mildly American South accent. "Look, do you think I *want* to do this, Mrs. Hosein?"

Across from him, Yasmeen Hosein, a middle-aged Trinidadian woman of some girth, scowled menacingly. With her pin-straight flat-ironed hair and make-up two shades lighter than her aubergine skin, she gave the impression of a hastily prepared cadaver. She was also overdressed—in a bejewelled ensemble and sparkly platform slippers—for such a casual daytime encounter.

"So why you doing it, then?" she grunted. "You wukkin for yourself, ent? A enter-trep-e-near. Is YOU callin the shots, not so, Mr Garth?" She stabbed an index finger at him, causing her silver bangles to toll as if sentencing death.

"That's my point," Garth replied. "I'm the boss. This is *my* YouTube channel. You're a performer on *my* show. And as your boss, I have tried to reason with you, Yasmeen—"

"Who name so? Boy, I old enough to be your mudder. Have some respect, eh. Is Mrs. Hosein to you."

Garth bared his palms in surrender. "Sorry, I didn't mean to offend. But I just had a meeting with your Trade Ministry—the Minister her goddam self. They're not happy, Mrs. Hosein. We gotta bring our numbers up or they'll nuke us right outta their marketing network."

Yasmeen fixed him with a vacant stare. "Me eh understand one thing you say dey. All I know is: you summon my tail to this fancy hotel, make me dress-up and put on cologne-water, only to tell me you firing me. And *I* must have sympathy for *you*, Mr. Garth?"

"I don't want to fire you. You're good at this 'nara' thing. I wanna keep working with you, if you would just follow orders."

Mrs. Hosein shifted her weight from one buttock cheek to the other, then pointed her lips toward his war-torn face. "Following orders never save you from that," she said, causing Garth to crimson with humiliation, for she was more correct than she knew.

Boisey, sensing his time had fully come, made to step out from the waiter's station.

But Bamboo said, "No. Let we mind we business and don't get involved,*oui*."

A sudden breeze doused the bamboo patch in yellow *poui*

blossoms, and the *Poui* said, "Not getting involved is what caused this whole mess in the first place. I say we vote. All in favor of our intervention?"

A great gust followed, and the entire tree canopy convulsed: coconut trees were creaking, palm fronds were rustling, the flamboyant rattled deliriously. Then *Poui* inquired again, saying, "All opposed?" and nature became eerily still and silent, except for the clacking of Bamboo.

Immediately, Boisey effervesced himself to the table side. "Sir? May I clear?" he said.

Garth nodded and requested the check.

Boisey bent toward the table, but Yasmeen, much unaccustomed to being waited upon, said, "Oh God, let me help you, nah, boy," and began gathering up the soiled dishes. "This fella here want to fire me, y'know," she said as she scraped food from one plate to another. "So tell your boss, I lookin for work. A lil small money, I go cook *real* curry for allyuh—not that long-water gravy what allyuh feeding people here."

Boisey reached for the tower of plates and cutlery, inclined them ever so lightly, permitting a knife to slip forth and land upon the terrazzo floor with a tremendous clatter. Immediately, he dropped to his knees and said, "So sorry, mea culpa, ma'am," even as he allowed Yasmeen to retrieve the fallen utensil first.

"Is alright, man. Calm yourself," she said. "It wasn't no cutlash." Stretching, she offered the knife by its silver hilt. Boisey enclosed her entire hand and held her in his gaze, longingly, peering into her eternal soul through the lattice of her mortal flesh. Her face twitched, then settled into furrows of confusion. Her hand trembled as, in the twinkling of an eye, and without the knowledge of Garth, Boisey's message was conveyed: *Arise and come with me. Where I go you will go and, for today, your people will be my people. I will show you where they are buried, and I will give you the desire of your heart.*

Then, Boisey prised the knife from her grasp and gave a slight bow. "Thank you, ma'am," he said, with the innocence of a lamb and the cunning of a serpent.

He departed then, returning to the waiter's station, to print out the check. Behind him, however, he heard Yasmeen saying to Garth, "Something not right with that old man. I feel he from Tobago or Moruga. My pores raise when he touch me. I feel he does *deal*."

"Deal?" Garth said.

"Yes, *jadoo*... *obeah*... black magic, nah. Anyway, back to you, Mr. Garth. I think you forgetting that this job have a higher purpose to me than just money."

"No, I get it: you thought your sister's kids would see the vids and come find you. I remember. And I kept my word: The Nara Guru YouTube channel is all about you. And we've grown so much, thousands of followers, but—"

"But I must only work in a dark dingy room under my house. I not good enough for studio and bright lights and thing. And I must only wear *duster* and *orhni*. I not supposed to uplift myself and take lil pride in my appearance... do the hair, wear nice clothes... no, I not classy enough for them standards dey. I's not folks, too."

"Look, you don't understand how social media works. I tried the studio, didn't I? But the viewers aren't biting. *They* don't like the 'uplifted' you, Mrs H. It's not... uhh... *real* enough."

"*Humph!* So, exposing to everybody the kinda hard life I tryin to escape... daiz the 'real' you want?"

"If you could just think of it as a costume?"

"Mr, Garth, listen-me good. I gone through too much things

in my life, I come too far, to put back on that 'costume' as you callin it. Either this job taking me forwards, or it carrying me backwards. But it cannot do both same-speed."

Hearing this, Garth leaned toward Yasmeen, elbows on knees, hands clasped, and confessed. "I've found someone else. Another lady, who's willing to do things the way the viewers want. She even has a killer Caribbean name: Miss Pussin. I'm supposed to meet her later today but—"

"Gi'she the work. I don't want it. And tell she Yasmeen Hosein from McBean Village, the *real* Nara Guru, say, 'Plenty howdy, and Congrats.'"

III

And at once, Yasmeen arose and left the Sky Deck. She waddled, for some time, throughout the labyrinth of the hotel, seeking a path to the parking lot. And although she was in fact lost, she sensed her steps were being ordered, for whether she turned to the right or to the left, the ears of her heart detected a voice saying, "This is the way; walk in it." She could not have known that in the staff restroom near the kitchen, Boysie tarried, patting his low afro, straightening his bowtie and name tag, awaiting the very moment when she would pass by in a cloud of cologne-water.

He stepped forth. And after she had greeted him with much excitement, she begged to be shown the way. "Certainly, madam. It would be my pleasure," he said.

Again, Boisey took her hand, this time wrapping it into the crook of his white sleeves, as he led her eastward, past a font filled with silver and copper coins, often used by guests as a wishing well. Then, Boisey and Yasmeen ascended the winding stairs, and emerged at the mouth of the cavernous lobby, where four doormen of the establishment patrolled. One of them, the youngest, approached Boisey, saying, "Yeah, Faddah. Tanty need a taxi, or wha'?"

"No, I come with one," Yasmeen said as she scanned the parking lot. "A black car. Lord, I was so nervous 'bout this meeting, I clean forget to take the driver name and number. I wonder which part he is?"

Immediately, while she was still speaking and looking up the hill to the left, a black vehicle rolled from its parking spot to the right of the lobby and came to a halt before her.

"Mrs. Hosein," a voice spoke from within the car, and she answered, saying, "A-A! Look he reach. Ok, thanks for everything, Boisey. And you keep good, eh. Don't let them bitches wuk you too hard."

At this, Boisey opened the back door and offered his other hand to assist Yasmeen as she, in her platform slippers, traversed the sloped curb. Finally, when she had fully entered the vehicle, he shut the door, waved goodbye and said, with a wry smile and in a still small voice, "See you soon."

But lo, Yasmeen did not hear him, for she herself was speaking. "Driver! Oh gosh, this hotel big till it stupid, *oui.*"

The driver was Anand Gopaul, an East Indian man in his late twenties who had been blessed with a long suffering disposition. He contorted himself to assist Yasmeen with her seatbelt, and as he did so, his muscular arms were visible below the short sleeves of his white shirt-jack. Truly, she felt safe with him. But to safety was added another feeling, pressed down and shaken together within her bosom: the unfamiliar sensation of being treated as precious cargo by a man, rather than as a beast of burden.

Moments later, through dark sunglasses, Anand peered at Yasmeen in the rearview mirror and said, "So where to, ma'am? Home? Or..."

"You mean I could go somewhere else?" she asked, and Anand was moved by a deep compassion.

He replied, "Yes, ma'am. Mr Krüger said to take you wherever you want," as he raised all the windows, ensconcing them together and conjoining their fates for the afternoon.

"And who payin for that?" Yasmin asked, still disbelieving.

"Him."

"Is so?" she said, delighting in this small yet meaningful opportunity to exact reparations from her Judas. "Well, pass 'round the Town, nah. Lemme see how Pordahspain does look on a Friday. I only come up-this-side... must be twice... in my whole life."

Anand drove out of the hotel. As they went down from the mountain along the curves of Lady Young Road, Yasmeen gazed at the treelined precipice, seeing but not perceiving the jubilance of the trees. She did notice, however, the Sahara-dust haze which blunted the sun's rays, ruddied the skies. and hovered over the vast green carpet of the Queens Park Savannah. Anand merged into one of the roundabout's lanes, then fell into pace with the puttering van of a scrap-iron vendor whose roof-mounted speakers cried out to the city, "*Buying scrap-iron! Old-battery buying!*"

"Any place in particular you want to see?" Anand asked, above the noise. "We on the Savannah now, so I could show you The Magnificent Seven buildings, if you want?"

No answer came, so he spoke again, "Ma'am?"

Again, Yasmeen failed to answer. For her thoughts had drifted back to the covenant Garth had made with her, and she remembered the former things that had passed between them.

Many months before, writhing in pain, Garth had sought her when the doctor recommended by the hotel had failed him; and Garth had come to her bawling like a wet-*bamsee* baby; and it was *she* who had told him he had *nara*, and it was she who had anointed him with coconut oil made with her own hands, and had rubbed him—three days in a row, she had rubbed his belly—until the muscle strain had healed. And he had said that the world needed to know of her and her miraculous gift.

Once more, and in a louder voice, Anand spoke, "Excuse, ma'am."

It was then that Yasmeen heard him, and replied in a quivering voice. "He fire me, y'know. That sonofabitch. After he know how much that YouTube work mean to me. After he did promise to make me go viral and make everybody in Trinidad see me."

"Sorry to hear that," Anand said, switching out of the innermost lane, which was encroached upon by Savannah coconut vendors plying their trade.

"But is *he* turn out to be the damn virus," Yasmeen said.

"Yeah, that's a hard-luck, ma'am." Anand then switched to the outermost lane, readying himself to suggest a walk in the Botanic Gardens, beyond those bronzed gates, if his passenger so agreed. Never in his life had he met an old lady who didn't like flowers, and whose mood would not be improved by strolling among them.

But Yasmeen ignored his suggestion, and continued: "You better watch yourself, Mr. Driver... mind that *neemakaram* fire you, too. These white people don't have no conscience, son. Them does just come here and full-up their cup like is a wedding we invite them to. And they never satisfy, they does take and take, and ask for container to carry home too. Daiz how them-so does move."

"You preach there, Tanty," Anand said, recalling some of

his own experiences with foreign clients, including Mr. Krüger himself. "But… I guess business is business."

The traffic light turned red. While a handful of joggers crossed in front of the vehicle, Anand propped his elbow on the door, pinched the furrow between his eyes and said, "Ok, ma'am. Well, we've been 'round the Savannah twice now, sooo… you make up your mind yet where you want to go?" Their circling had made him dizzy, it seemed; his eyes were beginning to play tricks: the flamboyant trees along the perimeter of the Savannah appeared to be reaching their gangly limbs toward the vehicle, and the *poui* that had been empty the first time around was now covered in pink blossoms. What was happening to him?

"Just drive, nah, man!" Yasmeen said. "My head hot right now, I can't think straight. Too-besides, it only have one place in Town I woulda like to go, but you wouldn't want to go dey… in your fancy vehicle… to get your wheel mud-up and thing."

"Where it is? Tell me?" Anand said eagerly.

"The cemetery."

"Which one? Peschier Cemetery here in the Savannah? Or Lapeyrouse? Them is the two where all the tourist does want to go." Over the years, he had in his spare hours done much reading and research on these places, in the hope of showing his foreign clients a better time and, perhaps, earning a better gratuity. However, he vowed now to accept none from this old lady; lifting her spirits would be its own reward.

She rifled through her purse while mumbling, "Boy, none of them name sounding familiar. But where the paper gone, Lord? I had it *chook* in my wallet so much years now, from the time that woman call and give me the information."

"Describe the place. You ever went before? You remember how it look?"

"Ah! I find it! Praise God! It name Western Cemetery. That near?"

"Yeah, that's in St. James. Five, ten minutes tops,"Anand said, though he was surprised, for no one had ever asked to be taken to *that* cemetery. He scoured his mind for what, if anything, he had gleaned about the place in his research, and could only recall that it had, in colonial times, been part of Terre Brulée estate owned by the illustrious Stones. But, as far as he was aware, no one of consequence was buried there.

"Why there, though?" he asked Yasmeen. "Is a special grave you looking for? If you don't mind me asking."

"Boy," Yasmeen said and gave a lengthy sigh which, to Anand's eyes, was matched by the great heave of a samaan tree up ahead. He shook his head to dispel what *must* be double-vision, wrenched the sunglasses from his face, and accelerated away from the Savannah, merging off in the direction of Maraval.

"Is my sister,"Yasmeen admitted. "She did livin up-this-side and we did loss contact, and so we never know when she pass. We only find out afterwards when one of she neighbor-them did get my number and call. And the chirren just scatter after she gone. I always feel so guilty 'bout that. Daiz why I did want the viral thing so bad, nah. I did want somebody see me and make contact... if they still around."

"Trinidad full of situations like that. Sad, real sad," Anand said, as his fingers death-gripped the steering-wheel. Ignorant, though he was, of the hurtful details of this old lady's situation, he knew full well his own agony. Can a child forget the woman who nursed him? Or lack compassion for the womb that bore him? No, the memory of his own mother's murder at the hands of his father remained as if inscribed on the palms of Anand's hands: him, at twelve-years-old sitting blank-faced on a couch, hugging his two crying sisters, while in the room's far corner, a neighbor pleaded with police to be allowed to keep the children, and the constable in turn pleaded "procedure"and "the law"—which meant "orphanage."

Immediately, Anand understood the connection he had felt, all morning, to this old lady: they had endured similar ordeals. And he knew exactly what his wife would say if he told her about the strange things he had just seen: he was being called, by God, not only to deliver this old lady to her dwelling place, but to deliver her to her lost family—as no one had been able to deliver him to his own. This drive was a pilgrimage.

Anand cleared his throat, then spoke in a sober tone. "Ma'am, I been listening to all what you say. I want you to find your people. You don't need Mr. Krüger. *I* will help you."

"How you mean?" Yasmeen startled and grabbed the back of his seat.

Her bangles were still chiming in Anand's ear as he replied, "I mean, if is viral you want, just do a Live. That's how people does go viral these days. Facebook, Instagram… do a Live on your phone and talk to the screen like is whosoever you trying to find. And other people will watch and share and thing, if it look sincere."

"Oh God, no," Yasmeen protested. "I 'fraid to talk on mic and thing. With the YouTube work, I didn't used to have to say nothing—just rub people belly."

"Don't hurt your head,"Anand said, with a confident chuckle. "When my wife want to go Live with she lil cooking and thing, I does write down all what she goin and say, like a script, nah. I could do that for you, too. But you just have to practice sayin it natural, natural—not like you reading."

"Boy, me eh know… " Yasmeen said, for something in her

innermost being had begun to stir like surf-driven and tossed by the wind. Could she trust this young man? Could she trust herself? She was what she'd always been: an uneducated country-bookie. Would people make fun of her speech, her accent? Worse yet, would she betray signs of the guilt she still felt concerning her sister's death? Would she start blubbering like an idiot on screen?

Then Anand spoke, deciding the matter for her. "We go do it, Tanty. I will be right there with you as you talking, and I will give you instructions-and-thing in what to say and how to say it. Don't frighten." Then he lifted his eyes above the hills, to regard the now ominous Western skies, and added, "*Humph.* Watch that cloud. We getting some rain."

IV

And it came to pass that while Yasmeen and Anand had been circling the Savannah, the servant had ascended the mountain behind the Hilton Hotel and had re-entered the wilderness.

Immediately, as he broached the treeline, the waiter's garments rended themselves and fell from him and he stood naked. In appearance, his form remained human and his legs remained straight, but his feet became cloven hooves that gleamed like burnished bronze. And his neat afro was no more: from his head sprouted two horns the color of iron; and his hair turned grey and became *jataa*, flowing forth like many rivers, into dreadlocks of great length. And from the gully above his lip emerged a clump of silver hair, which then spread like a lichen to cover his face then cascade downward, becoming an old man's beard. He gave a whistle, and at once there appeared beside him a black pothound, lean but well-muscled and with a glint of daring in its eyes, as stray dogs nourished on the refuse of the city are wont to be.

"*Bonjour, vieux Papa*," growled the dog, to which the man-beast answered in a thunderous rumble, "*Bonjour, Duvalier*," as he wrapped and tied his dreadlocks, forming a crown of silver upon his head.

After this he spoke one word, "*Allez*." Then he and the dog took off running. And like war horses, so they ran. Each went straight ahead, westward; they did not turn as they moved, the trees simply bowed and parted to make straight their route. And as the dog ran—never ahead nor behind, but always at heel, looking up at its master then back at the path—its head moved so swiftly that it appeared to be three heads, and its tail whipped like a *mapepire* serpent. And as the man-beast ran, the forest filled with sound: the stomping of royal stallions, the rumbling of chariots, and the clatter of a thousand wheels within wheels, raising a great cloud of dust that preceded them as they galloped along the spine of the Northern Range.

And the people dwelling in the foothills saw the cloud, but they understood it not. Only Anand saw the cloud and suffered a twinge of panic that it might threaten his mission of deliverance. For is it not written that, "He who has cocoa in the sun must look for rain"?

And yet, as the vehicle approached the Bournes Road intersection, a mere stone's throw from the Western Cemetery, Anand found himself in a dilemma where the thing that he wanted to do—proceed straight toward the cemetery—he could not do; and instead he heard himself saying to his passenger, "I go drive up Fort George real quick, so you could see the canons and the whole city-view and thing." Without waiting for Yasmeen's response, he turned right and ascended Bournes

Road, then turned left, and was halfway across Terre Brulée Street when Yasmeen exclaimed, "Wait, wait, wait! Stop here a minute and put down the glass, nah?"

Anand did as she asked.

She stretched forth and pointed to the hedge in front of a wooden house so old Anand assumed it might be original to the Terre Brulée estate named in his research. "Ohhhh gorm, look they have a *rojo*, the double red hibiscus. I eh see one since I was a lil gyul in Barrackpore. Lord, I can't leave without a piece to plant. I wonder if anybody dey home?"

Anand made to get out of the car. But then, an even older Indian woman stepped from behind the hedge. She wore a simple cotton house dress, and held pruning shears in both hands, as if her last snip had been interrupted. Following Yasmeen's gaze to the flower, the woman said, "You like it, eh?" and gave a proud toothless smile.

And straightaway, through the car window and over the fence, the women began chattering about the beauty, rarity, and medicinal benefits of the plant. And it was agreed between them that, after the cemetery, Yasmeen would return to collect a cutting which the old lady promised to set in a pot of moss. "By then, I might be resting," she said. "But my great-nephew, Sheldon, go be home. Just call for him by the small gate."

Yasmeen was elated. And, listening to these two old ladies, Anand's heart knew a satisfaction and a very great tenderness that he could not explain, except to think that this detour was all part of his divine calling for today. No matter what happened next at the cemetery, even if Mrs. Hosein didn't find her sister, she had something to anticipate afterward—she'd have a real living thing to take home. There was no need, therefore, for the further delay of a trip to the fort, Anand decided. So, at the end of Terre Brulée Street, he went down Fort George Road, back to the main road upon which they had only minutes ago been traveling.

V

He entered Western Cemetery by its wide-open gate. Wooded hills encircled the back wall, but in one area, the trees had been cleared and modern concrete townhouses jutted intrusively, their windows and glass doors glinting like paparazzi lenses in the sun. The place seemed empty except, in the near distance between two graves, there lay a black stray-looking dog and beside it, a worker in coveralls and tall rubber boots kneeled, trimming grass with a small cutlass. Had the worker's face not been hidden under a big floppy hat, surely Yasmeen and Anand would have recognised him and cried out, "Look Boisey from the hotel!"

He had awaited them eagerly with patient endurance, half-heartedly tapping blade to soil, and singing softly his favorite old-time calypso, one about making love in the cemetery.

Duvalier, uninspired by the serenade, had remained on all fours beside Boisey, his head resting on his front paws, his eyes closed. Suddenly, as Anand's vehicle crossed the cemetery's threshold, the dog raised its head and uttered two quick barks. Boisey neither flinched nor looked in the direction of the dog's interest. Instead, he reached across, stroked the animal's head, shushed him, while Anand's car crawled to a halt along the cemetery's internal road. Only when the second car door slammed did Boisey turn and sit on his haunches, pushing his hat out of his eyes, to observe the newcomers. "The sign by the front say the Muslim section is over this side," Yasmeen said, standing beside the car, holding her handbag in one hand and mopping her face with a rag.

Duvalier, who was forbidden to speak in public, whined with impatience.

"Calm down," said Boisey, "She will find it."

Then a blast of wind accosted the visitors, dishevelling their hair, disturbing their clothes, anointing them with petals and leaves of every description. While they shielded their faces from the risen dust, the sky changed from its garment of flannel grey to its earlier sackcloth of orange haze.

"You want me go with you?" asked Anand.

"No, son. I feel this come like a private family matter. I hadda handle it by myself."

"Is true. I understand." Anand nodded but his eyes conveyed disappointment.

Noticing this, Yasmeen at once explained herself. "You see: if I find my sister, I eh sure how I go react. And if I don't find she... well, Lord help me... after all this up-and-down today."

"You go find she. Just do your thing, take your time. Talk to your sister, woman to woman. And if you feel up to it, you could even do the Live right there. Where your phone?"

Yasmeen thrust her bag into Anand's hands, making him her caddy while she rummaged through, then emerged with her Telus-branded smartphone. She offered it to Anand.

"Your children send this from Canada, nah?"

"Yeah, it nice, eh?"

He tapped into Facebook and showed her the button which would allow her to "go Live." Then he said, "So, you go'head, Tanty. I waiting here."

"Okay, well..." She turned, waddled a few steps but kept looking back, while he nodded and kept shooing her forward. And yet she tarried.

"Hear what," he said as he went to her. "I think you too nervous to talk good on a Live. Let *me* do some videos, instead. A long shot of you talking to the grave, then a close-up of you reading something we could write-up together quick. Then I go stitch them up as one video, real emotional, and we go post that. Bound to score. Okay?"

Yasmeen agreed. She turned from him then and walked with a determined pace toward the array of simple green and white headstones. Anand remained at the car, holding her phone and handbag like two dumbbells he was about to curl; while at some distance, Duvalier panted and Boisey smiled expectantly.

Unsteady in her platforms, Yasmeen picked her way through the uneven terrain around the graves, consulting her paper, occasionally stooping to read headstones, some of which were obscured by overgrown grass. So absorbed was she, that she remained unaware of being watched by the man and dog, who had transposed themselves from the front of the graveyard to a patch of grass near the back wall.

When she was still a little way off, Duvalier growled.

Boisey scolded him, saying, "*Tais-toi, chien!* Next time, they will send you back as a gnat if you don't learn to control yourself. Yes, she has done bad things. But He makes the sun to rise on the virtuous and the fallen… like you, *non?*"

When the dog whimpered, Boysie's face softened. He scratched the dog's ears and said, "Alright, alright. Let's give her some help," then, cupping his hands around his mouth, he blew in Yasmeen's direction.

Immediately, she misstepped in her platforms, stumbled and broke her fall by grasping the rounded top of a gravestone near the cemetery's wall. Something on the face of the stone caught her eye. This grave was clean—someone had obviously been paying to keep it so—so she had no trouble reading, with eye and index finger, the metal plate affixed to the concrete headstone.

At once, she shot upright, exclaiming, "I find she!"

Anand called back, "You find she?"

Pointing at the grave, she answered, "Here!"

Anand leaned across the trunk and propped his right hand, which cradled the phone. He engaged the camera, lined up his shot, zoomed in, then called out. "Okay, go'head! I recording!"

Yasmeen turned to the gravestone, touched it, and emitted an obvious sigh. She bared her palms, then lifted them to frame her head, as if someone was threatening to shoot her if she moved.

Anand, who was unfamiliar with the Muslim prayer movements to commence *salat*, whispered to himself, "Yessss, that's gold, flippin gold. All we need is a lil cry now."

Gaze fixed downward, Yasmeen clasped her hands over her chest, and seemed to freeze in that position for a while.

"Come on, Tanty. Do something dramatic, nah," Anand muttered. She bent forward, in a stiff bow, as if reading the gravestone again. "Now, now… gi'we the meltdown. Viral things."

Then she straightened and just stood there, with arms limp at her sides. "I give up, *oui*."

Anand shut off the camera and turned away from Yasmeen. He resolved to turn back again only if he heard her bawling.

And it was at that very moment that she, unseen by him, sank to the ground and prostrated herself before the grave.

He, meanwhile, returned to the driver's seat and lowered himself heavily, with one leg in and one leg out of the car. A strange restlessness gnawed at the edges of his previously good mood. He stashed the phone on top of the dashboard and looked around the cemetery, which still appeared empty except for the man and dog who were now in a different spot, just sitting in the grass.

"*Humph!* Government workers, eh? Watch how he lounging… like he have nothing to do." As Anand spoke, though, his hands began itching as they sometimes did when he was nervous. He kneaded them against the steering wheel. Then, he reached into the glovebox, seeking a piece of paper upon which he might scribble a short script for Mrs. Hosein. He spotted the small bible kept in there at the request of his wife. He remembered that secured within the sanctity of its leaves was the only evidence he had of his life before the orphanage. He slid it out: a photograph of himself cross-legged on the floor, flanked by his sisters. Their mother, young and pretty, light-skinned, with grey eyes and long black hair, reclined in a hammock behind them, casting an adoring gaze. He flipped the photo over and read their names and ages, handwritten on the back.

He thought of how he had hardened his heart against his sisters after they'd both been adopted, and he'd been left behind. He recalled how he had counseled himself, saying *Boy, everybody born alone and does dead alone, so let them people go.* He reflected, with some remorse, on the day when the nun had found him in the workshop and said that his paternal "grandmother" was waiting in the office and had something important to tell him, and he, refusing to go, had cussed like wind and declared that he wanted "nothing to do with the bitch that make that sonofabitch," meaning his father, Shiva.

Being with Mrs. Hosein today was making him see that perhaps bad-mind was too heavy and cumbersome a thing to tote into old age. It could *bowsie*-back your soul.

For the first time in years, Anand prayed. "God, I know you send me to help this old lady find her people. I trying. You could see that, right? But I kinda wondering if maybe you planning to help me find mines, too? I know, I gave up on some of them long time. I know, I never really believe it was possible to find the others. But if you's really the kinda God like how people does say, I don't see what could stop you from forgiving me… and finding them. Amen."

VI

Yasmeen wept. Facedown on the grave, clutching and rolling her forehead from side to side, as if the grass was but a bedspread, as if there was no risk of being punctured by thorns. And she made intercession to God, with groans and utterances too deep to be put into words.

But Boisey comprehended them: *Oh God, Oh God… Salma… Salma… meh sister… meh one sister… Oh God…* is what Yasmeen's spirit cried.

And Salma did also comprehend. And she came to stand at the right of the gravestone, peering down at her wailing sister, although Yasmeen could not discern her appearance. This Salma, eternally in her mid-twenties, pretty and long-haired, with grey eyes and skin so light it shone like the sun, was clad in a floor-length dress so radiant and exceedingly white as no launderer on earth could whiten. The expression on her face, however, was one of barely restrained pain.

In a lilting voice, she spoke to Yasmeen without being heard. "I here, Yaz. You don't know it, but I here. I always been close, *gyul*."

Then Yasmeen groaned: *Oh God, Oh God… it shoulda been me,*

Lord… it shoulda been me.

"Yes. Ever since we small, you did want to be me," Salma said.

Then, slapping the earth like a *tabla* to accompany her ululations, Yasmeen continued: *Oh God… it shoulda been me lying down here. It shoulda been me who he did marrid and lead 'way like bison. Me, who he advantage for all them years.*

Salma shook her head disbelievingly. "Why you crying, Yaz? When I did want to leave him, you say no. You say you had no room for me and my chirren. You say it go shame Ma and Pa if I went back in the village. Remember?"

Then Yasmeen rose to her knees, and looking to heaven, she finally spoke in a loud voice, saying, "Allah, forgive me, but it shoulda been me who the man kill."

"But, my sister, it come like is you hand 'im the cutlash," Salma said in a sweet voice which only increased the brutality of her words. "Is you-self sharpen that *pooyah* and put it in he hand… when you did decide to tell 'im the truth, after you did promise that you woulda lie for me."

Then Yasmeen trailed her hand across the face of the gravestone, and speaking to it in the same manner as Anand had encouraged her to speak to the phone screen, she sought to lift the yoke of guilt that had burdened her for so long. "Is meh daughter that did answer the phone. Is she whey say you was never by we that weekend. I grab the phone, but I didn't know what to do. I panic. I sorry, Salma, I just panic. And nothing I was sayin, the man was believin. Is like he was expeckin it. Like he did already know where you went that weekend."

Salma's face was cleaved by a spasm of agony, and all the splendor departed her form. Tears upon her ashen cheeks, she gripped her own elbows and rocked, averting her gaze from Yasmeen, and looking to Anand, still seated in the parked car.

Her son, her only son, her firstborn. He who had from birth been her confidant, he upon whom she had laid the weight of her pain. He whom she had bound to act as protector over her other children. And he who, on the morning of reckoning, when Shiva had stretched forth his hand and raised a cutlass to slay her, had defended her against his own father. Oh how bitterly she mourned the boy he could never have been in that household! Oh how she rued the sin that had scattered all her children among strangers! She had followed them, always hovering near, but in all those days of wandering the Earth, her sin remained ever before her, and she had been affiicted by the memory of her nakedness in the arms of her lover, during that last weekend of mortal life. Did her children know? And did they despise her for not being a divine mother, immaculate and chaste, content to be husbanded only by God's love?

In desperation, her eyes sought Boisey.

He nodded, as if acquainted with everything she had ever done in life, and then he offered a smile verdant with meaning: *The only unforgivable sin is that of impenitence.*

Salma's luminescence returned—flickering, at first, but then she became herself again. She resettled her attention upon Yasmeen, who was now saying to the gravestone, "I did try to call you, to warn you. Over and over, I really try, Sally. But you never answer."

Salma knelt then and made herself eye-level with her sister. "I believe you, Yaz. I never wanted 'im, y'know. They did force me… you know that. I wish you coulda find a way not to be so jealousfull."

Yasmeen's head drooped and she spoke to her soiled hands, saying. "I wish he did never walk in Tanty Nazroon shop. I wish we did never meet—"

"No! Don't say his name!" Salma exclaimed. "...that bloody Shiva Gopaul." Salma's entire form sagged, and her aura sputtered in wary anticipation. And truly, on the left side of the grave, her also-dead husband, Shiva, now stood in charred garments and reeking of smoke, like a city in ruins. In an uncertain voice, he said, "Salma, please... forgive me, nah, girl?"

But Salma did not respond. She continued staring straight ahead at her unseeing sister, whose crying had now waned to a quiet sniffle and an occasional shake of the head.

Shiva clasped his hands and continued, "Salma, please. I sorry for everything. I shoulda never listen to meh father-and-them. I wasn't ready to marrid. I wasn't ready... And you was just a innocent lil girl, too good, too pure for me... and I did feel so bad about what I was doing to you..."

Finally, Salma turned her head to glare, across the breadth of the grave, at her husband.

"You lookin like shit," she said.

"Yes! Yes, I's a shitload of shit. I can't explain how much I hate myself. I always did hate myself, but I was too coward... so I did try to hate you instead. You and the chirren and..."

Yasmeen's voice interrupted him. "One last thing, girl," she said to the headstone. "I want you to know why I wasn't there for them-chirren. Ma and Pa did over-shame how the scandal make papers-and-thing. But I wasn't shame. Is just... how I coulda face them-chirren? Eh? When it come like is me whey kill they mother and father? How? You had nice neighbors. I say better a good neighbor whey close than a bad sister whey far."

At once Shiva crossed the grave, to shovel his hand at Yasmeen face.

"You bitch, you! What kinda sister you is, in truth? What kinda aunt?"

"Shiva," Salma said, but he ignored her and continued shouting at Yasmeen. "Allyuh fuckin-Mohammed-people just forsake my chirren!"

"Shiva," Salma said again.

He looked at her then. "She know what we chirren been going through? She have any fuckin idea how that boy suffer?" With a sweep of his hand, he indicated Anand.

"Just shut up!" Salma said. "Is *you* who cause this. All you ever do in your life was make people suffer. So just go back wherever you come from! Go stink-up your own grave!"

"What grave!" He flung his arms heavenward then let them fall upon his tousled head. "My mudder burn me, girl, and throw me in the sea… but it feel like I still burnin now. Is a constant, silent heat. So cruel and so keen to keep burnin. I need you to forgive me, girl… I beggin… please, please…"

And it was then that Boisey thundered in a voice filled with hailstones, "Shiva!"

Whipping around, Shiva saw the man in coveralls, a little way off, standing with the dog at his side. He called to Boisey, "*You* could see *me?*"

And Boysie replied in the spirit, "Yes. Leave her and come."

Shiva took off then, charging toward them, and as he drew nearer, Duvalier growled and his flanks tensed for action: *Oh how good and how pleasant it would be to devour this sonofabitch!*

VII

At the grave, Yasmeen continued to pour forth her heart. And to the flat face of the gravestone, she confessed a multitude of things: that Salma's daughter had once come to the house in Barrackpore, that she had mistaken the girl for a ghost because she looked so much like Salma, that she had allowed Ma—a griefstricken old lady—to convince her that the girl had come to "cause bacchanal" and lay claim to the house and land. And eventually, Yasmeen admitted, "I just couldn't face the girl. She and them strangers… some creole people she did come with… they was watching me so hard. I did feel like they know everything. I run back upstairs same-speed. I was too shame."

And as Yasmeen spoke, it was as if the briars and thorns which had grown up between her and Salma over the years were being pruned away, bit by bit. And Salma glowed brighter and brighter, her aura expanding in length and breadth and height until it encompassed Yasmeen too; and they became what they had been every night as children: two sisters snuggled under one warm spread. Then slowly, but with conviction, they both stood and lifted their hands to their earlobes, as if listening for some message to come from the heavens. But it was Yasmeen who said aloud, "Allah, I beg you: make exception. Receive my Salat al-Janazah now, while I still alive and could say it, with my own lips, for my sins and the sins of my sister and our poor family."

Separately, yet together, they prayed in whispers.

VIII

The dog's gnashing made Shiva stop short. He glared from man to animal, then back to man. "Wait, allyuh alive or dead?"he asked of Boisey, who chuckled and replied, saying, "Both. Just like you. Come, don't be afraid."

Then Shiva, advancing cautiously, asked, "So… you's God then?"

"Sort of," Boisey shrugged and said, "I am many, we are a legion: 'I am god, hero, philosopher, demon, and world'—which is a long-winded way of saying that I am not."

"Yeah, whatever," Shiva said with an impatient flick of his hand. "But how you know me?"

"We know you better than you know yourself, Shiva. And you were incorrect, earlier: you did not always hate yourself. We were there when you started."

"What the hell I hearing now?"

"We watched over you for a time," said Boisey, inching toward Shiva, as one would approach a forest deer. "But we did not do enough. We let our sympathies divide like branches, because we fore-knew Godfrey and pitied him. But we should have warned you that he was no 'friend.'"

"Godfrey? The lil buck from Guyana?" Shiva asked, then indicated the sisters, "What this... all this mess...have to do with Godfrey? He alive?"

"He lives," answered Boisey, who had finally negotiated himself within arm's length of Shiva. "But we should've stopped you from going with him. We were there that night. In the mangroves, near the jetty. When he uttered the hex upon your generations, we wept brine, because we knew you had heard him, and we knew that every curse and every blessing is quickened in the ears."

And immediately, Boisey grabbed Shiva, trapped him in a bear hug while whispering in his ear, "But a word of forgiveness restores life."

And Shiva began to wrestle with Boisey. Spewing curses and all manner of expletives, he wrestled, ignoring Boisey's admonition, "We will not let you go until you forgive us!"

Then Boisey tripped him, and they both fell to the ground, but Shiva went face first into the dust. The dog rushed in, snapping at one ankle while Boisey grabbed the other. Shiva kicked, ripped grass, pounded soil, determined to win and to keep possession of the bitterness that had been his one true friend from birth. But Boisey remained sovereign in strength. He flipped Shiva over, onto his back, and tried to pin him by the shoulders. Still, Shiva would not give in, his hands flew everywhere, he knew not where they landed, all he knew was that the impact had turned his knuckles into hot coals. Then, as the bout prolonged, Shiva decided that he was no longer fighting to win, he was fighting to lose. He kept flailing, lashing out, hoping Boisey would strike him in the head so hard that he would die a second death, a more noble one, against an enemy his own size.

But lo, Boisey pinned him and said, in a voice both urgent and without exertion, "Be still."

Shiva's entire being fell limp. The dog scampered off.

Boisey spoke again. "You have seen Hell, Shiva. You know it is nothing more than a state of eternal guilt, wherein dwells *The* Unforgiven and The Unforgiver too. Will you not come out of that abominable place?"

Panting and weak, Shiva said, "Ok, ok, I forgive you, man… God… whatever-you-is… but only if you agree to make Salma forgive *me*."

Boisey took his knee from Shiva's chest, and sat to one side, saying, "She did, a long time ago. But you should have kept your distance today, for *you* are yet unhealed."

Shiva arose slowly and with a creaking noise, as if his form was but a pile of dry bones coming together, bone to bone. "Well, I want to heal things," he said. "I want to go back in time and heal everything… for everybody. I want to un-marrid Salma and let she choose for she-self."

Boisey shook his head in refusal. "It was written of this in the book."

"No? Well then, I want to at least go back and un-kill us."

"Would you un-born your children, too? Would you un-joy their joys? Would you have them un-see all the beauty they've seen, un-love all their loves? To change the past, dear boy, is to annul *their* triumph: their choice of hope over despair, and light over darkness. Would you reverse the alchemy by which their inheritance of iron shackles has been refined into bangles of gold?"

Shiva jumped up and began pacing. And as he spoke, he alternated between pulling insanely at his own hair, and pointing at Anand, who could be seen through the open car door, talking on the phone.

"So, you's God, but you didn't stop me, back then?" Shiva complained. "You coulda save me, Salma, the chirren—all of we—even this… this Yasmeen. But you never stop me then, and you don't want to help me now. Man, you's a useless god!"

And Boysie stood then, his face radiant, as he said, "But Shiva, ye are gods. All this time wandering in darkness and you still haven't learned? Salma has learned. You are immortal, son. Your thirty-nine bitter years were but a teardrop on the face of Eternity. Even now there are many choices you can make… if you believe that you have them. Salma has made her choice."

"What choices? Show me them? I dead! Stop talkin a setta parables and show me one single choice I have, nah?"

Boysie held Shiva in a piercing stare and revealed what had been hidden since the foundation of the world. "What do you want to be next, Shiva? Lion, dragon, manicou, flower, water? Behold, we were sent this day to set this question before you and Salma. So choose now: what do you want to be?"

And Shiva stood for a while, hands on hips, chewing the inside of his cheek thoughtfully, before asking, "What she choose?"

"Bird. So she can go to the children, at any time, and sing to them."

Shiva turned to study Salma at the grave.

IX

The sisters were still praying in whispers when, suddenly, Anand's voice could be heard, growing louder as he came closer. "Tanty! Tanty!" he called.

Yasmeen swiveled to see him running toward her with a phone in his outstretched hand.

"Is Mr. Krüger," he said. "He want to talk to you. I think he want to…"

Anand arrived, and his eyes fell upon the gravestone. All the color and excitement in his face drained away, as he read there the same name written on the photograph he had just been holding: *Salma Mohammed-Gopaul, 26 years.*

With a thumb press, Anand ended the call and pointed at the gravestone. "This… this name here… this is *your* sister?"

Yasmeen gave a puzzled frown and said, "Yes. This is my lil Salma."

Then Salma herself crossed the grave and stood, still unseen, in the gap between her son and her sister. With eyes serene as doves and a smile like a victory banner, she placed one hand on Anand's trilling chest and the other on Yasmeen's stooped shoulder.

Anand gripped his temples and began walking in a circle, spinning like a mahogany pod in the wind. "I can't believe it, I just can't believe it," he kept saying, while Yasmeen kept asking, "W'happen, boy? You ok? Tell me, tell me, nah. What wrong?"

And not far away, Shiva stood watching them, as he announced his decision to Boisey. "A tree. That's what I want to be. Right there." He pointed to the bushy hillside, just beyond Salma's grave. "So, wherever she go, for however long, she could always come back and rest she-self lil bit. And in between, I could shade she grave. And every time she come back, I could always *jai-mal* she with flowers, over-and-over, like I marridin she again-and-again... but this time, with real love."

And Boysie was much pleased at this answer, for he knew that sin, though forgiven, is not without consequence. And he foresaw what Shiva could not yet understand: that whether or not Salma returned to him, once rooted, Shiva would have to live out his days, like every other tree upon the hillside, in fear and trembling. The townhouses would multiply, the city would encroach and, day after day, Shiva would live as Salma had once lived, wondering with great unquenchable dread: *When cometh the blade?* And surely, it would come; in the end, a blade would speak, and it would not lie.

Finally, Anand stood still. He dropped Mrs. Hosein's phone into his shirt-jack pocket and offered his hand to her. "Come, Tanty," he said. "Let we go back by the car, so we could sit down comfortable and talk. I have something to show you. I hope your heart good."

Mrs. Hosein took his hand. Together, they pivoted away from the grave and walked slowly, arms entwined, her leaning upon him, toward the car. And as they walked, Anand waved at the man in coveralls, who had never moved from the grass and was still sitting, unperturbed.

Suddenly, a kiskidee landed on the gravestone, puffed its brilliant yellow breast and warbled its eternal query, "*Qu'est-ce qu'il dit?*"

Boisey, pointing to the orange blossoms of a tall tree just beyond the wall, replied to the bird. "He said, 'Make me an immortelle.' Now, will you stay or leave him, daughter?"

And immediately, the tiny bird took flight, mounting on

outstretched wings like an eagle. She soared toward the hazy horizon, traveling over the sea and its arches of aquamarine. Those waves, those ancient of waves, they had witnessed Jayanti's arrival and had been waiting over generations, waiting more than watchmen for the morning, and expecting this other Gopaul's departure. So now, as Salma glided above them, they rendered a joyous oblation: a thousand beads of water, like grains of sifted sugar tossed carelessly into the island's golden sky.

All that is harsh and dissonant in my life melts
into one sweet harmony—and my adoration spreads wings
like a glad bird on its flight across the sea.

Rabindranath Tagore, Gitanjali

ACKNOWLEDGMENTS

Earlier versions of the stories in this collection first appeared in the following publications: "Sundar Larki" in *Daughters of Latin America*, and "Terre Brulée" in *adda*.

This book was inspired by both direct conversations with the elder women in my family, as well as overheard conversations among them as they went about their "ordinary"lives. Thank you, Ayesha Mohammed (Ma), Zuliman Sultan (Tanty Zalay), Amena Bocas (Tanty Zan), Linda, Nora, Janet, and Vera. I also appreciate the support and input of my cousins, Marcia Gonash- Abdool, Naylah Hosein-Rabilall, T'shura Maraj and Lezlee Maraj.

For some stories, I relied heavily on the knowledge of Dr. Visham Bhimull, Jameel Bisnath and Mitchum Weaver, all of whom answered my texts and calls with passionate explanations of our Indo-Caribbean history, language and culture. For the Trinidad patois aspects, I am grateful for the advice of Miss Julia from Paramin and Nnamdi Hodge.

My beta-readers truly stepped up with insightful and candid feedback: Anuradha Singh, Ira Mathur, Melanie Lewis, Roslyn Carrington, Jenn Leiker, John Blanchfield and Ruel Johnson.

However, it was my editors, Michael Lowenthal and Hester

Kaplan, and my agent, Clare Alexander, who supported and pushed me to produce the best book I could, under daunting circumstances. Thank you, everyone.

And, of course, all glory and honor are yours, Elohim.

Main Sources

1. Bahadur, Gaiutra. *Coolie Woman: The Odyssey of Indenture*. University of Chicago Press, 2014.

2. Borges, Jorge Luis. *The Aleph and Other Stories*. Translated by Andrew Hurley. Penguin Classics, 2004.

3. Chatterjee, Sumita. "Indian women's lives and labor: the indentureship experience in Trinidad and Guyana, 1845–1917." PhD diss., University of Massachusetts Amherst, 1997. https://hdl.handle. net/20.500.14394/11248.

4. Gayen, Chanchal. "Siparia Mai: An Illustration of the Tangibility Factor in Faith by Hindus in Trinidad." *Journal of Adventist Mission Studies* 9, no. 1 (2013): 31–44. https://dx.doi. org/10.32597/jams/ vol9/iss1/5/.

5. Harlan, Lindsey. *Religion and Rajput Women: The Ethic of Protection in Contemporary Narratives*. University of California Press, 1992.

6. Korom, Frank J. "The Transformation of Language to Rhythm: The Hosay Drums of Trinidad." *The World of Music* 36, no. 3 (1994): 68–85. http://www.jstor.org/stable/43562828.

7. Library of Congress. "20 Years of Service: Post-9/11 Veterans." Veterans History Project Collection. Launched on September 10, 2021. https://www.loc.gov/collections/veterans-history-project-collection/serving-our-voices/wars-in-iraq-and-afghanistan/20-years-of-service-post-911-veterans/.

8. Mahabir, Joy. "Alternative Texts: Indo-Caribbean Women's Jewelry." *Caribbean Vistas Journal: Critiques of Caribbean Arts and Cultures* 1, no. 1 (2013). https://caribbeanvistas.wordpress.com/mahabiralternativejewelry1/.

9. Mahabir, Kumar. *Indian Caribbean Folklore Spirits*. Illustrations by Aneesa Khan. Chakra Publishing House, 2010.

10. Pande, Amba, ed. I*ndentured and Post-Indentured Experiences of Women in the Indian Diaspora*. Springer Singapore, 2020.

11. Parkes, Fanny. *Begums, Thugs and White Mughals: The Journals of Fanny Parkes*. Edited by William Dalrymple. Sickle Moon, 2002.

12. Rocklin, Alexander. "Obeah and the Politics of Religion's Making and Unmaking in Colonial Trinidad." J*ournal of the American Academy of Religion* 83, no. 3 (September 2015): 697–721. https:// www.jstor.org/stable/24488181.

13. Roopnarine, Lomarsh. "Interview with Patricia Mohammed: The Status of Indo-Caribbean Women: From Indenture to the Contemporary Period." *Journal of International Women's Studies* 17, no. 3 (June 2016): 4–16. https://vc.bridgew.edu/jiws/vol17/iss3/2.

14. Sarkar, Barnali. "Murderous Ritual versus Devotional Custom: The Rhetoric and Ritual of Sati and Women's Subjectivity in Amitav Ghosh's Sea of Poppies." *Humanities* 3, no. 3 (2014): 283–298. https://doi.org/10.3390/h3030283.

15. Williams, James. "The Warau Indians-of Guiana and vocabulary of their language." *Journal de la Société des Américanistes* 20 (1928): 193–252. www.persee.fr/doc/ jsa_0037-9174_1928_num_20_1_3647.

www.ingramcontent.com/pod-product-compliance
Lightning Source LLC
Jackson TN
JSHW021853141225
95340JS00001B/1

* 9 7 8 1 6 3 2 4 6 1 7 6 6 *